A Red Ridge Pack Novel

End of Lies

Sara Dailey & Staci Weber

THE BEGINNING OF THE END

The Red Ridge Pack is in danger, and not from "normals" finding out that werewolves live in their midst. This time it's one of their own, the beautiful Kendall Stuart. Treachery, ambush, murder. An alliance with an opposing wolf pack. For a young woman set on vengeance, nothing is too much. This time she's not going to fail.

But Kendall will be challenged. Arrayed against her and the Crescent Hills pack will be all those who survive the initial attack. Led by Cami Moore, as crafty as ever, the resistance will organize, infiltrate, strike where it hurts most. But first they must learn which hearts are true. Like Gavin Reed. Cami can't figure out if the hunky, six-foot-four stranger wants more to kiss her or kill her, and where his loyalties lie. Something's been building between them since the moment they met, and soon it will come an explosive conclusion.

A Red Ridge Pack Novel

End of Lies

Sara Dailey & Staci Weber

www.BOROUGHSPUBLISHINGGROUP.com

END OF LIES
Copyright © 2014 Sara Dailey & Staci Weber

Digital edition created by Maureen Cutajar
www.gopublished.com

ISBN: 978-1-941260-55-5

For Jill Limber.
You are truly respected as an editor, but more importantly, truly loved as a person.
We are blessed!

ACKNOWLEDGMENTS

This series would never have been possible without a lot of support from our families. Many thanks to our parents, in-laws, sisters, husbands, and friends for keeping us going.

A special thanks to Shari Hassell for finding all of our typos and mistakes. To Jordan Mantell, whose poetry has added so much to this series.

To Boroughs Publishing Group. Thank You! Michelle, Jill, and Chris, we are so grateful for all that you do.

Last but not least, a big thank-you to all the fans of the Red Ridge series. What a ride!

CONTENTS

To take what is mine,
You must be fierce.
Fierce like this circle of ours
Which runs deep, don't you see?
Deeper than the ruby flow beneath its shell
Deeper than this broken, miscarried endeavor of yours
Within your blood-soaked misfortune
You have but unlocked sleeping eyes,
You have brought forth the shine,
A radiance of which you could never endure,
A light, love, and brilliance has been conceived
Beating hearts, bled together, and joined forever
By a glory of which you will never see
A breath you shall never breathe.

—Jordan Mantell

PROLOGUE

The tension inside the Tahoe made the full-size SUV feel as tight as a Smart car. Drew Barnes, Crescent Hills' next alpha and currently a prisoner, was sandwiched between Aiden and Luke in the second row of seats. From the steely expressions on their faces, it appeared as it they were hoping Drew would try something stupid so they could end him for good.

Luke was especially hopeful; he had more reason than most to want Drew Barnes dead. Drew had nearly killed Luke's true mate, Scarlett, less than forty-eight hours ago, and even though she was now safely sitting in the backseat behind him, Luke had vowed vengeance. But that was all before the call.

Everything changed when a phone call from Kendall threatened the safety of the Red Ridge Pack, the pack that exiled her and her mother after Kendall's unthinkable betrayal.

Nothing about the night sat well with Red Ridge's new alpha, Cade Walker, but what choice did he have? The Crescent Hills Pack, Drew's pack, had abducted his mother but was willing to trade her for the safe return of Drew, their future alpha. Cade had already lost his father today. He wasn't about to lose his mother too—even if that meant driving to an empty parking lot in the middle of the night with a storm looming in the near distance.

As they pulled off the highway and into the deserted lot of the Santa Fe Valley Mall, Cade reminded everyone to follow his lead and above all else to keep themselves safe. He leaned over and kissed his true mate, Alli, before opening the door to face his rivals.

With Drew as their only leverage, five of the Red Ridge Pack's newest leaders, Cade and Alli; their brother, Aiden; the new enforcer, Luke; and his mate, Scarlett; stood face to face with the Crescent Hills Pack.

The moment Noel Walker saw her son, Cade, she began walking in his direction. When no one tried to stop her, Cade released his hold on Drew, and he all but ran into Kendall's welcoming arms. However, Cade barely had time to notice as his focus was on his mother now standing before him. She reached out and pulled her only son into her arms.

Mother and son stood embracing each other as the heavy rain broke through the storm clouds above, neither wanting to let go. Noel finally pulled herself from Cade's arms. She stood before him with tears falling down the torn expression on her face. Her troubled eyes met his as she whispered, "I'm so sorry, son."

Time slowed to a crawl as confusion crossed Cade's face. Shaking his head, Cade pleaded, "No. Mom...no. Please don't do this." But as Noel backed away from her son and into the arms of the Crescent Hills' Fixer, Brian Reed, the truth was revealed. She had committed the ultimate crime. Her treachery was confirmed and written all over her tear-streaked face.

Cade stood there frozen in shock with his pack members by his side. It wasn't until several pairs of headlights began glowing one by one in the parking lot that they knew this was all a set up.

Holding his arms out wide, Cade motioned for his crew to retreat. Luke, understanding Cade completely, grabbed Scarlett's hand and tugged on Aiden's shirt. Swiftly, they made their way back into the Tahoe and tore out of the parking lot. Cade had barely made it back out onto the highway before Aiden shouted from the backseat, "They're definitely following us."

The tension once again filled the SUV, but this time, it was laced with insurmountable grief. Cade, mindful of the wet roads, gradually picked up speed, but the truck and SUVs chasing them didn't appear concerned about the road conditions.

When the truck pulled up alongside them, Scarlett gasped at the sight of her father behind the wheel. Immediately, Luke took her hand, offering his mate what little comfort he could. Scarlett's father was behind this all, but Luke knew she wasn't at fault for any of what transpired here tonight.

"Fuck!" Aiden shouted as the truck clipped the side of their SUV in an attempt to run them off the road. He was looking for the "oh-shit" handle in the back when his phone started ringing. He was tempted to ignore it, but once he saw that it was his true mate, Teagan, he answered.

"Baby, it's a trap! It's a trap!" she yelled.

"I know. Things went crazy wrong…wait…how do you…"

"Don't come home!" Teagan warned cutting him off. "They've taken over. The Crescent Hills Pack…they came onto the estate in big Jeeps, and they had guns, and…they…they've already shot two guys. Oh God, Aiden…I'm scared!"

Aiden couldn't breathe as the words fell from his lips. "I'm sorry I'm not there, but I'll find a way to get to you. I'm so sorry. Just do what they say and stay with my parents. I love you, baby."

Those were the last words spoken by Aiden before his entire body jerked forward and his phone flew out of his hand.

Cade couldn't do anything to avoid the truck from slamming into them again. Upon impact, the Tahoe crashed through the bridge's guardrail and dove over the side. In a matter of seconds, they were all trapped inside the vehicle and sinking into the freezing water below. Then the SUV disappeared into the darkness with Cade, Alli, Aiden, Luke, and Scarlett still inside.

CHAPTER 1

Cami

One hour before the invasion

8:17 p.m. It had been twelve minutes since Cade, Alli, Aiden, Scarlett, Luke, and a person with his wrists tied and a pillowcase over his head piled into Marcus's Tahoe. Thirteen minutes. Staring out of my upstairs bedroom window, I contemplated, mulled over, dwelled on, and worried over whatever could possibly be going on. One thing was clear. Some serious shit was going down, and no one, besides the select few who hopped in that SUV fourteen and a half minutes ago, knew about it.

Living on the edge of the estate had its benefits, and over the years, I'd learned early on how to use this prime location to my advantage, especially since I was *blessed* with the most overprotective, most overbearing parents this pack had to offer.

By the age of three, my window seat had become my place, the spot in my home where I could almost always be found. I watched people come and go, girls and guys run off to their secret rendezvous, parents argue, pack members talking to themselves, and just about every other ridiculous thing people do when they think no one's watching.

I didn't need rumors or gossip; I saw it all firsthand. But, that wasn't always a good thing. For example, I would rather not know that a group of my closest friends took off into the night seventeen minutes ago with someone who most definitely looked to be a prisoner, a prisoner who appeared to be about the same height and build as Drew Barnes, the Crescent Hills Pack's next alpha.

A light rap at my door shook me out of one of the many bad scenarios playing through my mind, and I had to swallow back the lump in my throat before I could answer her. "It's open." I knew it was my mother. It was her knock.

She poked her head in and smiled. "Hey, honey." She stopped and tilted her head to the side, giving me the once-over. "You okay? You look kind of worried or something."

God, it sucked having a mother who could read me like a book. I'd swear she was psychic if I hadn't actually gotten away with a whole lot of shit that I pray on a regular basis she never finds out about. I shook my head, ignoring that sinking feeling deep in my gut and said, "No, I'm fine. Just tired I guess."

"Okay well, the elders are meeting over at the lodge for an informal gathering. Nothing to worry about. Just with the meeting canceled earlier and Marcus still bedridden, we have some things to discuss. Your father and I shouldn't be gone long. You sure you're okay?"

Sighing, I glanced back out the window. "I'm fine, Mom, really. I'll see you when you get home." With another smile, she shut my door, and I watched from my spot as she and my father got in their car to drive down the street toward the lodge.

After twenty-six minutes and no sign of their return, my nerves were getting the best of me, and I considered calling Shari just to have someone to share in my concern, but I quickly decided against it.

I wasn't sure if I should tell anyone what little I did know. I figured Cade would inform everyone at the meeting what was going on, but when it was canceled and it was obvious that my parents, two of the highest-ranking members on the council, had no idea about

Drew and Brian's involvement in their pack's plan to take over our pack, I decided to keep my mouth shut, at least for now.

I wasn't sure how much more to the story there was, but after I witnessed Cade shoving who I could only assume was Drew into to his father's Tahoe, I knew there had to be more going on than any of us knew about.

After several more minutes of staring out at the nothingness below, I noticed Becca and Shari wandering down the sidewalk. Knowing the only reason they'd be down this far was to visit me, I hurried downstairs to greet them at the door. Before they could knock, I opened the door and smiled, trying to appear as if I wasn't completely freaking out on the inside.

As soon as they saw me, both girls laughed. "How in the hell do you always know when we're coming? You have a sixth sense, don't you?" Shari teased.

Becca playfully shoved Shari aside so she could come in first as she noted, "You know damn well poor, little Cami never leaves her window seat. She's like Rapunzel or whoever that princess was who was locked in the tower." I didn't bother responding.

Becca didn't even realize she was being a bitch half of the time. After all, she grew up being best friends with Kendall Stuart, the wicked bitch of the west. As a result, I usually cut her some slack.

I followed behind as the girls made themselves at home. First stopping by the kitchen, we grabbed some plastic cups, ice, and a two-liter Coke, and then headed up to my bedroom. After we were all inside, Becca locked the door and proceeded to pull a full bottle of Malibu Rum out of her bag. "Our parents should be out for a while. Why not take advantage of it."

While the girls played bartender, I purposefully stayed away from my seat in the window and instead curled up in the chair in the corner. I wasn't in the mood for any more of Becca's snide comments and it was killing me not to be on the lookout for the return of Marcus's Tahoe.

With drinks in hand, the girl-talk began, and I tried my best to appear interested and comment when expected. Before long, they were speculating on whether or not Luke and Scarlett were hooking up. I drifted off in thought, wondering what had happened between them after I'd left the other day.

When Scarlett admitted her father pushed her to hook up with Luke in order to convince him to back Aiden for alpha, Luke seemed completely crushed. But it only got worse when Scarlett confessed that her dad and Drew, who was posing as her brother Gavin, had also abducted Luke's father and that it was all part of a plan to take down our pack. Luke looked ready to explode when he forced Scarlett to leave because of her betrayal.

"Hello? Earth to Cami," Becca snapped. "Are you even listening? I asked how you felt about them hooking up. I mean, weren't you two together like just a couple of weeks ago?"

I started to answer but stopped when the sound of a car caught my attention. No, not the sound of one car. Several. My pulse began to race and that sinking feeling in the pit of my stomach was back with a vengeance. Something was wrong.

Perking up in my chair, I listened intently to the sound of vehicle after vehicle pulling onto the estate. Concern registered across the faces of Becca and Shari, and simultaneously we all rushed to the window. Three large, black SUVs followed by several old-school Jeeps lined the street below. Without a second thought, we all dashed down the stairs and out the front door just in time to witness several men and women carrying machine guns and other automatic weapons exit their vehicles.

We froze on the steps of my porch and watched as others from our pack did the same. Suddenly, a booming voice sounded through a bullhorn. "Members of the Red Ridge Pack, I implore you to go back into your homes. Do not panic. Do not run. Do not shift. Or you will be shot on sight."

For the briefest of moments, my legs felt like lead weights, but as soon as people from my pack started flying every which way as they ran for cover or to fight back, I took off toward the lodge, knowing I needed to get to my parents. Becca grabbed Shari's hand and pulled her along in the direction of her home.

Complete chaos erupted as the invaders shouted warnings when our pack began to flee, but it lasted only seconds before shots were fired. Gunfire blasted out over the breakout of pandemonium.

Instinctively, I hit the ground along with most of the other members of my pack, and as the gunfire ceased, the voice from the bullhorn spoke again. "This is my final warning. On my word, you will slowly rise to your feet, calmly walk to your homes, and remain inside until given further instructions."

My body lay flattened against the ground, but I lifted my head just enough to take in my surroundings. At least twelve vehicles lined the main road of our estate. Those in Jeeps stood from inside their vehicles with their weapons trained on the members of our pack. Several others, all dressed in military-looking garb and camo, held large automatic weapons, and in military fashion they surrounded their vehicles and moved with precision in order to cover the area to ensure that no one from our pack posed a threat.

My heart pounded in my chest and drummed in my ears. My breathing was labored even though I tried desperately to gulp in the air that my lungs were begging for. I couldn't go home. I'd be all alone. I needed to get to my parents. Then and there, I decided that when the mystery voice gave the word, I'd slowly make it over to the lodge and pray they would assume I was heading home.

I waited. Silence filled the air, and I could only assume that whoever was in charge wanted to make sure we were all under control before he allowed us to move. Without warning, the voice sounded again. "Do not try to be a hero. Do what I say, and no one will be hurt. Again, do not run, do not shift, *do not* make any movements toward my men. They have been given instructions to shoot to kill anyone who steps out of line. Slowly and calmly, rise to your feet, walk to your homes, and go inside now."

Before I moved, I waited a moment longer to see what the others would do. My pack did as they were told. Slowly, we rose to our feet and began to move. I'd only made it a few feet toward the lodge when four armed men from my pack charged out of one of the houses and began firing at the intruders. Immediately guns were turned on them, and shot after shot rang out until two of our men threw their guns down in surrender while the other two were dead before they hit the ground.

Chaos ensued once again as our pack ran for cover, but I couldn't move as I watched in horror as the other pack took twenty-five-year-old Jason Maxwell and twenty-three-year-old Jeff Bowers into custody while two others I couldn't identify lay dead in the middle of the road.

Suddenly, I was yanked out of my stupor when I was pulled into the dark space between two houses. Fear filled my bones as I turned to face my captor. It was the very last man I expected to see. Phillip Stanton, Luke's missing father, stood before me with a younger guy in a baseball cap next to him.

Frantically, Phillip explained, "Cami, listen closely. I need for you to get this guy to your house. Put him in the safe room and make sure nobody finds him. His name is Gavin Reed, Scarlett's real brother, and his presence here must remain a secret. There is no time for me to explain. Just get Gavin to safety, and if anyone comes to your home, make sure they do not find him under any circumstances. Do you understand?"

My eyes darted back and forth between the two of them as I nodded my head. "Okay, but what happens next? What the hell is going on here?"

Phillip looked back out at the street as he answered, "It's the Crescent Hills Pack. I have no idea what their next move will be, but for now, we need to do what they say before we lose any more men. Just get Gavin to your parents' safe room. I'll try to contact you if I can. I'll do what I can to distract them. Now go!"

Phillip pushed us off into the direction of my home just before he raised his hands, walked toward one of the Jeeps, and announced, "My name is Phillip Stanton. I am this pack's Enforcer. I would like to speak to whoever is in charge."

We didn't stop to see their response. Instead, together, Gavin and I turned toward my home, made our way inside, and locked and bolted the door behind us.

CHAPTER 2

Gavin

If things didn't look like *Red Dawn* circa 1984 outside, watching this girl in action might have been pretty damned entertaining. She looked like she was on a mission running all around her house. I watched as she grabbed her phone from her purse, a set of keys that were hidden in the back of the freezer, and one of those accordion folder things that was rigged up under the kitchen sink. From the look on her face, I could tell that this girl meant nothing but business. I understood that. Hell, with things as bad as they were at the moment, I sure as shit appreciated it.

I was startled out of the trance by the snippy tone of her voice. "Dude? Come on! Get your ass over here."

A little scared of this crazy chick, I hurried her way. She was standing in the doorway to the master bedroom with her hands on her hips looking incredibly impatient with me, and—truth be told—a little sexy. I followed her into the walk-in closet inside the master and stood back while she felt along the back wall for something. A moment later, I heard the click.

The girl—shit I wished I could remember her name—glanced over her shoulder at me and smiled. It lit up her entire face and made her look even more beautiful than she already did. In any other situation, I would have unleashed my mad moves on her, but I guess I'd just have to save those for another time, like, I don't know, maybe when my crazy pack wasn't holding hers hostage with machine guns.

She pushed on the back wall, and it opened. Using the freezer keys, she turned a lock and then punched some numbers into a keypad, which unlocked a hidden door. As she walked in, I stood back and watched as she flipped on the lights and put the folder down on the table in the center of the room.

"Okay, so, the pantry is stocked, and so is the fridge. Make yourself at home. I will be back as soon as I can," she said as she walked back past me. The whole insane situation combined with not remembering her damn name was completely freaking me out, and I couldn't seem to keep myself from reaching out to stop her. As soon as my hand touched her shoulder, she whipped around to face me.

"Sorry, I didn't mean to scare you," I muttered, holding my hands up in surrender.

"You didn't scare me," she snapped right back.

Her fierce little attitude made me want to smile, but I held it in because something told me that this girl was not someone to be messed with. She wasn't nearly as tall as my sister, Scarlett. In fact, she was kind of tiny by were-standards, but beyond that, she shared all the typical werewolf traits: long brown hair, big chocolate eyes. But there was something definitely special about her, something that was uniquely *her*. She was a fiery little thing; that was for sure.

"Thanks for doing this. I'm Gavin, by the way. It's nice to meet you," I finally managed to say as I held out my hand.

The irritated scowl dropped from her face and a stunning smile replaced it when her hand met mine. "It's nice to meet you, Gavin. I'm Cami. But I gotta go. Stay here until I get back," she ordered before she turned and shut the door to the safe room.

I removed Luke's hat and jacket and took a good look at the room I was stuck in for God only knew how long. For such a small space, it had everything you would need in case of an emergency, or hostile invasion by a pack of desperate, money-hungry werewolves. There was a small kitchenette off to the right with a mini fridge, microwave, and small sink. A bistro table and two chairs sat in the middle of the room. Toward the back, there was a loveseat, a coffee table, and a television.

The two closed doors lining the right wall piqued my interest. When I opened the first one, I was surprised to find a decent-sized bedroom. I was kind of worried that all six feet, four inches of me would be sleeping on that little loveseat, but I guess if this place was built to protect their alpha, it would at least have a bed. There was a full-sized bed pushed against the wall on the far side and a set of bunk beds on the opposite side.

After quietly shutting the door, I moved on to secret door number two, which led to a small bathroom. It really was like a small, tastefully decorated apartment...hidden away inside someone's closet behind a serious lock and security system.

Sure, it was comfortable, but it was small, and the longer I stood there, the smaller it got. Not to mention, it was driving me insane not knowing what was going on outside. I had always known that my pack was capable of something like this, but now that it was actually happening, it just seemed too crazy even for them. The one thing that I just couldn't wrap my head around was how Nathaniel and my father convinced the rest of our pack that this was the right thing to do.

The more I thought about the fact that some of the guys that I grew up with were now outside the walls of this house wielding machine guns, the more I needed something to take my mind off of it all, so I sat down on the loveseat and looked around for a remote control for the TV. I found the TV remote, the DVD remote, and one that didn't seem to go with anything.

After turning on the Discovery Channel, my curiosity got the best of me, and I started messing with the foreign remote. I couldn't help myself. Remotes are just part of the male DNA. At first, the TV went to snow, but after pressing a few more random buttons, the picture became clear, displaying several different images from cameras all over the estate. Apparently, the mystery remote controlled an extremely high-tech surveillance system. Needless to say, I was thoroughly impressed.

The large-screen TV showed six different locations all around the estate simultaneously, or I could shift the view to show one camera at a time. I'd finally gotten the hang of it when Cami's doorbell rang and scared the shit out of me.

Holding my chest to keep my heart from leaping out, I was struck by the fourth image on the TV. It was Clayton, our pack's enforcer, standing on the doorstep of someone's home. Clayton could interrogate a major terrorist and cause him to beg for mercy within minutes without even breaking a sweat himself. The man didn't know the meaning of "taking it easy," and it didn't matter if it was a male or a female. He always got what he came for no matter the cost.

I wasn't sure if Clayton was on the doorstep of this house or not. All I could do was hope that whoever just rang the doorbell was not him. After shuffling through a few more screens, I'd finally landed on one that showed the inside of Cami's home and gave me a direct view of the front door, just in time to witness her unlocking it and pulling it open.

CHAPTER 3

Kendall

Drew hadn't let go of me since Marcus Walker's Tahoe sped off into the night. As soon as they were gone, I'd pulled him into his car and proceeded to remind him of exactly what he'd been missing since he'd been gone. His lips and hands were everywhere as I enticed him with my moans of encouragement.

His lips trailed down my neck as his hand found its way down the front of my unbuttoned jeans. "Baby, I've missed you so much. I want you so bad right now. No one can see us. Come on, baby. I need you."

I pulled away to look into his eyes. "I love you, Drew Barnes. I can't wait to get you out of here so I can show you just how much." I nipped at his bottom lip, and he responded by pulling me into his lap so that I was straddling him, and then he ravished my mouth with his.

Did I love Drew? Who the hell cared? He was a means to an end. An end that was happening at this very moment. So yeah, I guess it was fair to say that for that reason, I loved Drew Barnes a whole hell of a lot.

His phone ringing over the Bluetooth in his car interrupted his frenzied attempt to get me out of my pants, and we both turned to look at the touch-screen display to see who was calling. His father's name flashed across the screen, so I moved back to my seat so he could hit the answer button on his steering wheel.

Before he could even say hello, his father's thunderous voice filled the air. "Drew, you can head to the Red Ridge Estate now. The ambush went just as planned. There were very few casualties, and they are now completely under our control. All of the elders have been detained, and we are accounting for the rest of the members as we speak."

Just listening to the news got my blood pumping. The Red Ridge Pack was going down, and just as I'd envisioned not all that long ago, I would soon be their new female alpha. They may have thought they'd seen the last of me, but I couldn't wait to show them that I was back with a new alpha by my side. Screw Cade Walker and his half-breed bitch!

As Drew pulled out of the mall parking lot, he asked his father, "What about Cade and his group? He sped off with Allison, Aiden, Scarlett, and Luke. Have you heard from Brian?"

After bellowing an order for someone to make sure that Phillip Stanton was locked in the cell, he replied, "Yes. Brian reported that during the chase, the Tahoe collided with his vehicle, slid on some ice, which caused it to hydroplane. The vehicle went over the side of the bridge and into the water."

Holy shit! My hand flew over my mouth, and Drew cut his eyes toward me before he said, "And…"

"We have some people searching for survivors, but we aren't expecting to find any," his father answered, his voice completely void of emotion. "You and Avery get back to Red Ridge and find me as soon as you get here. I'll tell you more once you arrive."

A mix of emotions I didn't quite understand bubbled up inside. In all honesty, I wasn't sure what I was feeling, but I threw my arms around Drew's neck anyway, pretending I'd felt nothing but unbridled joy, and kissed him repeatedly all over his cheek and neck. "Those fuckers are dead, and Red Ridge is ours! I can't wait to see the look on the rest of their faces when they realize I was a part of this. Kendall Stuart is back, bitches!"

"So, it's Kendall now, huh?"

"Yeah, no more, Avery. It's Kendall from now on."

Keeping one eye trained on the road, Drew leaned my way, and I grabbed his face and kissed the life out of him. The car swerved onto the shoulder, and we both laughed. Drew ran his hand all the way up my thigh and rubbed me hard between my legs as he practically growled, "God, baby. I can't wait to get you alone. You're going to be screaming my name all night long."

Spreading my legs a bit wider, I threw my head back and cooed, "Promise?" Thinking of everything that had just gone down and recalling all I'd been through to get to this point made me want to pull over and show Drew just how *thankful* I was, but as soon as his car turned off onto the dirt road that led to the estate, I couldn't wait to get there. My lavish gift of appreciation would have to wait.

When we pulled up to the entrance of the estate, we stopped in front of a few large SUVs blocking our path. Several men armed with automatic weapons guarded the area, and one of the pack members, whose name I'd never bothered to learn, came over to our car to look inside. "Mr. Barnes, Miss Stuart, head on in. Your father is expecting you."

Drew looked my way and shot me a wicked grin. "Well, Kendall *Avery* Stuart. Welcome home."

CHAPTER 4

Cami

I knew they'd come, but it didn't stop the complete and total breakdown that was happening inside of me as soon as the doorbell rang. Though it felt as if my intestinal tract had tied itself in some type of intricate Boy Scout knot, I shook it off and prayed I could play it cool in front of the mammoth of a man standing on my porch.

Planting a scowl on face, I opened the door just enough to peer out and asked, "Can I help you?"

Without hesitating, the man pushed his way inside, allowing three more men I hadn't seen at first to enter as well. "Are you Cami Moore?" the ginormous freak of nature asked.

Trying my damnedest to keep my voice calm and even, I replied, "How about I tell you that as soon as you tell me who you are and what the hell is going on here?"

Practically growling, the manimal stomped toward me, effectively backing me up against the nearest wall. "Who the fuck do you think you are, little girl? I'm the one asking the questions, so unless you want your parents drawn and quartered outside of the lodge where they are currently being detained, then I suggest you lose the attitude and answer my question."

I couldn't stop myself from visibly trembling and swallowing back the lump of pure and utter panic lodged in my throat. When he shot me a wicked grin from several inches above me, it felt as if my already tiny frame was shrinking in fear, and I found myself wishing

I could sink back into to the wall just to get some distance from the man I would now forever consider the spawn of Satan.

Was this guy for real? The evil glint in his cold eyes told me that I wasn't exactly in the position to find out, so I nodded my head. "Yes, I'm Cami."

Taking one step back, his shoulders relaxed a bit. "Well, good. Since we got that out of the way, allow me to introduce myself. My name is Clayton Lathom. I'm the Crescent Hills Pack's Enforcer, and these men are searching your home to make sure that you are not hiding anyone. We are in the process of accounting for all of the members of your pack. Are you here alone?"

Again, I nodded my head but didn't dare ask any questions, even though I was dying to know if my parents were okay. The spawn shifted his attention to the men scouring my home and then back to me. "I recommend that you stay put. It would not be in your best interest to move."

I sure as shit wasn't going anywhere as I watched him join his men in the search of my home. All I could do was pray that I'd left no clue in my parents closet that would make them suspect that there was anything beyond those four walls in there. As long as I didn't screw up by leaving the clothes parted or something fishy, I was certain there was no way they could tell that there was a hidden room.

After several minutes, the spawn was back. He opened the door for his men to exit and then gave me an assessing glare. "Cami Moore, your parents are safe. They are being detained at the lodge along with the rest of the elders. If you would like to keep them and yourself alive, you need to remain here, follow any instruction given to you over the course of the next few days, and give our pack your full cooperation. If you can do that, you should be fine. We will be giving your pack more information soon. For now, just be patient and stay inside. Now hand over your phone. My men have already confiscated any other devices that you could use to communicate with others, such as your family's laptops and tablets."

I pulled out my phone from my back pocket and stuck it in his outstretched hand. Then without waiting for me to respond—not that I'd planned to anyway—he walked out the door and shut it behind himself. After several deep breaths, I finally managed to make my body move, so I locked the door, dragged my anxiety-ridden body over to the closest chair, and collapsed.

I had no idea how long I'd sat there in a motionless daze. It was as if time had stopped, and I'd been sucked into some kind of black hole of insanity. The realization of everything that had gone down tonight finally had the chance to come crashing down on top of me, and I was suffocating under the weight of it.

I was alone, my parents were being held hostage at the lodge, and Cade and the others were somewhere out there stuck on the outside of our new prison. And now there was a guy locked in our safe room, a guy who was not only a member of the Crescent Hills Pack and apparently the *real* Gavin Reed, but the one person who would surely bring a shit-storm of trouble down on me and my family if his pack found him here.

A shuffle from behind me caused me to jerk up from my seat and turn around. Gavin stopped dead in his tracks and held up his hands in surrender once again. What was up with this guy? Did he think I carried a concealed weapon or something? He shot me a truly swoon-worthy smile, and for the first time, I noticed just how devastatingly gorgeous the guy who was previously hidden underneath a baseball cap and bulky coat actually was.

Gavin's dark hair was styled in a messy, purposefully imperfect faux-hawk that accentuated the heart-stopping features of his face. His chiseled cheekbones, dark eyes that held more mystery than the Bermuda Triangle, and perfectly kissable lips completely caught me off guard. Not a good thing considering the fact that this guy was a member of the pack that was currently holding us hostage. If my guard needed to be anywhere, it was up. Way, way up. But that didn't stop my wandering eyes from traveling down to take in the rest of this beautiful creature standing before me.

He was much taller than any other wolf I'd ever met, and while he was lean, he was by no means skinny. His strong, broad shoulders and thin waist created the perfect Y shape, and I didn't have to see it to know that some rock-hard abs were hidden beneath his t-shirt. By the time my eyes made it to the baggy, worn jeans that hung just right on his lean hips, I found myself fantasizing about what it would be like to wrap my arms around his slim waist and have him envelop me in his long, sinewy arms.

"Cami? Are you okay?" Ensconced with obvious amusement, Gavin's voice interrupted my PG-13 thoughts.

Shit! I was staring! Probably with my mouth hanging open. Snapping out of it, I tore my eyes away from his holy hotness and somehow managed to locate the piece of my brain that reminded the rest of my body that this could-be male model standing before me was still kind of the enemy. Okay, maybe not the enemy, but definitely trouble.

In an attempt to cover up my momentary journey to the land of raging hormones, I snapped, "What the hell are you doing out of the room? I told you to stay there! Do you want to get us all killed, you ass-monkey?"

Gavin took a few steps back and his smile faltered, but the look in his eyes revealed he was still amused by the whole situation. I, on the other hand, suddenly wanted to knock the smug look right off his face.

"Did you just call me an ass-monkey?"

I hopped up from the chair, grabbed the sleeve of his shirt, and started leading him back to the safe room. "Yeah, I did. And you need to get back in the room before your scary-ass enforcer comes back and threatens to chop my parents into pieces again!"

Gavin came to an abrupt halt, causing me to stumble backward a bit. He grabbed my arms to steady me before he practically roared, "He did what?"

His touch shot stupid little tingles down my arms, and the concern on his face was annoyingly sexy. God, I needed to get a freakin' grip! Pulling myself out of his grasp, I huffed and continued toward the master bedroom. "Yes, drawn and quartered, to be exact, in front of the lodge. Now can we please just get to the safe room? I think we need to talk!"

Gavin didn't speak again until we were locked safely behind the hidden door. "Are you okay? Did Clayton threaten you? I'd like to say he's all bark and no bite, but that would be a lie."

His fingers grazed my arm as he spoke, which somehow managed to set my cheeks aflame. I moved away before he touched me again, fearing he could set my entire body on fire. "Not really me, but he really did say that if I didn't cooperate he'd hurt my parents. His men checked the house to make sure I was alone and took my phone and all of our other electronics. Then he said if I stayed inside and followed orders I would remain unharmed. So you wanna tell me what you're doing here and what your twisted pack is up to?"

Gavin walked over to the small couch and sat, spreading his long legs out and leaning his head against the wall behind him. "Well, let's see. I'm here because my sister wasn't returning my phone calls or texts and I panicked. I thought your pack had found out what Scarlett was up to and that she was in trouble. So, I snuck into the cell under our council's board room, found Phillip, stuffed him in my car, and drove here in hopes of using Phillip as a means of getting Scarlett back."

Getting the feeling that I needed to sit down for the rest of this, I grabbed a chair and dragged it across the room to sit near the couch. No need to sit too close. There was room on the couch, but I needed some distance.

He lifted his head to see what I was up to before he sighed, let his head drop back again, and continued. "So as you can imagine, I was kinda shocked to find out that it was Drew, not your pack, who had Scarlett. Drew attacked her and left her for dead. And she would have died too if Luke hadn't found her in time. Anyway, I handed Phillip over, and Cade and the rest of them decided it would be best to keep my presence here a secret while they figured out what to do next. Then Avery called Cade and offered to trade Cade's mother for Drew, so they all left to make the trade and well, here we are."

"Wait, they have Cade's mother? Does Marcus know? And who is Avery?" This was just getting more and more convoluted by the second.

Lifting his head and looking me directly in the eyes, Gavin said, "I don't know how to say this… I'm sorry, Cami, but Marcus is dead. And yes, my pack has Noel. And Avery is Drew's girlfriend, but Cade knows her. He called her Kendall."

CHAPTER 5

Gavin

I watched as the confused look on Cami's face changed from complete shock to a ridiculously sexy scowl. She leaned back in the chair and one by one put her long, lean legs up on the coffee table in front of her. I tried not to stare, but damn, she had the most gorgeous legs on the entire planet.

Definitely on the petite side for a werewolf, Cami was probably only about five-foot-five but somehow seemed to have legs for days, and while she was an average height for a human female, were-females were usually a good five inches taller. But what Cami lacked in height, she made up for in attitude. The girl was like a feisty ball of fire, and for some reason, it was a major turn on.

As if on autopilot, my eyes continued to roam up her legs to her slim waist. The image of my hands splayed across her flat, toned stomach flashed in my head, causing my breath to quicken, and as I continued my silent study of all things Cami, I was struck by what she was wearing.

Obviously, she was not expecting company, and it was no wonder her legs looked so long. She had on these little, soft-looking purple pajama shorts and a barely there yellow tank top without a bra.

As if she sensed my wandering eyes, she crossed her arms over her chest, but when she took a deep breath and that tiny tank strained against the swell of her full breasts, I had to look away before the tightening beneath my jeans became too much to handle.

Tearing my eyes from her chest was almost painful, but it was where they landed that caused my body to react even more. She had the sexiest lips I'd ever seen. They were full and pouty and covered in a sheer red gloss. Lost in thought, she wetted her lips with her tongue, and I had to fight the urge to find out if that lip gloss was cherry flavored.

I should have looked away, but that was a lot to ask, and suddenly I was torn. Between those lips and the outline of her tits through that tank top, I wanted nothing more than to pull her onto the couch with me, on top of me, but I knew that probably wasn't the best idea even though my body was begging me to give it a shot.

Cami's voice interrupted my internal struggle. "I should have known Kendall wouldn't be able to stay away from here for long, but I can't believe she's already figured out a way to dig her claws in another future alpha. God, she's such a crazy bitch!" She looked over at the TV and said, "I wonder if she's here. I see you figured out the video surveillance system my dad installed."

My guilty eyes jumped up to meet hers, and I could only hope she didn't notice I'd been sitting here imagining her naked. Shifting in my seat, I cleared my throat and grabbed the remote. "Not really. I pushed some random buttons on this thing, and it just came on."

Cami stood up, grabbed the remote from my hand, and pulled her chair over to the large table on which the TV sat. Grabbing the other chair, I followed her over to the screen, and she started showing me all the places around the estate that could be seen from the hidden cameras.

I was trying really hard to pay attention to everything she was showing me, but everything about her was so distracting, like the faint smell of her body wash, her bare shoulders and the hint of cleavage peeking out of her top, and the way her perfect ass filled out her tiny shorts. But it was the sadness that crept into her eyes when she mentioned her parents being locked in the cell below the lodge that caused my chest to tighten. It was obvious she really cared about them and was worried sick.

It made me wonder how I'd feel if my own father was the one locked up. Would I be worried? Upset? Maybe, but the truth was that he would deserve it. I dug my phone out of my pocket and looked at the screen. He had called several times, and I knew he wouldn't stop until I answered. Unfortunately, I had yet to come up with a story to tell him that would explain my absence. It wasn't like I could say, "I'm right here, Dad! Look out the window!"

"You okay?" Cami asked.

"Yeah, sorry. I was just thinking about my father. He's called a few times, but I didn't answer. He'll just keep calling until I pick up."

"So, answer next time. You're going to have to talk to him at some point."

I rolled my eyes at her and immediately felt stupid and childish for it, but she obviously hasn't spent much time in my dad's presence. To say he was a scary man was an understatement. "Sure I'll just tell him that I stole back Phillip to trade him for Scarlett. Oh, and his little pal Drew tried to kill his daughter, who, I almost forgot, mated with his rival pack's newest enforcer," I said, knowing full well I was being an ass, and as soon as I looked into her eyes, I immediately regretted it.

"Luke mated with Scarlett?" Cami asked, her small voice almost a whisper.

She looked hurt, and it made my stomach clench. Did she have feelings for Luke? I had no right to feel jealous or possessive, but damn…I did.

"I can't believe it," she muttered, more to herself than to me. Cami stood up and moved over to the little sofa and rested her head in her hands. I had no idea what to say, or if I should say anything at all. Hesitantly, I walked over and sat down, careful to make sure I wasn't touching her.

"I just can't believe it," she repeated. "The guy that has never been serious about any girl ever…mated? What are the odds?" Cami lifted her head and let out a small chuckle.

"Sounds like you two have a history?" I prompted.

"No comment," she fired back.

Obviously, that line of questioning wasn't going to get me anywhere, so I shifted tactics. "So, should I worry about this Luke guy with my sister?" Luke had already proven he was a good guy, who loved my sister, but I was hoping to see if her answer would reveal how she really felt about him.

"Oh no, I didn't mean it like that. Luke is a great guy…the best, actually. Your sister's a lucky girl," she confessed before completely changing the subject. "So, let's think up a story for your dad."

I smiled and gave her a friendly pat on the knee—except my body's reaction to touching her leg was anything but friendly.

"Are you in school? We were actually supposed to go back tomorrow. Guess that isn't happening now," she said.

"Yeah, I was home from college for the holidays. Hey, that would work," I answered just as my phone began to buzz. I looked at my phone. "Speak of the devil."

Mentally preparing myself for an ass chewing, I hit the accept button and said, "Hey Dad."

"Where the hell are you?" His gruff tone actually made me flinch.

I glanced over at Cami, who appeared to be struggling to hear, and since I wanted her to trust me, I put the call on speaker.

"Oh, I'm at John's. What's up?" I asked as I focused on Cami nervously picking at her nails.

"Who the hell is John?" my dad demanded, forcing my attention back to the call.

"My roommate…John."

"Why are you in Albuquerque? You weren't supposed to leave yet."

"Dad, have you heard from Scarlett?" I asked avoiding his question.

I was sure my dad would lie to me, but I needed to hear his excuse. He knew that I would do anything for my sister, and he wouldn't hesitate to use my feelings for her against me.

"She's with me…in Red Ridge," he lied without missing a beat.

I caught Cami's attention and raised my eyebrows. "Oh yeah? Put her on. I need to talk to her real quick."

More lies poured from his mouth like it was second nature. "I'm at the lodge, and she's at the house that we're staying in. Why don't you go ahead and head this way. You don't have to be back to the dorm for a couple of weeks. Come and stay here with us until you have to go back to school."

I was used to my dad lying. I was used to him being an asshole. What I wasn't used to was the anger boiling up inside me when he lied to me about the safety of my little sister. Did he seriously not give a shit that his daughter was missing?

"Not going to happen. Look Dad, I don't want to be involved in anything you have going on with the Red Ridge Pack. I already told you that. Tell Scarlett to call me, and then maybe I'll think about coming for a visit. Until I hear from her, I'm staying with John."

"Gavin, you listen to me and you listen good. Get your ass to Red Ridge NOW! I don't want to hear any of your shit right now. All I want is you on this estate!"

Honestly, I had no idea how to respond, so I looked over at Cami. Keeping my eyes on her, I said in the flattest tone I could manage, "I already told you; it's not happening, Dad." Then I ended the call.

CHAPTER 6

Kendall

When we arrived at the estate, we headed straight for the lodge to meet up with Nathaniel, Brian, Noel, and a group of other high-ranking members of the Crescent Hills Pack. Memories came flooding back as we drove down the main road, and I wanted to kick myself when unwelcomed tears welled up in my eyes. I turned my head to look out the passenger-side window, hoping Drew wouldn't notice.

Screw this pack, screw Cade, screw my old so-called friends. Screw them all. They all turned their backs on me, so sure they'd never have to see me again. Not even Becca tried to contact me after I was banished. Well, I couldn't wait to see them now, to see the looks on their faces when they realize that the girl they exiled not all that long ago would soon be in charge.

Drew pulled up in front of the lodge, and as I reached for the door handle, he placed his hand on my other arm to stop me. "You sure you're ready for this, babe?"

Thankful I'd discreetly dabbed away my unshed tears, I slapped on the fake smile I'd perfected over the years and said, "More than ready. Don't worry, baby. I got this."

I may have looked calm and cool on the outside, but butterflies on crack invaded my gut the moment we stepped inside the lodge. After checking in with one of the team leaders of the takedown mission, we were directed down to the jail below the lodge where Drew's father, Brian, and Noel were located, already hard at work pumping the council for information about the pack's business. Crescent Hills needed money quickly, and they didn't seem to be wasting any time.

All heads turned our way as we entered, and passing the cell full of leaders of my old pack brought new meaning to the term *if looks could kill*. But as uncomfortable as I felt, I refused to let them see me crack, so I donned my best you-ain't-seen-nothin'-yet smile and waved.

Nathaniel nodded in greeting as we approached. "Our men are finishing up accounting for all of the Red Ridge members now as well as confiscating all of their communication devices. They are meeting back here when they are finished, and we are keeping their elders here for now."

Drew responded, but I didn't hear him as I found myself in the midst of a serious staring contest with Noel Walker. The bitch started eyeballing me the moment we walked in, and I'd be damned if I'd look away first. She was no longer the alpha female here, and the quicker she realized it, the better. She was either going to submit, or I would be staring her down all damn night.

Drew and his father's conversation continued, and I heard something about Drew's mother staying back in Crescent Hills with the rest of the pack and someone needing to find Nathanial, Drew, and me a suitable place to stay, but with my concentration elsewhere, I only caught bits and pieces.

Then suddenly, a familiar voice rang out, immediately tearing Noel's attention away from me. "Noel, you treacherous whore! How could you do this to *your* pack?!"

My head snapped to the side but not before Noel turned to look first. It was Madelyn Moore, Cami's mother. She always did have a mouth on her. With all eyes on her, Madelyn continued. "Marcus is sick and bedridden, and you—"

Madelyn was cut off by the sound of Nathaniel's booming, wicked laugh. Nathaniel turned to face the cell and stated, "Well, I guess now is as good a time as any...I regret to inform you all that your alpha is dead. But let me assure you, it wasn't at the hands of my pack. The blame for his death lies with his wife, your alpha female, Noel."

As gasps and cries of confusion rang out from the prisoners, Nathaniel glanced over at Noel and shrugged as if to say, *Sorry, but someone needed to take the fall.*

Her face paled and her eyes filled with tears as she turned away from the elders of her pack.

I almost felt bad for her...*almost*. What did she expect? She meant nothing to the Crescent Hills Pack. They needed her to fulfill a job, and now that it was done, she was no longer of any importance.

Cami's father, James, walked over to the bars of the cell nearest to Noel and asked, "So what about your own son, Noel? Where is Cade? Did you kill him too?" A snicker escaped my lips, and I immediately covered my mouth. Noel's head snapped my way just before she grabbed my arm and dragged me up the stairs and outside.

When the door closed behind us, she snapped, "Who the hell do you think you are, Kendall? You need to wipe that smirk off your pretty little face before I—"

Yanking my arm from her grasp, I piped up, "Look, bitch, you're nobody. You mean nothing to me or anyone else; you have absolutely no power here anymore. So don't stand there and act like you have any control over me. You are no longer the alpha female. You're just the Fixer's whore and a traitor who turned on her own pack. If you think for one second that you will ever be anything more than that, then you're even dumber than I thought. And I'd watch what you say to me from now on. I will be the alpha female of this pack soon, and you will be answering to me."

Before she could respond, I turned around and stormed off into the lodge. I didn't need to hear what she had to say. It didn't matter. She didn't matter.

CHAPTER 7

Cami

After the phone call from his father, Gavin and I had been surfing through the surveillance screens for the last few minutes trying to get a handle on what the Crescent Hills Pack was up to now. His nearness was practically killing me, and I debated on going upstairs to change clothes. I felt naked standing next to him in my skimpy PJs, and if he didn't stop checking me out, I was going to either punch him or pounce on him. Damn my trampy hormones.

We were searching for the camera that showed the cell below the lodge when Gavin landed on a screen that made me gasp. "Wait! Stop! Go back!"

"What is it?" Gavin asked as he switched back to the previous screen.

It was really *her*. I knew Kendall was back, but something about seeing her here sent chills down my spine. It appeared that we had just caught the tail end of an argument. But what the hell was Noel doing outside with Kendall? Why wasn't our alpha female in lockdown with the rest of our pack? If only this thing had sound...

"Cami...?" Gavin prodded.

"It really is Kendall Stuart, isn't it? I just can't believe it."

"Who is that woman she just left standing there? Looks like Avery—uh, Kendall just told her off or something."

Gavin was right. Kendall had been right up in Noel's face, no doubt doing her famous *I'm the lead bitch here so back the fuck up* speech. Now Noel was just standing there looking lost in the aftermath of Hurricane Kendall. Without taking my eyes off the screen, I said, "That's our alpha's wife, Noel Walker. And I'd pay good money to find out why she's out there instead of locked in the cell with the rest of council."

Gavin sat back in his chair and turned toward me. His heated gaze sent my mind to a place it shouldn't be, and it irritated the shit out of me. With a constant gleam of playfulness combined with a hint of intrigue there, I could easily get lost in the dark recesses of his tempting eyes. Crossing his arms over his chest, he asked, "So, tell me about Avery…or Kendall, or whatever. What'd she do to get banished?"

I had some questions of my own about how Kendall Stuart ended up with the next alpha of Crescent Hills, but he needed to know just how low this girl would stoop to get what she wanted. "You want the short version or the extended version? She's a piece of work, to say the least."

Gavin's laugh made me smile. "That I already know. How about the version somewhere in between?"

"Oh, where to start? She was with Cade for a long time and was determined to be the alpha female of this pack. In fact, she thought it was a done deal, and it kind of was. But then Allison came to town, and Kendall's best-laid plans went to shit. Cade fell hard for Alli, who ended up being his true mate. So, in short, Kendall hooked up with this crazy guy named Dylan, and they kidnapped Alli to weaken Cade and planned to kill him. But it didn't work out so well. Cade found them, Dylan got killed, and Kendall got banished. And that was the last I'd heard about her until now."

Gavin's eyes went wide. "Holy hell! I knew she was ruthless, but I'd have never guessed she was capable of that. I wonder if Drew knows."

"Well, if he does, then he's as crazy as she is. Okay, now it's your turn. How did she end up as a member of the Crescent Hills Pack?"

Gavin shrugged and looked away. "I don't really know. She just kinda showed up one day. When we first met, she actually tried to hook up with me, but as soon as she realized that being with the son of the Fixer didn't really amount to much, she sought out Drew and pursued him like a lioness in heat. But even after she managed to stake her claim as the next alpha female, she never really stopped coming on to me behind Drew's back."

"What?" I practically shouted. I guess it was my turn to be shocked. Was he actually telling me he'd been messing around with the evil bitch hell-bent on taking over my pack?

As soon as the word left my mouth, Gavin sat up in his chair and reached out to touch my knee, but I moved away before he could make contact. "No Cami, don't get the wrong idea here. Kendall means nothing to me."

Oh, this was just getting better and better. I shot up from my chair, now fuming. "So, what, it was just a casual hook-up whenever Drew wasn't around? Maybe you should have mentioned this earlier. I'm pretty sure Phillip wouldn't be protecting you if he knew you were screwing the enemy!"

I stalked off across the room, but Gavin was hot on my trail. "Cami, don't leave. That wasn't what I meant. Just listen to me, damn it!" I stopped just in front of the door, turned around, and crossed my arms over my chest. My death-to-Gavin glare must have had the desired effect because he took a few steps back before he continued. "That came out all wrong. There is and never was anything between Kendall and me. She may have tried, but I never wanted anything to do with her. I mean it."

I didn't know what to believe. Everything was just so screwed up, and it didn't help matters that his pack was to blame. How the hell was I supposed to trust him? Finally, I decided it was time to ask the question I should have asked a long time ago. "What is your pack really doing here? I mean, what's their endgame?"

Gavin shifted his weight from one foot to the other as his gaze fell to the floor. "I really don't know."

"What the hell do you mean *you don't know*? Your father is like the freakin' ringleader!"

"Look, I don't know what their endgame is. All I know is that my pack is in a lot of financial trouble because one of our members drained the pack's bank account and took off. Our business suffered because of it, and we ended up having to refinance our land and homes in hopes of turning things around, but it didn't work out. So, now it's in foreclosure and we are losing everything. Our alpha came to my father with a plan to take over your pack's land and business and that's all I know. I don't know what happens next."

The truth was, after they got what they needed there wouldn't be much hope for my pack. Either we join them, if that was even an option, or they kill us. And the guy standing before me was still one of them; that, I needed to remember.

My hand was on the doorknob, and I almost left, but the fear that had been brewing inside me all night was quickly turning into anger, a raging, boiling anger that would easily consume me if I'd let it.

When I looked up and my eyes met his, everything I'd been holding back began spewing out of my mouth. "You know, I just love how you keep saying *we, we, we*! It's quite telling, really. Here I am protecting your ass, risking my life and my parents' lives for you! I don't even know you, but you've made it pretty clear that you're one of *them*! You're all *my* pack and *your pack,* blah, blah, blah. So what the hell am I doing here with you? The fucking enemy!"

"Whoa! I am not the enemy here! I was just trying to be honest with you and tell you what I knew, so don't stand here making accusations about shit you don't understand! I can't help who my father is, and I certainly can't control his actions. And I think it's safe to say that after today, they are no longer *my* pack! So you need to slow your fucking roll!"

Oh my God! He was so frustrating! Slow my what? What the hell did that even mean? I turned the knob and opened the door to keep myself from yelling at him. Otherwise, I was going to go bat-shit crazy on his ass. Before I walked out, I warned, "Just so we're clear, if it comes down to outing you or protecting the people I actually care about, I won't hesitate to throw you to the wolves. Pun intended. And you need to stay in this room. I mean it, Gavin. You put me in danger, and I'm done with this shit. I'm outta here."

Once the door was shut and locked behind me, I sank to the floor right there in the closet and let the tears fall that I'd been struggling to hold back in front of Gavin. The last thing I needed was to let him see me cry.

CHAPTER 8

Gavin

I was jolted awake by the shrill sound of my cell phone ringing. The room I was sleeping in was pitch-black, so I had to feel around on the nightstand for it. I held the phone up to my face and squinted to see who was calling me so early in the morning. Not recognizing the number, I answered hesitantly. "Hello."

There was just silence, and I almost ended the call when I heard her voice. "Gav?"

"Scarlett? Is that you? Where are you?" I asked sitting up in the bed and grasping my phone in both hands. I held my breath and waited to hear her voice again, silently praying my ears hadn't been deceiving me the first time.

"Gavin...it's me. God, it's so good to hear your voice," she said and I could tell that she was crying. "Gavin...Dad...Dad tried to kill us. He ran our car off a bridge and left us to drown in the freezing water. Can you believe it, Gavin? He actually wanted me dead," she cried, and I could hear her mate, Luke, comforting her in the background.

I knew what she said, but I was having a hard time digesting it. My father tried to kill his own daughter! Just saying it in my head made me want to strangle the life out of the man. A heavy, weighty feeling settled over me, and I had to push my covers off just to try and alleviate some of it before it crushed me. I stood up and began pacing back and forth in the small bedroom.

"Are you okay, Scar? Please tell me you're okay. If you're not okay, I swear to God I will kill that son of a bitch. I just might anyway," I said as I wiped away the tears that were pooling in my eyes.

"We're all fine, but it was horrible, Gavin. Cade's Dad's Tahoe sank so fast, and the water was so cold. We saw them search the water, but it was so dark, and it was raining really hard, so they gave up pretty quickly. For now, they probably think we're all dead, but when they don't find our bodies, they're going to know that we're alive."

"Where are you?" I asked.

"Staying at a motel outside of Red Ridge."

"Good. Stay there. Don't come here. Things here are crazy. I'm hiding in a fucking safe room built into somebody's freaking closet."

"What? Why?"

"When our pack attacked, Luke's dad, Phillip, handed me over to Cami. She's been hiding me in a safe room that her parents built. I was beginning to go crazy not knowing where you were. Of course, our lying-ass father told me that you were here on the estate. He thinks I'm staying with John until the dorms open back up for the spring semester," I explained.

"Oh my God, Gavin. I can't believe any of this is happening." There was some shuffling in the background and muffled voices, and then Scarlett said, "What? No...fine," to someone else in the room with her. "Gavin, okay...listen, Cade wants to talk to you. He needs to know what's going on there, so I've got to go. I love you, Gavin," she said before handing the phone over to Cade.

I told Cade all about what had been going down on the estate in as much detail as possible. We agreed that my presence should remain a secret and that we should communicate daily through this number, so we can figure out what to do. As usual, Cade was all business and the call ended all too soon, but there just wasn't much we could do as of yet.

I knew Cami was going to want to kick my ass for not waking her up to speak with Cade, so as soon as I ended the call, I made sure to check the video surveillance before leaving the safe room and to find her.

Even knowing that Cami and I were the only two people in the house didn't stop me from tiptoeing up the stairs and looking over my shoulders like Jason Bourne as I hunted down Cami's bedroom. After trying two other doors, I'd finally found it.

Cami was sleeping so soundly that it killed me to have to wake her up. I didn't realize that she could be any more beautiful, but I was wrong. Asleep, her face was not just stunning, it was angelic. The tempting red lip gloss was long gone from her lips, but the swollen, sleepy, natural look nearly brought me to my knees. I would have given my left nut to be able to crawl into that bed and wrap her long, sexy legs around me, but if I did, she would probably tear my right nut off with her bare hands. Maybe I could live without one nut, but definitely not both.

Hell, it might have been worth it. I'd never been more tempted.

As if she sensed me watching her, her eyes shot open, and her icy glare landed on me. "What the fuck are you doing out of the safe room? Are you freakin' deaf or just really that stupid?" Cami yelled as she sat up and clutched her covers up to neck. I jumped back from the venom in her voice. I hate to admit, but I was a little scared to open my mouth and say anything. I knew how bad this looked, me standing over her watching her sleep. Now, she probably thought I was a Chester for sure. I had to tell her though. "I just got a call…"

That certainly got her attention. She was out of the bed and standing right in front of me in less than a second. With her hands on her tiny hips, she snapped, "And?"

Man this girl was something else. "It was Scarlett. They are all safe, and they're staying in some motel outside Red Ridge."

"That's great news," she said and then frowned. "Why don't you seem happy about that?"

I didn't want to tell her the rest. I didn't even want to think about it. It was just too humiliating to admit that your own father, the man that raised you, could do something so heinous, but she deserved to hear the truth. She was risking her own life and the lives of her family by hiding me here. The least I could do was tell her everything I knew.

"Cami, it was my…" I started but was silenced by the ringing of the doorbell.

Cami and I both looked at each other like we had been caught doing something naughty. Without making a sound, Cami wildly motioned for me to get back into the safe room. I ran out of her room with her right behind me and down the stairs. As soon as I was inside the safe room, Cami motioned for me to be quiet and locked me inside.

CHAPTER 9

Kendall

First thing this morning, I collected my girls, Shari and Becca, to see how they were doing, but mostly to see their reaction when they realized that I was here with the Crescent Hills Pack and that I would be the next lead female of the pack. To say they were shocked would be an understatement.

Both of their parents had the nerve to tell me that it wasn't a good idea for them to come out, but after I reminded them that decision was no longer theirs, they didn't argue. They were not in charge here anymore, and the sooner they realized it, the better.

Now we were all standing on Cami's doorstep waiting for her to answer, and I couldn't wait to see the look on her face when she saw me standing here. After a couple of minutes, I rang the bell again…and again. "What the hell is taking her so long?"

In her infinite wisdom, Shari replied, "Maybe she's still sleeping."

"Really, Shari? I would have never thought of that one on my own. And here I'd forgotten how freakin' brilliant you are." God! The truth was I'd forgotten what a know-it-all she was. Duh! Like I couldn't have guessed that Cami was still sleeping on my own, so I added, "It's called a rhetorical question, dumbass."

Shari didn't get a chance to apologize for being an idiot because Cami finally decided to open the damn door. She stood there gawking with wide eyes and raised eyebrows. Not a good look for her. Before she had the chance to speak, I threw my arms around her and gushed, "Cami, I'm so excited to see you again! You've missed me, haven't you?"

After a few seconds, she wrapped her arms around me too, but only half-heartedly, and whether she realized it or not, her reaction spoke volumes. It wasn't like I was offended or anything. It simply reminded me just how fake the little bitch could be.

I pulled away and asked, "Well, aren't you going to say anything?"

She slapped a fake smile on her face and let out a nervous giggle. "Sorry, Kendall. I'm just a little shocked. What are you doing here?"

Returning her phony grin, I draped one arm around Becca and the other around Shari and then asked, "Well, aren't you going to invite us in or are you going to make us stand out here in the cold?"

Cami took a step back and swept her arm to the side. Of course, I took the lead as usual, and my minions followed. It was kind of like déjà vu, and I couldn't stop a little smirk from forming on my lips.

Locking the door behind her, Cami asked, "Seriously Kendall. Do you know what the hell is going on here?"

I just kept walking into the living room and then took a seat on the couch. Crossing one leg over the other, I sat back and watched as my girls took their seats as well, but Cami just stood there in front of us with her hands on her nonexistent hips. Skinny little bitch. Jeez, I forgot how much she irritated me too.

When I didn't answer her, she raised her eyebrows again and tilted her head to the side. I suddenly wished I had my phone out so I could snap a pic and show her how ridiculous she looked. Just to wipe the stupid expression off her face, I finally responded. "Come on, Cami. Calm down. Smile for God's sake. I'm back! Don't ruin it with your prissy attitude. I'll tell you all about it, but first, why don't you go get us all something to drink? I'm totally parched."

She huffed and then headed toward the kitchen. Becca leaned over and whispered, "Gah, she's so annoying. Ever since she hooked up with Luke, she thinks she's all that. Don't worry about her, Kendall. Shari and I are thrilled you're back."

I looked over at Shari, and she smiled and nodded. I could hardly believe my ears. Little miss virgin finally gave it up to the biggest player in the pack. What a freakin' moron! "Cami hooked up with Luke? Seriously? What, did he dump her like yesterday's trash when Scarlett came to town? She should have known that the next hot piece of ass that came along would catch Luke's attention. Poor, pitiful Cami. I kinda feel bad for her…well, not really." We all laughed until Cami came traipsing back in with her hands full of a pitcher of tea and four glasses.

Placing everything on the table in front of her, she snapped, "There! Now what's going on?"

Becca immediately poured me a glass and then one for herself, leaving the other two sitting there for Shari and Cami to serve themselves. Now that's why I loved Becca. Her actions were bitchier than her words sometimes.

I watched as Cami finally gave in and sat down, and after taking a drink, I figured it was time to let the girls in on what was about to go down here. "Okay, so obviously you've figured out that I am now a member of the Crescent Hills Pack. After I left here, I ditched my bitch of a mother. She was going to get me nowhere fast, so I hooked up with the CH, and they were more than happy to let me join them. Honestly, I had no idea they were planning to invade Red Ridge until just recently."

I paused for effect, trying to look as innocent as possible, before I continued. "Anyway, they just need the land and money or something. Apparently, someone screwed up royally and we are losing our land. So, here's the deal, girls. They're not looking to hurt anyone. As long as you stick with me and follow orders, you'll all be just fine. I think they're going to give everyone the opportunity to join them or leave. In fact, I'm pretty sure they plan on gathering everyone for a meeting soon."

Cami sat back and crossed her arms over her chest before she said, "So, what, we are all just supposed to sit back and let Crescent Hills take over everything?"

"Yeah, pretty much. It doesn't appear that you guys have much of a choice, does it? But don't worry. I haven't gotten to the best part. I'm with Drew Barnes, the alpha's son, which means I'll be the alpha female before long and everything will be just the way it should have been before the Wrights weaseled their way into this pack. And we will all be together again. It will be just like old times!"

CHAPTER 10

Cami

After an excruciatingly long forty-five minutes, I was more than ready for Kendall to get the hell out of my house. I could only keep up my *oh-I'm-so-glad-you're-back* façade for so long, and Kendall had a special gift for reading people. If she hadn't seen through me already, she surely would soon enough. It was one of the things that made her the ultimate mean girl. She could sense weakness and fear, and intimidation was her most valuable weapon.

If the whole situation weren't so screwed up, I would have found it all quite entertaining. Shari and Becca both looked scared shitless, but I'd have to guess for completely different reasons. Becca spent the last couple of weeks trying to hook up with Drew. She thought she sealed the deal when she made out with him at the New Year's Eve party, and then when he wasn't all over her the next day, it only made her try harder. I had no idea how far they went, but I wouldn't be surprised if it was all the way. Becca didn't give up all that easily.

Shari, on the other hand, obviously didn't want to be sitting there with her old BFF. Sure, she wore the smile and followed along just like she used to, but it wasn't because she was happy Kendall was back. I knew Shari better than that. She had changed a lot since Kendall left, and now she was merely trying to survive the situation, just like me.

Sensing that Kendall was growing bored of our little get-together, I decided it would be a good time to pull her aside before she left. I wasn't sure if she'd be willing to part with any more information than she'd already shared, but I figured it couldn't hurt to ask.

Once we were out of earshot of the other girls, I asked, "Are you being straight up with us, Kendall? Is your pack really going to let us decide whether we want to stay or leave? Just like that?"

She cocked her hip to the side and tilted her head. "Would I lie to you, Cami? You know you can count on me to keep you safe. As long as you stick by my side, you'll be just fine." Then she tucked my hair behind my ear and whispered, "Just be thankful you're with me. No one will touch you, and once this is all over with, it will be just like it used to be. You, me, Becca, and Shari. You'll see."

I didn't reply. I just stood there and looked into her eyes trying to gauge if she actually believed the words that were coming out of her mouth or if she was just as full of shit as she used to be. I couldn't tell, but it didn't matter. Either way, I knew that it wouldn't be as simple as she'd said.

After a quick hug, Kendall made her grand exit with Becca and Shari following close behind. I almost threw up in my mouth when Kendall turned around, did her signature Betty Boop move, and said, "Kisses!"

Before the door closed, I caught Shari's attention. She simply shrugged, but the expression in her eyes confirmed what I already knew. She was just playing along, treading water, trying to figure out what the hell to do.

I waited a minute or two before I ran upstairs to look out my bedroom window to make sure the coast was clear. Then I hurried back down to the safe room to talk to Gavin. He was staring at the surveillance screens when I entered, but was at my side within seconds as soon as he saw me. "What did they want? What did Kendall say?"

I took a step back because his nearness always seemed to knock my senses off kilter. "She said to stick with her and everything would be okay. That her pack would give us all the option to stay and join Crescent Hills or leave. And of course, she didn't fail to mention that she was with Drew and would be the next alpha female once this was all over with."

Running his hands through his hair, Gavin shook his head and sighed. "It's all bullshit. She's lying. There is no way that is ever going to happen. They may allow a few to stay, those who somehow manage to prove their allegiance to CH, but other than that, I can't believe they'd just let you all walk away. It would be too much of a risk. Red Ridge could regroup and try to take back what was theirs."

My heart pounded so hard in my chest that I could hear it drumming in my ears. He was right, and I knew it, but the alternative was just too hard to swallow. They only had one option then, not two. "So, are you saying what I think you are? Is your pack going to kill us all?"

Gavin turned away, unable to look into my eyes. He knew it as well as I did. His pack was ruthless and willing to do whatever it took for the livelihood of their people. Even if it meant the total annihilation of another pack.

My eyes filled with tears, and I didn't want to think about it anymore. If I did, I'd break down for sure, and I couldn't let him see me cry. Instead, I walked past him into the small living room and sat down on the couch. I leaned over, placing my elbows on my knees and blocked my face from Gavin's view. "So, what were you going to tell me earlier? What happened to your sister and the rest of them?"

I didn't look up but heard him walk over and felt him sit down next to me, close but not close enough that we were touching, though his knee was only centimeters away. I may have been imagining it, but it was like I could feel the heat radiating from his body, and that mixed with his masculine scent was a heady combination. Suddenly,

I wasn't thinking of hiding my unshed tears anymore. I kept my head down to conceal the deep blush covering my cheeks.

After a deep intake of air, Gavin said, "It was my father. My own father. That bastard, he…" His voice trailed off, and I instinctively looked over at him. He too was hunched over with his head in his hands, but he was breathing hard, in and out, as if he was trying to calm himself down. I knew I should keep my distance, but I couldn't stop myself. No, that wasn't true; I could have, but I didn't want to.

Moving over, I filled the small gap between us and ran my hand up and down his back. After a few seconds he looked up, and the pain in his deep brown eyes caused my stomach to clinch. Only a moment later, he turned away again, but didn't finish his thought. "Just get it out, Gavin. Whatever it is. Just say it. It's okay," I encouraged as I moved my hand back and forth to stroke his broad shoulders.

His head fell back into his hands as he finished what he had to say. "It was my father. He chased their car and ran them off a bridge. The Tahoe crashed into the water. They all got out unscathed…But, he tried to kill them. He tried to kill my sister. And for now, he thinks he did. He thinks they're all dead."

CHAPTER 11

Gavin

"I need to be at that meeting," I said under my breath, but obviously Cami heard me because she gave me her best *oh-no-you-don't* stare. "I'm not stupid. Of course I know I can't go, but it would be nice to hear what's going on for a change," I explained.

Cami's eyebrows shot up as she turned the television on and brought the lodge up on the main screen. "Oh my God! I completely forgot. The lodge is the only place on the estate wired for sound. Why didn't I think of that earlier?" she asked herself, clearly irritated that she failed to remember that very important bit of information.

"Seriously? How do you forget something like that?" I grumbled, trying my best to sound frustrated, but the effect this girl was having on my body made angry hard to pull off.

Shooting me an icy glare, she replied, "I know, I know, but I'm not usually the *Mission Impossible* spy girl here on the estate. We're lucky I even know any of this is down here. My parents only just showed me right after my sixteenth birthday. Before that, I didn't even know any of this existed."

"Well, I guess should count myself lucky then."

Once Cami figured out how to control the sound, she sat back in her chair and stared at the screen. "There, now you will be able to hear everything."

When I didn't reply, she turned my way and asked, "Hey, are you going to be okay here? You have everything you need?"

"I'll be fine, Cami," I assured her. "Promise me something?"

Cami stood up, and her hand went straight to her hip as her head tilted to the side. Once again, her intoxicating eyes met mine, but she didn't say anything, and for a moment, I lost all thought. Something serious sizzled between us every single time our eyes locked. Well, I felt it, and I could only hope that she sensed the same crazy chemistry I did. If not, then she probably thought I was a total creeper. Realizing that she was waiting for me to say something, I quickly added, "Be careful. You can't trust any of them."

Cami rolled her beautiful brown eyes at me as she turned to leave, and I swore I heard, "Duh," pass those luscious lips of hers.

Once Cami was gone from the safe room the air fell flat, and I needed a cold shower. If I was going to be confined here with Cami for much longer, I had a feeling I would be spending a lot of time standing under the cold water, so I might as well get used to it.

I settled down in front of the television with some pretzels and prepared myself for the spectacle I was about to watch. Scanning the lodge, I noticed the Red Ridge members were sitting together in a small area off to the left and being eerily quiet for a pack that had just been through hell. I half-expected them to be shouting and making demands for their release. I assumed that they were afraid of what would happen if they spoke up, especially since they were still surrounded by armed guards.

Finally, I spotted Cami squished between the two girls that had shown up here with Kendall earlier. I figured she'd be sitting with her parents, but they were set apart from the group, along with Phillip, and they were being guarded by Justin Maples, a hothead who wouldn't hesitate to put a bullet in someone's brain for looking at him the wrong way.

My own pack seemed to have already made themselves at home as they took up most of the space in the lodge, forcing RR to fit in one tiny side area. I cringed when I noticed Drew sitting at the front with one arm draped over Kendall's shoulder, but his eyes were on

Lacey Campbell, a girl who'd be down on her knees in front of him in a second given the opportunity. What a prick.

It wasn't long before Nathaniel walked up to the podium to address the crowd with Clayton and my jackass of a father at his side. Nathaniel turned his attention to the members of the Red Ridge Pack, cleared his throat, and began immediately. "First off, let me commend you all for your patience and obedience during this arduous time. I want to be straight with you and gain your trust. Therefore, I'm afraid I have some bad news to deliver. As you know, your alpha has been very ill. Unfortunately, he took a turn for the worse and has passed away."

When the members of the Red Ridge Pack instantly exploded into screams and sobs, Nathaniel gave them a moment before he continued. "Believe me when I say you have our deepest sympathies." *Bullshit!*

As I looked around at the faces of the devastated pack, my heart ached for them. There was a time when I would have grieved over the loss of our own alpha, but not anymore. I'd seen and heard too much. And when he opened his mouth to tell his next lie, I nearly fell out of my chair.

"Without leadership, you are left in a vulnerable position, so vulnerable in fact that we were able to just walk right onto this estate and take over, but that is not why we are here. Members of Red Ridge, let me assure you, we are here to help. We want you to join us…accept us. Accept me as your new alpha, and we can become the biggest and strongest werewolf pack in the country," he announced.

One brave pack member stood and said, "We do have leadership. Well, we will. Marcus's sons, Cade or Aiden, one of them will step up and take command."

That one remark started the uproar that led to Nathaniel clearing his throat dramatically once again. When that didn't work, he roared, "Settle down!" a bit louder than necessary. When the rival pack members calmed themselves, he continued. "That brings me to the second piece of bad news. Cade was driving his father's Tahoe late last night. It must have been the bad weather that caused him to lose control of the SUV. Our men witnessed his car drive off Old River Bridge and into the river below. I'm sorry to say that inside the Tahoe were Cade, Aiden, Luke, Allison, and our own Scarlett. It pains me to say, there were no survivors."

I saw Phillip drop his head into his hands, and then the woman a few rows over shrieked and covered her mouth with her hands. The younger girl next to her dropped her head and turned into the woman, who wrapped her arms around her. Their pain was real and raw, and as the tears rolled down their cheeks, I realized they must have been Aiden's mother and mate. The mother had just been told, in front of everyone, that both her children were dead. The man next to her, surely Aiden and Alli's father, wrapped his arms around the both of them as they wept, and then his shoulders shuddered too as they all sobbed together.

I was suddenly ashamed to be watching them. There I was, sitting back eating pretzels while they were living through a nightmare that I knew was untrue. I had to turn away from the screen. It was too intimate…too personal. Seeing them suffer, seeing Phillip, who had been nothing but kind to me, tormented by the news broke my heart into pieces.

Ignoring everyone's pain, Nathaniel began to explain how joining the Crescent Hills Pack was completely optional. He actually told them that if they refused to join them that they could leave without any repercussions. I knew he was full of shit. There was no way he would ever just let them leave. I really hoped that they didn't buy any of that crap. Nathaniel even went as far as to promise to appoint a few Red Ridge members to his council of elders.

From the looks on their faces and the blanket of silence in the room, it was easy to see that no one gave two shits about pack politics. They had just found out that people they loved and respected were dead. No one in that room was worried about anything but that—well, except my pack members of course.

Our alpha gave a Cliff's Notes version of what was to come, telling Red Ridge that housing arrangements would be made over the next few days and that CH would be taking over the business end of their pack, but who knows if anyone from Red Ridge heard a thing he had said. Tears flowed, heads were in hands, faces were either completely blank or overcome with anguish.

Finally, Nathaniel began to wrap up his speech. He picked up the gavel and announced, "One more thing." Everyone's head popped up like they were expecting even more bad news. What they heard brought angry scowls and hateful glares toward the alpha. "Until the next meeting, you are not allowed to leave your homes. At that time, we will have plans of how we wish to proceed from here on out. In the meantime, you will be given one hour of guarded recreation time each day beginning tomorrow, and you will receive further instructions via the intercom system. Thank you for your patience. This meeting is adjourned."

CHAPTER 12

Kendall

Immediately following the meeting, all of the members of the Red Ridge Pack were sent back to their homes with the exception of Phillip and Cami's parents. Apparently, they didn't feel comfortable having the enforcer loose on the premises; and well, Cami's parents, I would have to guess they just wanted to teach them a lesson for their outbursts toward Noel. So, instead of sending them home with everyone else, the three of them were sent back to the cell.

Nathaniel called a brief meeting in the lodge with our pack where he handed out assignments. Mostly, he directed which men were to guard what and where, but Drew was instructed to gather a small group of people to conduct random searches of homes and to map out the estate to look for weaknesses in their security. Noel was told to draw up temporary living arrangements for our pack members who were here on the estate. She proceeded to ask some of the other women to help but intentionally left me out. Shocker!

In the end, I was left standing there with nothing to do. I was supposed to be a leader here. I knew this land just as well as Noel, and I was the one who would be leading by Drew's side soon, yet I was left out of everything. That was *so* not okay, but I decided it would be best to keep my mouth shut, and I promised myself to continue to do so, at least until I got Drew alone.

I waited patiently until everyone dispersed and went about their business and then tried to grab Drew's attention before he ran off with his men, but it was like he was deliberately ignoring me. Before

I knew it, I was hanging around in the middle of the lodge alone, so I gathered my purse and stormed off toward the house we were staying in.

On my way out the door, Noel, who was off in a corner with her little helpers, caught my eye and smiled. Fucking smiled. That bitch! She was so going to regret that shit. Screw these people. Just to prove that being left out didn't bother me, I smiled back, waved, and said as sweetly as possible, "You all have a good night. I'm headed home to take a nice, long bath. Don't work too hard now."

To my surprise, I hadn't been home long when Drew showed up. As soon as he walked in, he saw me on the couch and headed my way. He leaned down, slid his hand up my shirt, and tried to kiss me.

When I turned my head, he moaned. "Come on, baby. What's wrong? I don't have much time, and I want to taste you so bad. Don't hold out on me."

He continued to feel me up, not caring in the least that I was pissed off. Well, two could play that game. I pulled him down on the couch and crawled over to straddle him. He leaned up for a kiss, but I pulled back and flashed him a wicked grin as I rocked my core against him until I felt him harden beneath me. His hands grabbed my hips, and he guided my body to grind harder back and forth against his length. His eyes rolled back in his head as he whispered, "Baby, I want you so bad."

I leaned in and sucked on his earlobe until I felt him shudder, and then I replied, "Go fuck yourself, Drew." Then, I got up and wandered into the kitchen to make myself some tea. He was so stunned that he didn't even try to stop me, but that only lasted for a moment. He jumped up off the couch and followed me. "What the hell was that, Kendall?"

Turning to face Drew, I shrugged and replied, "I don't know. I guess I'm just not that into it. Maybe I just have too much going on right now...Oh wait! That can't be it because I have nothing going on! Nothing! I'm supposed to be the alpha female soon and no one has bothered to include me in anything!"

Drew took a step toward me and threw his hands up in air. "Seriously? That's what this is about? You're throwing a little tantrum because you feel left out. Get a freakin' grip, would ya? I don't have time for this shit!"

"A tantrum? What do you think I am? A fucking toddler? And don't tell me to get a grip. I'd be a major asset if you'd let me. You could have easily stepped in and given me a role here. This is *my* pack, and I know more about these people and this land than anyone!"

In two large strides, Drew was right up in my face, his nose practically touching mine. He yanked my hair, forcing my head back to look up at him. "Did I hear you right? Did you just say that Red Ridge is *your* pack?"

My eyes went wide as I realized my mistake. "No! Baby, that's not what I meant. I promise. I didn't mean it like that!"

Drew didn't let go of my hair and had me pinned against the counter with his body. With his free hand, he ran his fingers over my hips and then down the front of my pants. "That's what I thought. Now if you're finished throwing your little fit, turn around and bend over so we can finish what you started in there."

*****

It wasn't long before I'd locked myself in the bathroom and hopped in the oversized bathtub for a nice, long soak. I needed to clear my head. When Drew had finished with me, he zipped up and walked away, leaving me standing in the kitchen all alone. No goodbye, no kiss, no assurance that he'd be back. I shouldn't have been surprised.

I knew what I'd gotten myself into when we'd made our relationship official. He could be rough and mean and would most likely never be faithful, but if I wanted to lead this pack, sacrifices would have to be made. Besides, I should have known better than to tease him in the first place.

My eyes were closed and I lay back in the bubbly water, relaxing and enjoying the silence. But no matter how hard I tried, one face refused to stay out of my mind. I'd tried to ignore my feelings since I'd first laid eyes on him, but he never strayed far from my thoughts, and I couldn't stop wondering where he was and why he wasn't here…couldn't stop wishing he was here with me now.

I dried my hand with the towel near the tub and grabbed my phone. I scrolled down to find his name and pushed send before I had the chance to talk myself out of it. After a few rings, it went to voicemail, but I didn't hang up. I needed to hear his voice even if it was just a recording.

"This is Gavin. You know what to do. But I don't check this shit, so text me. Laters."

CHAPTER 13

Cami

My mind was in one big cloudy haze of FML. I needed to talk to my parents and Phillip, all of whom were shipped right back down to the underground cell immediately following the bullshit meeting. And of course, I needed to get to the Wrights too. They all needed to know that their children were alive and safe outside of Red Ridge, but yeah, that didn't happen. And poor Teagan. She and the Wrights were almost instantly lost in the crowd on the way out, and I was shoved off in the other direction by a couple of the CH guards.

I wandered around after the meeting for a lot longer than I should have and knew I was asking for trouble, but I just couldn't go back to that house yet. Everything was so screwed up, and my brain was somehow in overdrive and lost in a tangled mess of what-ifs. I'd managed to avoid the CH guards for a while until I stumbled over some debris on an overgrown path and ran smack dab into one of them, who caught me by the arm to steady me. "You okay, Miss?"

I looked up at him and shrugged out of his grasp. "Yeah, sure. I'm just what-the-fuck-ever, you know?"

His eyes danced as he laughed at my response. Surprisingly, they were kind eyes, but he was the enemy, so I kept walking. He said something else, but I didn't bother listening and didn't turn back. After that, my head stayed down until I arrived at my front door. Before I opened it, I made sure to make plenty of noise in case Gavin was dumb enough to be out in the house in broad daylight.

The last thing we needed was for me to swing open the door and have someone passing by see him inside.

For once, Gavin was nowhere in sight, so I figured he might actually be in the safe room where he was supposed to be. I almost plopped down on the couch in the living room but had a strong suspicion that it would only draw Gavin out of the safe room and piss me off, so instead, I headed straight there to talk to him about the meeting.

I had barely taken a step inside before Gavin was practically on top of me. "Whoa, big guy. Back it up, would ya?" I tried to play it off, but every time the boy was near, my heart raced, and I had the urge to throw myself into his arms and wrap myself around his slender waist. And considering the just-going-through-the-motions mood I was in, being near Gavin could be dangerous.

He took one step back, just enough space to allow me to step inside, turn around, and lock the door. However, when I turned back around, he was right there towering over me, looking down at me with those deep, dark eyes and a cocky little smirk on his perfectly kissable lips. He was so freaking frustrating!

I huffed and pushed past him as I asked, "So did you hear everything? What'd you think?"

He followed me over to the tiny love seat and flopped down next to me, but this time, he threw his arm around the back of the couch, resting it on the cushions, not touching me but still too close for comfort. His scent, a mix of manly body wash and some unidentifiable yumminess, drifted my way, and before I realized what I was doing, I closed my eyes and inhaled deeply.

But my eyes shot open when I felt his fingers wrap around my shoulder and pull me ever so slightly toward him. In my peripheral vision, I could tell he was looking my way, but my eyes stayed focused straight ahead, too chicken-shit to look anywhere else.

His head fell back against the wall behind us when he finally decided to speak. "Yeah, I heard it all. And it's all bullshit. All of it. Do you really think they're just going to let you all just walk out of here? If so, you people are more naïve than I thought."

I jerked away from him as if his words had stung me and turned toward him. "Excuse me? *You people*? Are you freaking kidding me right now? Who the hell do you think you're calling naïve?"

Gavin actually had the nerve to reach for my hand, but I stood up and took a step back. He let out a frustrated sigh and ran his hands over his head. "No, that's not what I meant, Cami. Gah, everything I say just comes out all wrong. I'm just pissed they're actually feeding you that line of bullshit."

"And what, you're just worried we're all stupid enough to believe it? Is that it?"

"No…I don't know. I just don't know what to do, and I feel like I'm just stuck here, and I can't do anything about it. I want to kill my dad for what he did to Scarlett and for what he's doing now, but I can't, and it's driving me insane."

Gavin was up now and pacing back and forth, rage brewing in his eyes. I couldn't help but feel bad for him. He was kind of like a caged dog, but there was nothing I could do about it either. We were all stuck in a holding pattern until somebody figured out what to do, and our situation seemed more and more hopeless by the second. I mean, how long did we really have? What was his pack going to do? Line us all in front of a firing squad? Gun us down? They sure as shit weren't going to just let us walk away. Were they?

I walked over to the surveillance monitors and began navigating through the screens. "Look, I have to sneak out of here tonight and get to the Wrights' house. I can't get to Phillip, but at least I can talk to Lilly and Paul and Teagan. They need to know that Aiden, Allison, and the rest of them are safe. I can also check out the perimeter and see if and how I can get out of here so I can meet up with them. We have to do something. Who knows how much time we have?"

Gavin stopped in mid-stride and said, "What? Have you lost your mind? You're going to get yourself killed! You can't just sneak around out there. You certainly can't just sneak off the estate!"

"Well, I can't just sit here and do nothing. According to you, that's what's going to get us all killed! Besides, I've spent the last four years sneaking out of this house right under my psycho-Nazi parents' noses, and I know every secret path, hiding place, and escape route this estate has to offer. If anyone can do this, I can."

I didn't look away from the screen, but I heard Gavin's pounding footsteps heading my way. A second later, my chair was being spun around and I was facing him. He squatted down before me, his eyes pleading as he said, "You can't do this, Cami. It's too dangerous. Let's just wait for Cade. He'll call soon. He'll know what to do."

His hands held on to each of the armrests, caging me in. If I leaned in just the slightest bit, our lips would be only a breath apart, and if he met me halfway, I'd finally know what it would be like to taste him, to have his lips against mine, his tongue exploring my mouth, mine exploring his.

Desire rushed through me, and as if I wasn't in control of myself, my body began to lean forward ever so slowly. My eyes trained on his, I watched as Gavin did the same. The intensity in his eyes was scorching, and my entire body was on fire. But when his hand moved from the armrest to my thigh, something in my brain snapped.

Shit! I can't do this! What the hell am I thinking?

I jumped up out of the chair and asked, "You hungry? I'm starving! I'll go make us something to eat. You stay here. It's still light out. I'll bring it to you."

My sudden launch out of the chair had knocked Gavin on his ass. He just sat there, wide-eyed with his arms wrapped around his knees and watched as I fled from the room. Could I have made more of a fool of myself? I think not.

*****

I'd gone straight to the kitchen and made us both some sandwiches and chips, grabbed a couple of Cokes from the fridge, and then froze before I headed back to the safe room. I set my own drink and food down on the kitchen table and decided to just drop his off. I didn't need to be near him. In fact, I needed some serious distance from that guy. He made me crazy, and the last thing I needed right then was to lose my mind.

So, I opened the safe room door, walked in, and handed Gavin his dinner. Without another word, I turned and walked out. I grabbed my food from the table and headed up the stairs to my room. For the rest of the evening, I sat in my spot and watched from the window as the CH guards paced back and forth along the main road.

The sun had been down for hours, and I'd spent the entire time watching the guards: their path, their shift change, who was lazy and who was distracted easily. I perked up as soon as I saw a guard I recognized, the one with kind eyes. Then, I noticed a girl around my own age tiptoe over and hide near a tree. She caught his attention and waved him over. A broad smile broke out across his face, and I recognized that look immediately. He gestured for her to move toward the tree line and within a few seconds they had both disappeared. It was time to make my move.

CHAPTER 14

Gavin

"Goddamn her. What the hell is she doing?" I muttered to myself as I watched the screen showing Cami scaling her way down the tree outside her bedroom window. Ever since she mentioned sneaking out, I'd shamelessly been glued to every camera angle I could find that had a view of her home.

She was going to get caught and get herself killed. I briefly considered going after her, but what would that accomplish? Besides, she was obviously committed to being a complete moron since she was already out of the house and running off into the night. If I chased her down now, it wouldn't stop her. She would just be even more pissed off at me. Then, it would cause a scene and get us caught for sure. Damn her stubborn ass!

I hurried over to the surveillance screens and tried to find her on the cameras. If I couldn't go after her, at least I could watch and make sure she was as good at sneaking around as she claimed to be. As soon as I found her on one camera, she would disappear only to turn up on another screen a moment later. I wanted to strangle her for putting herself in such danger, but as I watched her make her way around the estate, my anger began to fade, and I was just flat-out worried.

Every time I lost her on the TV, I held my breath until I found her again. The very thought of her being caught made my stomach roll. If one of those guards dared lay a finger on her, he would have hell to pay. I'd always been the protective type, but the way I felt in that moment verged on obsessed…crazed even. I didn't want to watch the screen, but I couldn't look away either. With my eyes glued to the screen, I toggled through the cameras, trying to keep up with her.

But then my view was blocked for two freaking seconds, and she was gone. I'd started sweating, and in the time it took for me to pull my shirt over my head, she had vanished. My heart pounded in my chest as I searched camera after camera for any signs of Cami. It was complete torture to watch her purposely put herself in danger, but the not knowing, the not seeing her, was another kind of pain entirely.

The longer she remained hidden from sight, the worry I felt quickly shifted back to fury. Why did she have to be so freaking stupid? She could have waited until tomorrow. She would have had the perfect opportunity during their recreation time to speak with Aiden's family. It could have waited. She was just being reckless.

Frantically I searched camera view after camera view for any sign of her, for who knew how long before finally giving up and forcing myself to leave the screen focused on the Wrights' home and sit back in the chair to wait.

Thankfully I didn't have to wait long. Almost as soon as my back hit the chair, I saw her for just a moment as she rounded the corner from the back of the Wrights' home. As I let out a breath I hadn't realized I was holding, I was instantly assaulted with an array of emotions. I'd never been so pissed at someone, yet at the same time, so relieved that she was safe. I wanted to strangle her and then kiss every inch of her body. However, something told me she'd most likely be opposed to both.

Pushing those thoughts aside, my eyes toggled back and forth between the screen and the clock as I waited for her to re-emerge. After a few excruciatingly long minutes, she appeared on the screen once again, and I watched every step she took back to her house.

When I heard her slip back inside, I rushed out of the safe room.

She was in the kitchen getting herself a glass of water when I walked in. She read the expression on my face and said, "Just give me a second, Gavin, before you freak out on me, okay?" I leaned against the wall behind me and crossed my arms over my chest while she gulped down the cold water. I could tell she was flustered, but she wasn't getting out of this talk. What she did was foolish and unnecessary, and frankly, it scared the shit out of me.

"Come on," she said, knowing that I wasn't going to give up, and she motioned for me to follow her back into the safe room. Once we were locked safely inside the soundproof apartment, her shoulders sagged. "All right, let me have it."

I was about to lay into her when my phone began to ring, startling us both. I pulled it out and looked at the caller ID before pressing ignore and shoving it back into my pocket.

"What the hell were you thinking, Cami? Do you know what would happen if they found you sneaking around out there? Do you? Do you think they wouldn't kill you? What? Because you're young? Because you're female? Because you're beautiful? They would. My father would do it without a second thought. Why do you have to play the goddamned hero here?" I went on and on as she just stood there and took it. "Please make me understand why you had to put yourself at risk tonight. Why this couldn't wait until tomorrow?"

"I just couldn't," she whispered.

"You couldn't what?" I yelled and immediately regretted raising my voice at her when she looked up at me with tears in her eyes.

"I can't sit here while the people I care about are suffering. I can't just do nothing. I couldn't go to sleep tonight knowing that Alli and Aiden's parents think their kids are dead," she yelled back at me.

Without thinking, I pulled her to me and held her tightly. I brushed her hair away from her face and tucked her head under my chin. To my surprise, she didn't push me away. Instead, she let herself cry into my shirt as I gently rubbed her back. When her tears were gone, she pulled away. I lifted her face with my fingers until our eyes met. "Please don't do that again. I was just so worried about you."

"So worried," I whispered again as I pulled her back to me. Just then my phone began to vibrate, and I felt her body tense in surprise, but I didn't let her go. I knew who it was, and I couldn't care less about her text message. I just needed to know that Cami was okay, that she was unharmed.

I had a sudden urge to strip her bare and worship her body as I made sure there wasn't a mark on her silky skin. I couldn't stand the tension between us anymore, and if I didn't taste her soon, it was going to kill me. Letting my instincts take over, I took her face between my hands and leaned down to finally press my lips to hers when my fucking phone started up again.

"Just answer the damned thing," Cami said as she pulled away from me before our lips connected. I yanked the phone out of my pocket, silenced it, and tossed it on the nearby table. I didn't want to talk to Av—Kendall. Not now!

"Fine! Then, I will," Cami said picking up the phone. I knew she wouldn't answer it. That would be stupid and more than likely get us caught, but I didn't expect the look on her face when she saw who was calling me.

"Oh look, it's your girlfriend," she teased, but her voice, oozing with jealousy, betrayed her, and I couldn't help but smile. Cami was jealous. Over me. I liked that. I liked that a lot.

"She won't leave me alone. Drew must have pissed her off again," I said trying to explain away any doubt.

"Maybe you should talk to her," she suggested.

I tried to grab Cami's hand, but she moved out of my reach.

"No really, I mean it. Talk to her. Maybe she will tell you something that can help us. It couldn't hurt right?" she asked, making a good point. Kendall did always talk too much.

"You sure?"

Cami nodded and started to leave, but I grabbed her hand and said, "Wait. I'll put it on speaker." With that, I was rewarded by the most beautiful, wicked smile I had ever seen. Cami walked passed me and sat on the loveseat with those long, delicious legs all tucked up underneath her. I fell into the seat next to her as I answered the call.

CHAPTER 15

Kendall

So, I'd officially hit an all-time low. Yes, I, Kendall Avery Stuart, was truly pathetic, and I'd like to say that I wasn't ashamed to admit it, but I totally was. I'd called and texted Gavin entirely too many times and was quickly breaching stalker territory, but Drew never came back home, and I needed to talk to somebody. No, I needed to talk to *him*.

Before I'd hit send, I'd vowed it would be the last time I'd call until he called me back and then was rendered speechless when he actually answered. "Avery, what's up? Everything okay?" His voice was smooth and even and carried just a hint of concern. "Avery? You there?"

After a few more painful seconds of silence, I finally got my head out of my ass and remembered how to speak. "Uh, yeah. It's Kendall now, actually. I've decided to go back to my first name. Did you know Avery is my middle name? So, yeah…I guess you should call me Kendall now." I had no idea where that came from or why it mattered, other than the fact that I wanted to hear him call me by my real name. I wanted him to know my real name, who I really was.

"Okay…Kendall it is then. What's going on, *Kendall?*"

The playfulness in his voice made me smile, and I laid back on my bed feeling more relaxed now. There was just something about this guy…

"I just needed to talk to someone, you know? I wish you were here. Drew's being a total jerk, and I'm just so sick of him treating me like shit." This was by no means the first time I'd complained to Gavin about Drew, and I knew what was coming. Truthfully, it was the reason I'd called so many times. I needed to hear it.

"You know what I'm going to say, Kendall. You don't have to put up with his shit. You deserve so much better. There are tons of guys who would stand in line just to have a chance to treat you like a queen."

Usually, I said *I know* and left it at that, but tonight I was feeling bold. I couldn't explain it. Maybe it was because he wasn't here or because Drew really was being such a douche, but I finally got up the nerve to say what I'd always wanted to say. "Would you?"

"Would I what?"

"Treat me better?"

"Oh no, Kendall. We are not going there. Drew Barnes would probably order Clayton to chop off my balls for even thinking like that, and personally, I really like my balls. We both know you're not going anywhere, so don't toy with me like that, okay? It would only mean trouble for the both of us. But you know I care about you, right?"

My heart did a little fluttery thing in my chest, and I rolled over, gripping the phone like it was a lifeline to the one person in the world who might actually give a shit about me. I felt tears well up in my eyes, and I hated myself for letting him make me feel so damn vulnerable.

"Kendall? You still there?"

"Yeah, I'm here." My voice cracked a bit, and I had to swallow back the lump in my throat. "I'm sorry for bothering you with all of this. I just wish you were here."

"It's okay. You wanna tell me what's going on there? What Nathaniel is really planning?"

"You know Nathaniel. The man is ruthless. I think he will probably allow a few members of Red Ridge to stay. Just those who can somehow either prove their worth or their loyalty. Other than that, I'm guessing after he's gained control of their money and business, he'll just kill the rest of them."

There was a long pause before Gavin spoke again. "That's what I was afraid of."

Pretending I agreed, I said, "I know what you mean. It's just awful. Maybe if you were here—"

"You know that wouldn't matter, Kendall. Besides, I'm not speaking to my father until I hear from Scarlett. He says she's there and fine. Have you seen her?"

Shit! Freaking Scarlett! That bitch has to ruin everything. "Um, yeah. She's here. I haven't seen much of her though. You know she mated with Luke, so she's been uh…kinda busy, if you know what I mean." I laughed trying to make my lie more believable.

A nervous chuckle sounded over the line, and I breathed a sigh of relief, but it was short lived because I heard the front door slam. Drew must have finally decided to come home. Covering my mouth with one hand, I lowered my voice and said, "Hey, I gotta go. Drew's back. Talk to you soon?"

"Sure, Kendall. Talk to you soon."

CHAPTER 16

Cami

Last night was completely jacked up. No, this whole insane situation that has become my life is jacked up. My pack has been taken over, my parents are locked up, and we are all probably going to be executed any day now instead of going back to school, which is what we are supposed to be doing today. Yet, for reasons I couldn't explain even if I was being held at gunpoint, my brain can't seem to focus on anything other than the uber-hot werewolf locked in my parents' closet.

So, instead of contemplating my next move in the *CW* drama that has become my life, I'd spent all of last night and most of this morning pissed off about how the events of last night had played out. First of all, *yay*, mission accomplished. I'd actually pulled off my plan to inform Alli and Aiden's parents that their children were alive and well outside of Red Ridge. Unfortunately, there was no way to get to Phillip, and it was killing me to think that he believed his only son to be dead, but I could only hope he'd find out the truth soon enough.

Then, I made it back here, and Gavin was pissed off, but all sweet and worried too. And he almost kissed me. Almost! I wanted to take his damn phone and throw it across the room hard enough for it to shatter, and that was before I saw who was calling. Once I realized it was Kendall, it took every ounce of willpower in my body to not go bitchcakes on his ass right there with his phone in my hand.

Instead, in my infinite wisdom, I told him to answer it, and then I had to sit there and listen to them flirt with each other, which was bad enough, but after that, Kendall blurts out that their pack is most likely going to kill us all. Yeah, awkward, to say the least.

Once the end button was hit, it was pretty much the end of our conversation as well. I said something like, *Well, I guess now we know your pack is going to kill us all.* And he said, *I'm sorry, Cami.* To which I followed with, *Yeah, that pretty much sucks. I'm going to bed.* Then I stormed out of the room because…Well, that's what I do.

Now, I had to go downstairs and face him. Mr. Can't Listen For Shit was cooking breakfast, which both melted my heart and irritated the piss out of me. Why couldn't he just be a moody asshole who stayed in the safe room? No, he had to be all gorgeous and sweet, and all *I was so worried about you,* and all *let me stare at you while I undress you with my eyes* and shit. It was unnerving!

Before I headed his way, I put my hair up in one of those messy buns that was supposed to appear as if you just threw it up there on top of your head when truth be told, it took like four tries to get it to look perfectly messy. Then I brushed my teeth, swiped on a tiny bit of mascara, and put on my best cleavage-producing push-up bra under my tank top. Hey, if he was going to check me out, I wanted to give him something to look at.

After I was satisfied with my just-rolled-out-of-bed look, I trotted downstairs and into the kitchen. This time, when I wandered into view, I didn't look away when his eyes met mine, and I watched as his eyes slowly traveled down my body. His lips parted the slightest bit as his hungry eyes made their way back up. And just because I was feeling bold, I turned around and pretended to look for something on the table behind me, so I could give him a view of my backside in my very tiny sleep shorts. When I heard him suck in a short breath, I knew I'd gotten the reaction I'd wanted.

But as soon as I turned back around, he was back to busying himself with breakfast-making as if nothing had just happened. He cleared his throat and said, "There's coffee if you want it. And bacon over there on the counter. The eggs are almost finished."

I *so* didn't get this guy. There were times when he looked ready to pounce on me, but up until last night, he hadn't made a move. At one point last night, I'd even convinced myself that I'd imagined our almost kiss. I felt like shouting, "Good God, Gavin! Just do it already!" But then I worried that maybe I was reading him all wrong, and he'd think I was a crazy slut.

But the worst part…The worst part was the fact that I shouldn't even give a shit. Making out with Gavin Reed was the absolute last thing I should be thinking about right now. But I bet he's one hell of a kisser.

*****

It was finally "recreation" time, which really just meant that our pack was allowed to wander around in a designated area outside while armed guards watched our every move. We were given the "privilege" of being able to speak to one another, but the guards were listening, and if anyone spoke for too long or appeared to be trading secrets, they were quickly separated. All we needed were some orange jump suits, a basketball goal, and some free weights, and it really would be like prison rec time, minus the gangs and shit.

Nervous energy coursed through my veins, but if there was any chance of me spreading the word about Cade and the others being alive, I had to play it cool. I scoped out my surroundings and immediately noticed Lilly, Paul, and Teagan talking to Gage, Luke's closest friend. They all looked my way at the same time, and I knew immediately that they had told Gage. He jerked his head to the side, signally me to meet him over by a nearby tree. A guard had just made his pass, which meant Gage and I had at least a minute to talk before the guard came back by.

I meandered over, trying to appear as if I was in no hurry, and met Gage there just as the guard was making his way back toward us. Keeping his head down, Gage said, "We don't have much time, but listen. Stay away from Becca. I don't trust her. Talk to Shari. I'll tell Ryder and Sammy the news. We have to do something. Tell Cade we're in. Whatever it is. We're in. Got it."

I glanced over in the guard's direction. He was getting close, but we had a few more seconds. "I should hear from Cade soon. I'll let you know what he says as soon as I can. And Gage, I think I can get off the estate. We can get out of here if we need to."

Footsteps were upon us, but we were expecting them. "All right, you two. Move it on along. You know the rules." The guards shooed us away from the tree, so we parted ways, but I left feeling a bit more confident knowing that Gage was all in.

My eyes searched the area for Shari and found her easily, but with Becca attached to her hip, there wasn't much I could do. Damn Becca. That girl was going to be the death of me. I wandered over and waited around for Shari to break away from Becca, but it wasn't happening, and my time was running short. I'd noticed that Gage had appeared to have successfully talked to Sammy and Ryder, so at least that went as planned. Finally, with just a few minutes to spare, I heard Gage's voice. "Hey, Becca, come here for a second."

Her face lit up like a damn Christmas tree. You'd have thought he'd just asked her to prom. Letting out a girlie giggle, she scurried over and linked her arm through his. As Gage led her away, he turned back and winked at me. Thank you, Gage! Knowing my time was limited, I grabbed Shari's arm and pulled her away from prying ears. "Listen and don't freak out because people are watching. Cade and the rest of them are still alive." Her eyes went wide, and she let out a small gasp, so I squeezed her arm, hoping it would remind her to keep her cool.

"Shari, you cannot tell Becca. I don't trust her not to tell Kendall. I have a way to contact Cade, and I should hear from him soon, so hopefully we can figure out a way out of this mess. Can I count on you to work with us?"

"Oh my God, Cami. What are we going to do? Who all knows about this?" Her eyes were tearing up, and I knew we needed to end this conversation quickly before one of the guards noticed our path strategically avoided any contact with the CH men.

"I don't know yet, but the Wrights know. And Teagan, Gage, Ryder, and Sammy. As soon as I talk to Cade, I'll find you again at rec, but you have to figure out a way to get away from Becca. Got it?"

Shari nodded and was about to speak when a whistle blew, signaling our time was up. I let go of her arm, and we went our separate ways. Relief flooded my body as I headed back to my house. I could only hope that Shari could be trusted. One thing was for sure; Becca could not know about any of this.

As far as I knew, the only other person who knew about Gavin was Phillip. I hadn't told the Wrights, which meant Gage didn't know, and I intentionally left that part out when I spoke to Shari. If the time came that they needed to know, then I would tell them, but until then, I decided that Gavin's presence here should remain a secret.

When I got back home, Gavin was actually tucked away in the safe room for once, and I contemplated going in there to let him know about the progress I'd made this afternoon but quickly convinced myself that I needed a nap. The truth was that I needed some space, some time to think things through, and when I was around that boy, my brain just didn't function properly.

So, I bypassed my parents' room and headed upstairs to my spot and hung out in my window seat to let my eyes and my mind do their thing.

The next thing I remembered I was being jerked awake by the sound of Gavin's voice. "Cami, are you up there? Cade's on the phone."

I guess I did need a nap after all. As I wiped the sleep from eyes, I stumbled over to the stairs and found Gavin holding on to the railing about halfway up the stairs as if he didn't feel comfortable coming all the way up. With a half-smile, he held out his phone.

As soon as the phone hit my ear, I started to report the good news but was quickly cut off. "Hey, Cade. I made some progress today—"

"Cami, we have a problem. It's Aiden. I can't believe we didn't think of this before, but he's getting sick because…"

"Because Teagan's not there," I finished for him when he couldn't seem to find the words.

CHAPTER 17

Gavin

Not feeling real comfortable about eavesdropping on Cade's call, I went back to my little home after handing Cami the phone, but I knew something was wrong. Cade's voice was tense, and he was more demanding than usual. I was hoping that Cami would let me in on the news, but whether I liked it or not, I was still an outsider, so I wasn't sure she'd include me at all.

A few minutes later, when I heard the door unlock, a smile crept across my face, but it didn't stay long once I saw Cami standing in the doorway. Looking completely wigged out, she marched toward me, handed me back my phone, and said, "We have a problem."

"I figured. What's going on?"

"You know Aiden is mated to Teagan right? Well, he's there and she's here. And now he's getting sick."

"Already?" I asked. Cami didn't say anything. She just nodded her head. "Man, that's fast. That mating shit sucks."

Cami breezed past me and took a seat at the small table in the middle of the room. "No shit. We've got to a get a plan together. The longer Aiden and Teagan are separated the worse he's going to get," she said as she leaned back in the chair. "I know I can get her off the estate; it's just figuring out how to do it with no one realizing that she's gone. It'll be pretty obvious if one of the two humans on the estate goes missing."

"Yeah, I'd say that'd be kinda obvious. Maybe we sneak Aiden back on to the estate? He could stay here in the safe room too." I suggested.

"Oh, I just don't know," Cami huffed, stretching her arms over her head giving me the sexiest view of her tight little stomach. "Did I tell you that I was able to talk to Gage and Shari about Cade and the others today during rec time? And Gage was able to talk to Sammy and Ryder."

I felt my face grow hot as it twisted into what I could only imagine was one hella-angry scowl. Was she freaking insane? Putting us all at risk by blabbing about Cade in broad daylight with guards everywhere was beyond nuts. What if someone heard? Not to mention the fact that the more people that knew, the greater chance we'd have of getting caught. Unbelievable! I covered my mouth with my hand before I said something I'd regret and then moved as far away from Cami as I could in this small-ass room.

"What? Jesus," Cami asked.

I took a couple of deep cleansing breaths as she walked toward me. Then I turned to face her but continued to back away as the words just started spilling out of my mouth. "I can't for the life of me figure out why you would choose to tell everyone about Cade while surrounded by people who would kill you if they heard. It's just ridiculous! I get that you think that you're invincible, but don't you ever think about other people? The guards could have heard you. What if one of your *friends* tells someone else and word gets out to the wrong people? Or what they know gets them killed? How would you feel then?"

As I took a moment to catch my breath, I noticed the paling of Cami's complexion. Her hands were clenched in tight fists, and her jaw was even tighter than before. She opened her mouth to let me have it. "You're overreacting and being an ass. I've already told you that we have to do something. We can't just sit around and do nothing," she fumed.

I turned away from her and ran my hand through my hair, trying to get my temper in check.

"Don't walk away from me. Listen, maybe you don't have the balls to do anything about our situation, hell maybe you like being trapped in this little room, but I *will* do something. I won't watch my pack fall and do nothing," she yelled.

I turned back around and glared down at her little five-foot-nothing frame. "Are you serious? You think I like being trapped here? I'm not too scared to do anything. I'm just trying to be smart about this. The more people who know, the greater the chance of getting caught."

Her dark brown eyes shot daggers right back as she puffed up her chest like a damn blowfish and crossed her arms. "Stop acting like I'm a complete moron. I've kept my eyes open, and I've seen holes in your dad's security. There is a way off the estate. I just have to make my move."

Shit! Now, that freaked me out. What was she going to do? When I didn't say anything, she huffed and threw her hands in the air. "I can't talk to you!"

I have no idea what came over me, but as Cami walked past me, I reached out and grabbed her arm. She swung around to face me, and I couldn't take it anymore. I wrapped my arms around her tiny waist and crashed my lips into hers. I think I was just as surprised by my actions as she was, but I figured I might as well run with it.

I turned us around and backed Cami up until I felt the wall right behind her. I pulled my lips away for only a moment, but in that moment everything changed. I looked at her hooded eyes, her swollen lips, her chest rising up and down, and I softened inside. When I kissed her again, it was gentle this time, and I slowed everything down, taking my time feeling the warmth of her mouth.

Her lips parted, and I slipped my tongue past them so that I could taste her fully. Once her tongue found mine, my body melted into hers. I knew she could feel how much I wanted her, but I didn't pull back. I wanted her to know how much she affected me.

I ran my hands up and down her sides, letting my thumbs graze her stomach. I reached around and cupped her ass, pulling her even tighter against me. A small moan escaped our lips nearly simultaneously. It was that sound that sent us both into a frenzy of need. Finally, Cami put her hands on me. She slid her hands up the back of my t-shirt and dug her nails into my skin as she devoured my mouth.

I wanted to look at her again. I wanted to see all that need on her face and know that I put it there, but pulling away was the worst mistake. As soon as our eyes met again, she pulled her hands out of my shirt and pushed me away. I stumbled back, and we stood staring at each other for a moment before she turned around and walked out of the room without saying a word.

Holy shit! That kiss…that kiss was fan-fucking-tastic. I was so worked up I could barely walk, but I needed to see Cami, so I stumbled over to the TV screen. But I wasn't planning on spying on her in like a creeper way. I just needed to see her face, needed to know what she was thinking. When she pushed me away, I couldn't tell how she felt about what had happened between us. I couldn't read her, and I needed to know.

When I turned on the surveillance camera in her room she had just walked in. At first she looked angry, slamming her door shut and stomping over to her bed. She threw herself down and covered her face with her pillow. I wasn't prepared for the feelings that bombarded me when I saw how upset she seemed. Here I was completely amped, and she looked like she was crying into her pillow. My first instinct was to run up there and tell her I was sorry and that I would never do that again, but that would only make me look like more of an idiot.

So, I fell back into the chair simply devastated, but then I saw her begin to kick her legs around in the air. She looked crazy. I mean, she was lying on her back and kicking her legs around like a cockroach. I leaned forward, puzzled over what I was watching. Cami pulled the pillow off her face, and I couldn't help but laugh. She was smiling from ear to ear, and she looked so happy…perfectly happy as she clutched the pillow to her chest.

CHAPTER 18

Kendall

Bored out of my mind and looking for something to do, I was on my way to Becca's when I heard it. An earsplitting sound I never thought I'd actually hear stopped me dead in my tracks, and I watched as the CH guards froze as well and listened intently into their earpieces. The Red Ridge Pack's emergency sirens blared throughout the estate, and in all the years I'd lived here, I'd never heard them before.

It wasn't until people began to peek their heads out of their doors and the CH guards shouted orders for everyone to stay where they were until instructed otherwise that I managed to convince my legs to actually move. Needless to say, my insides were in total freak-out mode as I sprinted to the lodge to find out what was going on.

I busted through the door just as an announcement was being made over the estate-wide intercom for all members of the Red Ridge Pack to report to the lodge immediately. It appeared a search team was being assembled, so I hurried over to Drew dead-set on getting some information. "Drew, what's going on here?"

He sighed as if I was wasting his time and then grabbed me by the arm and led to over to a hallway. "Babe, I don't gotta lot of time here. Someone escaped. A Jake Larson? We figured a few members might be getting a bit too comfortable here, so after some of the houses were randomly searched we sent another guard or two to search again a few minutes afterwards, to see if we would catch anyone sneaking out. Of course, we targeted houses with guys like

Larson living in them. You know, rule-breakers, risk-takers. Looks like our efforts worked."

"So what now? Are you going out to find him? I want to go! I know this land better than any of you. I can help."

Peering over my shoulder to watch as the members of Red Ridge filed in, Drew let out a deep breath. "Look, they're bringing everyone in for a head count to make sure no one else has escaped. Then, they are sending them back home, with the exception of Larson's family, and putting everyone on lockdown until further notice. We will need your help here at the lodge."

I crossed my arms over my chest, but thankfully resisted the urge to stomp my foot. "You can't be serious. Why the hell can't I help with the search? I've lived here my whole life. You can't tell me that I wouldn't be an asset out there!"

Drew ran his hand through his hair and looked away. "Look, it's not going to happen. My father said no. He wants you here. He thinks you're just too close to this place...to these people."

"What? You know that's bullshit! Maybe you should tell your *father* to go screw himself!"

Before I even had a chance to react, Drew had grabbed me by my arm again and was dragging me further down the hall and then shoving me into a dark room. I heard him kick the door shut with his boot, but I could barely see a thing as my eyes tried to adjust to the dark. He forcefully spun me around until my back was shoved up against the door, and then his body was pressed up against mine.

He held my chin up in his hand and his lips were only a breath away when he finally spoke. "Listen baby, you know I can't do that right now. As much as I want to tell my father to go fuck himself sometimes, you know I can't. Do you hear me? Not yet. But soon, baby, soon, it will be me and you leading this pack. The largest pack in New Mexico."

Grinding himself against me harder, Drew whispered, "Do you feel that, baby? Do you feel how hard that makes me just thinking about it?" And then his lips were on mine, consuming me whole like only he could.

CHAPTER 19

Cami

Stumbling home in yet another daze of FML, I was terrified to return to the scene of the crime—I mean *kiss*. I'd stayed locked in my room all morning avoiding what was sure to be one hell of an awkward encounter until the emergency sirens began blaring throughout the estate. Thankfully, Gavin was smart enough to stay locked inside the safe room even though I was quite sure it was killing him. But, at least he had the luxury of the surveillance system on his side.

Once it was announced for us all to be herded into the lodge like cattle, I'd be lying if I said I wasn't completely petrified. Not once in my entire life had the emergency sirens gone off on our estate, and I couldn't imagine what could have possibly happened to trigger them. I guess I shouldn't have been surprised that I wasn't the only person in our pack who was plotting to escape. I mean, it wasn't like we're all a bunch of sheep around here, but it's amazing how easy it is to be ruled by fear, especially when your captors prove early on that they won't tolerate defiance of any sort. Two of our members *were* killed in cold blood that first night.

What I couldn't figure out was how on earth they figured out Jake was missing so quickly, but from what little their alpha told us, it didn't sound as though he'd been on the run for long. Within ten minutes or so, he had filed us all in, had his men make their head count, and informed us that Jake was missing but *would* be found before the day's end. Then, before we were dismissed, Nathaniel, in an eerily calm tone, informed us that we were all on lockdown until further notice, and if we took "one single, solitary step" outside of our homes that we would be shot on sight.

Gavin was waiting for me in the chair that sat in front of the surveillance screens when I opened the door to the safe room. The chair was spun around, facing the closet door, and his hands were locked behind his head. There was a smirk on his face, which was annoyingly sexy. He sighed, exposing a tiny sliver of his tight abs, and said, "So, we're on lockdown. Whatever are we going to do with ourselves?"

He was making light of the situation and…flirting? My God, how did he do that? My legs felt like Jell-O, and I wanted to jump on his lap and force him to kiss me again. But now was not the right time to be flirting. "This is not funny, Gavin! One of our members escaped and is probably going to be captured by your crazy pack and who knows what they'll do to him!"

His hands came out from behind his head and landed on his knees, but he kept his eyes on me. "I know, I know. I'm sorry. I was just trying to make you smile. You don't do it near enough, you know."

Then he smiled, not only with his kissable lips but with his dark eyes too, and it made me smile back. A stupid, girlie *oh-my-God-you're-so-hot-I-want-you-so-bad* smile, which made me hate him even more. Damn him!

With a quick pivot-turn towards the door, I said, "Anyway…I don't know what you're going to do locked in here by yourself, but I'm going to make myself something to eat. I'm starving. I'll drop you off some food in here in a few." I was determined to get the hell out of there before he shot me another panty-dropping smile, because I *would* actually jump in his lap like a crazed, lust-sick fool.

But no! Mr. Bound and Determined seemed bound and determined to make me as uncomfortable as possible today. Before I could even get out the door, he was on my heels following me out.

"What...I mean where are you going? You need to stay in there! Don't you ever do what you're supposed to?"

He glided past me, his body grazing right up against mine, his intoxicating scent assaulting my sensing, and said, "Now, where's the fun in that?"

He was going to be the death of me. And now I was following him! "Seriously, Gavin. You need to stay in there. You are such a pain in the ass!"

He came to an abrupt halt and turned around, causing me to run into him. I bounced off of him like a ball and stumbled back a few steps. He latched on to my arms to steady me, setting off every nerve ending in my body.

He smiled down at me again with that damn twinkle in his eyes. "How about this? I'll make a deal with you. You let me out of my little prison for a few minutes, and we make some lunch together. Then, instead of you dropping off my food, you actually eat with me, and in return, I will provide you with some outrageously entertaining company. I found some playing cards stashed in a drawer. I see a very competitive game of gin rummy in our future."

I took a step back, desperately needing some space before I did something stupid like, like I don't know, push him back on my mother's bed, strip him naked, and lick every inch of...*My God! What is wrong with me?*

Unable to stop them, my naughty eyes shifted toward the bed. Damn it! Finally, I started to speak, to tell him just how bad his idea would be, but Gavin quickly cut me off. "Okay, I can see you're hesitant." *Oh, if he only knew.* "But, before you answer, I also saw a DVD of *The Breakfast Club* in there. Come on, an '80s cult classic, a few exciting games of rummy, and stimulating conversation with yours truly? How can you pass that up?"

Before I had the chance to answer one way or another, Gavin turned and took off toward the kitchen. Without looking back, he said, "Did I mention I'm not taking no for an answer?"

CHAPTER 20

Gavin

Cami decided that she needed real food for lunch so she whipped us up some spaghetti with meat sauce. I would have loved to stay in the kitchen and watch her cook, but of course she threw a hissy fit about me being out of the safe room. So, like a good little boy I went back to my prison.

It was okay though; my imagination was enough to have me completely worked up. I pictured her in the kitchen wearing those tiny little sleep shorts with her thin pink tank top pulled snuggly over her ample breasts. I thought about her bending over to get a soda from the refrigerator. I watched in my mind as she oh-so-sexily popped the top, lifted the frosty can to her pouty lips and let the sweet, bubbly beverage fill her mouth.

I was so lost in my own Pepsi fantasy that I almost didn't hear Cami walk in carrying a plate full of spaghetti. Seeing her after that amazing daydream sent a wave of need through me that I couldn't ignore. When she handed me my plate, I took it in one hand and took her in my other. Pulling her to me, I put the plate on the table next to me and wrapped both of my arms around her and held her surprised gaze.

The look on her stunning face took my breath away as something real and equally mind blowing flowed between us. Cami dropped her eyes to my chest, breaking the intense connection between us, but I wasn't letting her off the hook. She had to have felt our undeniable chemistry too, so I took a chance and leaned in to whisper in her ear, "Look at me, Cami."

She took a deep breath and stepped out of my arms. "Are you trying to make a move on me, Gavin?"

There was a glint in her eyes, and I could tell that see was teasing me, so I went with it. "Hell yeah, I am. Baby, I've got moves you've never seen," I said, making her laugh out loud.

"Really? Do those moves include quoting Julia Roberts in *My Best Friend's Wedding*?"

"Huh?" I asked, feeling totally lame for unknowingly quoting fucking Julia Roberts! *Real smooth, man.*

"Never mind, lover-boy. I'll be right back," she said with a flirty smile as she turned to leave.

Cami returned not a minute later with her plate of spaghetti and two bottles of water.

We ate our meal with a weird silence filling the air. I tried to focus on the food in front of me, but it was hard to keep me eyes off of her, especially when I'd catch her eyes on me every now and then when she thought I wasn't paying attention. Whether she knew it or not, she looked like she wanted to jump over the table and devour me, which, in turn, made me hard as a freaking rock. I had to fight off the urge to shove everything off the table, spread her body over it, and taste every inch of her. Food be damned.

Every time our eyes connected, she'd smile and look away as if she was suddenly shy. The sweet, vulnerable Cami was such a contrast to her usual feisty self, and it was hot as hell, but truth be told, it confused the shit out of me too. Not that I cared. Confused or not, I wanted this girl. No, I *needed* this girl.

All too soon, lunch was over and Cami was taking our plates back to the kitchen. The fear that she wouldn't return punched me in the gut, so I followed her even though I knew I shouldn't. Surprisingly, Cami didn't yell at me for leaving the safe room. She did, however, shoot me her famous dirty look. I asked to help her with the dishes, but she refused.

"I've got it. There are some movies in the drawer under the TV in the safe room. Why don't you pick one out for us," she suggested. A huge goofy grin appeared on my face, and I couldn't have fought it if I'd tried.

"Any requests?" I asked.

"I trust you," she said with the sexiest damned grin I'd ever seen.

"Some movies? Holy crap," I said under my breath as my eyes scanned over hundreds of DVDs. I was trying to decide between a romantic comedy or a horror flick, both excellent choices for sitting really close together on the loveseat.

"*Texas Chainsaw Massacre* or *The Notebook*? I haven't seen either one," I said holding up both DVDs as Cami walked back into the safe room.

"No scary movies! We could make our own with a video camera right now. Don't you think?" she said as she settled down on the loveseat and tucked her long legs up under her.

"Yeah, I guess we could," I barely whispered as I put *The Notebook* in the DVD player.

I could hardly concentrate on the movie with Cami sitting so close. I would shift in my seat just to touch her, and when she would move and accidentally brush against me, I thought I just might die from the need to touch her again. I wondered if that was possible, if any guy had ever died from being so damn horny. I bet some poor sucker had.

I probably should just turn in my man card now, but at some point, I got completely sucked into that damn movie, and by the time the credits began to roll, I was one hot mess. I tried to cover it up. I tried to wipe the moisture from my eyes without being seen, but it didn't work. It was just one teeny-tiny tear that escaped, but dammit if she didn't see it!

"Awww, you big baby," Cami teased. When I looked at her, her face was streaked with tears of her own.

I gave her a playful shove then pulled her in for a hug. I was completely surprised when she didn't push me away.

Laughing at herself as she wiped her eyes she admitted, "I guess it got to me too, or maybe it's just all the stress. And I've seen this freaking movie like five times!" Cami looked up at me, and I couldn't stop myself from reaching up and wiping her tears away.

Time slowed as we sat there together. Cami bit down on her bottom lip just before she grabbed my neck and pulled my lips to hers, shocking the shit out of me. I wanted to be smooth, to kiss her gently and not like a sex-crazed teenager, but seriously, I had no swag when it came to this girl. So, I just gave in and went with what felt real. And in that moment, frantic need took over.

Lucky for me, Cami seemed to feel the same way. The built-up sexual tension between us sent both of us into a frenzy of touching and kissing and exploring. Cami whimpered once when I left her lips and again when my mouth trailed down her neck. The damned loveseat was entirely too small. Cami obviously agreed because the next thing I knew she was straddling my lap.

My breath caught in my throat when I opened my eyes to see Cami's mouthwatering cleavage right in front of my face. I captured her lips again as I let my hands run up her tank top. As I gently cupped her full breasts, Cami's head fell back giving me access to her neck. It was my turn to whimper as Cami readjusted herself, pressing against my erection. Needing to touch even more of her, I lifted the thin tank over Cami's head, revealing a white and hot-pink polka-dot bra underneath. Damn!

My breath hitched in my throat and for a moment, I just stared at her perfect tits, but Cami grabbed my face and forced my mouth back to hers. My hands acted on their own as they pulled her bra down, so I could run my fingers over her hardening nipples. When

Cami rubbed herself even harder against me, I knew that this loveseat would never work. I wrapped my hands under her ass and stood, lifting us both off the couch. Within seconds, I'd carried her into the bedroom of the safe house.

Immediately, Cami pulled my shirt off and pushed me back on the bed. Standing there in her bra, which was already halfway off, and those itty-bitty shorts, she shot me a sexy smile before she leaned down to kiss me again. As Cami climbed on top of me, I wrapped my arms around her and pulled her body against me. I rolled our bodies over so that we were lying on our sides, and then our eyes connected as Cami's hand slid down my stomach, causing me to shiver. I stopped breathing when she reached down to unbutton my jeans, but in that same moment, sirens began blaring throughout the estate. We both jumped so high I had to grab Cami before she fell off the bed.

"What the fuck?" I panted.

Cami's eyes went wide just before she shot up from the bed and ran to the couch to grab her tank top. "It's the emergency sirens again. That can't be good. I better go," she called before she ran out of the room without looking back.

CHAPTER 21

Kendall

Standing on the steps of the lodge, I watched as the CH search team dragged Jake Larson in my direction. His body was limp, yet he didn't look injured, which meant he hadn't been beaten for his crime against the Crescent Hills Pack...yet. My initial reaction to this sight simply piqued my curiosity, but the eerily triumphant look on Nathaniel's face made my skin crawl, and I quickly realized that these men had something far more sinister in store for poor Jake than a simple beating.

My entire body my jerked when a voice rang out over the intercom. "All Red Ridge Members, immediately report to the grounds outside of the lodge. I repeat, immediately report to the grounds outside of the lodge." *No, they wouldn't!* Slowly, I began taking steps back toward the lodge's door, away from the scene that would be unfolding before my eyes any minute now. Everyone here may think of me as an evil bitch, but even I didn't want to watch this.

A hand reached out and grabbed my arm. "Where do you think you're going? This is just about to get good."

Drew's wicked grin only served to worsen the sickening feeling in the pit of my stomach. "What's going on? What are you going to do to him?" I asked, unsure if I actually wanted to hear his answer.

He dropped his hand from my arm and shrugged as if something like this happened every day. "Guess you'll just have to wait and see. It should be a pretty good show, but I wouldn't stand too close to the action. It might get a little messy."

It didn't take long for the members of the Red Ridge Pack to assemble around the stairs leading up to the lodge. For the time being, Jake Larson was kept out of sight as they were directed to gather in a half circle in front of the building. They whispered among themselves, but all chatter ceased as soon as the doors of the lodge opened and Nathaniel and Brian dragged their semi-conscious pack member, who was bound and gagged, down the stairs and threw him to the ground at their feet.

Gasps and cries erupted from the crowd, but the Crescent Hills Pack was prepared. Its men lined the angry throng, armed and ready to attack if anyone stepped out of line. Nathaniel turned around and walked back up to the third step before he turned around again to address the group. "First, let me say, this is not something that I wanted to see happen. It was my hope that we could come together peacefully and work together as one. I am not a violent man, but I cannot ignore insubordination. My pack has done nothing but treat you well. We have promised to work together as one, to come together and join forces to become the most powerful wolf pack in New Mexico. All we have asked is that you give us time. Time to work through the transition. Soon, you will be given the opportunity to choose to stay here and join the Crescent Hills Pack or leave. The choice will be yours, but until then, you need to know what will happen if you choose to break my rules. Jake Larson chose to escape, and for that, he will be punished, and his family will be detained. If you choose to be a renegade, be prepared to face the consequences."

Nathaniel nodded his head at Brian as if to give him the go-ahead. Clayton walked over with some rope in his hand, and together, they picked up Jake, dragged him over to a nearby tree, and strung him up by his bound wrists. Jake hung from a thick branch as

Brian began his brutal assault. Punch after punch, kick after kick, Brian beat Jake to within an inch of his life. Blood poured from a deep gash above his eyebrow, and though his head hung lifelessly to the side, I would have guessed his entire face was already bruised and swollen. I'd be surprised if his cheekbones, nose, and jaw weren't all broken, along with every single one of his ribs.

It was a gruesome sight, but what really made my stomach churn was the look on the faces of the people who I had once considered my family. Some looked on wide eyed as if unable to look away while others covered their eyes to shield themselves from the nightmarish vision. Many held each other for support as tears rained down their faces. A few dropped to their knees and sobbed into their hands. The unfamiliar feeling of guilt was too much for me, and I found myself looking away.

After a few of the longest minutes of my life, a deep voice among the crowd rang out. "Stop! For heaven's sake, please stop!" It was Gage Isaacks. "We will listen. We will follow your orders. You have our word. Just please stop before you kill him."

Somehow Brian, in his murderous rage, heard him and halted in mid-punch. He turned his attention to Nathaniel to look for further instruction. Nathaniel nodded once, and Brian stepped away but didn't untie him from the tree.

Standing before the crowd, still on that damn third step, Nathaniel said, "I hope you all heed my warning. Jake will remain here to remind you all to do as you are told. That will be all. Go back to your homes. You are dismissed."

CHAPTER 22

Cami

I couldn't believe my eyes, couldn't believe the bloody scene unfolding right in front of me. People say that shit all the time, *I couldn't believe it, blah, blah, blah*...But, I really couldn't. I'd seen some horrid things since the CH Pack took over our estate, but this? To force us to stand here and watch as they brutally beat Jake half to death and then to leave him hanging lifelessly from that tree? When was it going to end?

Or, more importantly, *how* was it going to end?

After we were dismissed, I just stood there, unable to convince my feet to move. I watched as my pack mourned with their families and made their way back home together. I was alone. My parents were still locked away with Phillip in the cell beneath the lodge, and all I could do was pray that they were okay. There was nothing I could do, and in that moment in time, I'd never felt more helpless.

But that was exactly what the Crescent Hills Pack wanted. They wanted us to feel helpless. That was how they planned to break us. They needed to make us feel as if we needed them. Only then would a pack as strong as ours be willing to "join forces" as Nathaniel so eloquently put it.

And Holy Mother of God, it was working! He was breaking our pack! My eyes roved over the people of my pack as they slowly walked down the road to the homes. They were huddled together in little groups, holding each other in comfort with their shoulders hunched and their tears flowing. The realization of it all struck me so forcefully that bile rose up in my throat, and I had to fight back the urge to vomit right there. We weren't big, strong werewolves anymore. We were weak and vulnerable. Marcus Walker would flip the fuck out if he saw this shit.

Suddenly, my feet had no problem moving. I needed to get to Gavin. Less than an hour ago, I was wrapped in his arms, ready to…who knows what I'd been ready to do if those sirens wouldn't have sounded, but somehow, he made me feel things I'd never felt before.

Even with all of this madness going on around us, he awakened feelings inside of me that I didn't quite understand. He made me feel less alone. Like someone was here for me. He made me smile, made me laugh. He made me forget.

Within minutes, I flew threw my front door, locked it, and dashed into the closet of my parents' bedroom. My fingers fumbled over the numbers as I punched in the code, and as soon as I had the door open, Gavin was standing there waiting for me. His eyes were filled with so much sorrow and pain and anguish, and I knew they were reflecting everything I was feeling in that moment. He had seen it all on the surveillance videos, and along with all the pain, I could see the hesitation in his eyes as well. I could tell he wasn't sure how I was going to handle this. He wasn't sure what I needed right now.

Without breaking eye contact, he took one small, seemingly uncertain step toward me, but I knew exactly what I needed even if he didn't. I needed him. I threw myself in his arms and held on to him as if he was all I had left in the world. His entire body engulfed me as he let out a sigh of relief. "I'm so sorry, Cami. I'm so sorry." Gavin breathed into my hair and kissed the top of my head.

I buried myself in his chest just needing to be close to him. His long, strong arms wrapped tightly around me made me feel safe even if I was anything but. "Your alpha is trying to break us. That's been his plan all along. He wants us weak and helpless, so we will just roll over and let him take over. And it's working."

Gavin pulled away, but only so he could look down at me when he spoke. "I know, Cami. Nathaniel is ruthless and cruel. He always has been. And you're right. He wants your pack broken, and he'll stop at nothing to get what he wants. But you know what's been bugging the shit out of me? How he figured out that Jake escaped so quickly. I mean Jake couldn't have been gone long, right? It's like somehow my pack knew almost immediately."

"I know! I had that same thought! How could they have known?"

Turning his attention toward the surveillance screens, Gavin asked, "Is there any way to rewind the video or whatever and see if we can find out what happen when Jake escaped? We can look back and see when and how he left and then when the CH guards showed up."

I popped up on my tippy-toes and planted a kiss on Gavin's lips. "You're brilliant! You know that?"

A huge grin broke out on his gorgeous face. "Yeah well, that's what they tell me." He chuckled at his own joke, and it made me laugh. Somehow in the midst of this massive shit-storm, this guy could still make my insides all fluttery and lighten my heavy heart.

Simultaneously, we untangled ourselves from each other's arms and scrambled over to the chairs in front of the large screen. I grabbed the remote and scanned over the buttons but didn't see anything other than the same old buttons we had used to shift between the different cameras on the estate.

I looked over at Gavin, who was running his hand over a panel on the table below the screen. "Look, I think I found something," he said as he tried to get his fingernail under the lip of the rectangular panel.

How the hell had we not noticed that before? After a few failed attempts, I dug my nail beneath the lip and pushed it in and pulled up. It was kind of like pulling off the battery cover on the back of a TV remote. With the panel open, a whole new array of buttons where available for us to explore.

Gavin looked my way, his eyebrows raised sky-high. "Holy shit. Guess there's more to this system than we thought."

After at least an hour of trial and error, we finally figured out how to play back the video and found Jake's house from earlier that day. We played the video at a slow, fast-forward speed until the CH guards showed up at his house for a random search. As soon as the guards left, we located Jake and watched as he slipped out of the mudroom door, and then seven minutes later, the guards showed up at the door again for another "random" search.

"What the hell? Why did they go back?" I asked, more to myself than to Gavin. It's not as if I thought he'd have an answer.

But, Gavin was a whole lot smarter than I gave him credit for because actually he did have an answer. Or, a theory anyway. "Okay, so Jake's a tough guy, right? Kind of the rebel type?"

"Yeah, I guess. Why? What are you thinking?"

"Okay, so who else in your pack would you say is like Jake? You know, probably seventeen to twenty-five years old, defiant, guys who wouldn't just sit back and let all this happen. Maybe they are targeting guys like Jake. Keeping a close eye on certain people? It would make sense. I mean not everyone is going to follow the rules, right?"

"Oh my God. You really are brilliant. Okay so, let me think. Definitely Gage, Ryder, and Sammy. Some of the older guys who are friends with Jake, like Dane, Vince, Logan, and Nick. Let's go back and look at some of their houses and see if the CH guards did double checks on them."

Sure enough, Gavin was right. His pack was profiling certain members of our pack and trying to catch them breaking the rules. Obviously, it worked out in their favor with Jake, and now everyone was probably scared shitless. The Crescent Hills Pack had us right where they wanted us.

A thought suddenly occurred to me, and it was one I was quite sure Gavin wasn't going to want to hear, but in my mind, it was a good thing. I just needed to find a way to convince Mr. Pessimistic. I turned my body toward Gavin, placing my knees between his, and grabbed one of his hands, holding it between both of mine. I leaned in and said, "Listen, I know you don't want to hear this, but maybe this is a good thing. They are targeting guys. And I still need to get Teagan out of here. They aren't watching me."

Gavin started to interrupt me, but I cut him off. "Before you try to convince me that this is a horrible idea, just hear me out. We'll look at more footage. See if they've been watching me or the Wrights' house or any of the other girls. I'll be careful. I have to do this, Gavin."

With his free hand, Gavin pulled me into his lap and then wrapped his arms around me. "I don't want you to do this. I could go. They don't even know I'm here."

Snuggling into the crook of his neck I sighed. "You wouldn't have the first clue where to go."

"You can tell Shari at rec tomorrow what's going on. She could go. I could meet her and help her," he suggested, but his voice betrayed him. He knew as well as I did that it was a stupid idea.

I looked up at him and let out a small laugh. He poked me in the side and said, "This is not funny, Cami." But he was laughing too before he even finished his sentence.

"I know you don't want me to go, and as much as I love Shari, the girl would get lost in a walk-in closet. There is no way she could pull this off. I have to do this, Gavin. I know you're worried, but I'll be careful. I promise."

His laughter died and his eyes darkened. "I know. I just don't want to let you go." Before I could respond, his lips collided with mine. His kiss was hard and demanding and full of need. His tongue swept across my bottom lip, and my mouth opened to invite him in. I wanted him. All of him. I didn't want to let him go either. Not when I'd only just found him.

CHAPTER 23

Gavin

I wanted to drag Cami back into the bedroom and continue what we had started earlier, but I didn't want our first time together to be tainted by the memory of my father's brutality. Instead, I handed Cami my phone so that she could call Cade and get her plan moving. As much as I didn't want Cami to put herself in danger, I understood her need to do something to help.

"Thanks, Gavin," Cami said as she took the phone, and I knew that she was thanking me for more than just the phone. She took the phone over to the loveseat and sat down to make her call. I followed her over and lifted her legs onto my lap.

I listened as Cami replayed the day's horrific events to Cade, and although I wasn't trying to listen in, I could hear Cade's outrage. Mindlessly, I traced my fingers along Cami's outstretched legs. Cami was so sure of herself and her ability to get Teagan off the estate unnoticed, but I wasn't convinced. I wanted to believe her. I wanted to trust that she could do what she claimed she could, but after seeing Jake nearly beaten to death and left strung up on a tree to suffer, I wanted so badly to beg her not to risk it.

I knew that Teagan needed to get to Aiden. And I knew that as a human, she would never be able to do it alone. What I didn't understand was why Cami had to be the one to get her there. Cami didn't owe Teagan or Aiden anything. As far as I could tell, they weren't even that close. If they were related or best friends even, maybe I could understand, but they're not, and Cami's putting her life at risk to help them. I just didn't get it. Maybe I'm just an asshole or very un-martyr-like or whatever, but dammit, why Cami?

I wasn't sure if I could stay here and just watch. I knew I would go crazy waiting for her to return. Cami was supposed to get word to Teagan that she should be ready to leave tomorrow night. *So soon?* My stomach clenched at the thought of Cami leaving.

"Oww!" Cami whispered as she kicked her legs free. It was only then that I realized I had been squeezing the life out of her poor calf.

"Shit! Sorry!" I muttered. Moving to get off the couch, I leaned over and planted a chaste kiss on her lips. I needed to get a damn grip. If Cami was determined to go through with this plan, the last thing I wanted to do was fight with her.

As Cami finished going over the details with Cade, I grabbed a soda from the small refrigerator and stood in the kitchenette. I didn't want to hear anymore. I tried not to think about what would happen if she did get caught, but I couldn't help it. I certainly wouldn't be able to stay in this damn room and hide anymore. It was taking every ounce of willpower within me to do it now. If something happened to Cami, I would fight. I would fight my own pack, my own friends, and my own father if it meant keeping Cami safe.

"You okay?" Cami asked. I was so lost in my own head that I didn't even see her walking my way. Cami grabbed my soda and took a sip before placing it on the counter behind me.

"I will be all right," she reassured me. "Gavin, I can do this."

Taking her hands in mine, I took a deep cleansing breath and said, "I know you can."

That was all Cami needed to hear, I guess, because she wrapped her arms around me. We stood holding on to each other for a moment before she pulled away. "It's getting late. I'd better go and get some sleep."

"I wish you could stay with me," I blurted out before I thought about what I was saying. I meant it, but I knew that Cami staying here wasn't safe, and I didn't want to pressure her into sleeping with me.

"I wish I could stay too," she admitted, looking into my eyes and giving me a naughty little wink. "How about I go get ready for bed, and then I'll come back down for a while."

"I have a better idea. Sleep in your parents' room tonight."

"Gross! We are not messing around in my parents' bed," Cami replied with playful grin.

I pulled her to me and whispered in her ear, "I just want to hold you. Let me hold you until you fall asleep and then I will come back in here. Just for tonight."

"You promise me that you will come back in here once I fall asleep?" she asked.

"Promise."

*****

I listened as Cami's breathing became deep and even. When her arm that was wrapped around my chest relaxed, I knew she was sound asleep. It was time for me to leave, but I stayed awhile longer. The thought crossed my mind that this might be the only night I ever got to spend with Cami, but I tried to push it aside. Those thoughts wouldn't do me any good, and they certainly wouldn't make the next twenty-four hours any easier. I felt myself drifting into the warmth of her body, so before I did something stupid, like fall asleep, I kissed Cami's temple and eased out of the bed.

I looked down at Cami sleeping so soundly and made a silent vow. I would do anything in my power to make this girl mine and keep her safe. Anything.

CHAPTER 24

Kendall

The next day, at Red Ridge's scheduled rec time, I decided to sneak away from the house Drew practically had me locked away in and head over to see if I could catch Becca and Shari. I needed to try to gauge how they were handling what went down with Jake yesterday.

Thankfully, Nathaniel finally allowed his men to untie Jake from the tree this morning, but they had left him hanging there all night as a "reminder" to anyone tempted to disobey the new alpha's orders. And I thought Marcus was a douche bag. Nathaniel Barnes was an evil bastard, through and through.

Unfortunately, I was starting to realize that his son wasn't much better. Gavin had tried to warn me, but when I first came to Crescent Hills, I was so focused on clawing my way to the top that nothing else mattered. Drew was hot, and he wanted me. That was all that mattered. Sure, he was an asshole, but if I wanted to be the alpha female that was the price I had to pay.

It is the price I have to pay.

The only good news I'd been given since I'd gotten here was that my friend Natalie was coming to the estate today. She wasn't even really my friend. We were more like frenemies, but whatever. At least she would be someone to talk to even if she was a total bitch. Her father was the Crescent Hills accountant, so I could only guess that our pack was making progress on the financial end of things. Maybe the "merger" wouldn't take as long as I thought.

On my way toward the rec area, I pulled out my phone. Of course, no missed calls, no messages, no texts, nothing. I may have a new pack, but I'd never been more alone. Needing to know that someone out there gave a shit, I started typing out a text to Gavin when I ran smack dab into someone.

I stumbled back a few steps and looked up to find none other than the little, bleach-blonde domestic, Teagan Rhodes. Her eyes shot open in shock and probably fear, and I couldn't help but laugh. She tried to walk around me, but I stepped into her path. "Well, if it isn't Red Ridge's very own domesticated pet. Bet you're wishing you didn't get wrapped up with this whole werewolf bullshit now, huh Meagan?"

"It's Teagan."

Again, she attempted to move around me, but she wasn't getting away quite so easily. "Oh right. *Teagan.*" Just to be a bitch, I sniffed her and scrunched up my nose. "Sorry to hear about Aiden. That's so sad and all. I guess there's no reason for you to be sticking around once the Red Ridge members are given the option to leave, so you might as well pack your bags. Obviously, you won't be allowed to stay here. Crescent Hills doesn't do the whole domestic thing."

She looked up at me with glassy eyes, and I could tell that I'd gotten to her. But then she straightened her posture a bit, tossed those damn blonde locks over her shoulder, and said, "Hey thanks, Kendall. Good talk." Then, instead of trying to walk around me, she turned around completely and headed in the opposite direction. Unbelievable!

I tried to ignore her perfectly perky ass as I followed behind her to the rec area. Realizing my phone was still in my hand, I looked down at the half-written text and decided to erase it. In truth, it would just make me feel worse. I'd tell Gavin that I missed him, and he wouldn't say it back. He never did.

Seeing Becca and Shari up ahead caused my heart to race. Jeez, my emotions were all over the damn place today! When had I ever been nervous about seeing these girls? Never! That's when! I needed to get a damn grip.

Before they had a chance to notice me, I shoved my poor-pitiful-me attitude deep down inside and replaced it with a confident smile and made sure my shoulders were back and my head was held high. I was Kendall Stuart, dammit, and these bitches needed to remember it!

When I was a few feet away, they both turned my way as if they somehow sensed I was coming. Of course they smiled, but Shari's stupid grin seemed forced. Shocker! Refusing to let my own smile falter, I didn't let my old friend's pathetic attempt to pretend to be happy to see me faze me.

As I approached, I said, "Hey, girls! I've missed you two! Kisses!" Then I hugged and kissed them both on the cheek just like I used to.

While Shari seemed more than aware of all the stares I was receiving from people from my former pack, Becca was oblivious to it all as she gushed, "Oh my gosh, Kendall. You look great. I'm so glad you're here!"

I really did want to say something about Jake, tell them how sorry I was or whatever, but I didn't have a clue how to go about it, so I figured it was easier to just act like the whole thing never happened and hope that one of them didn't bring it up either. I opted to tell them about Natalie instead.

"Oh thanks, honey. You know I'd be hanging around more if I could. I've just been so busy." *Yeah right!* "I just wanted to stop by and tell you guys that my friend Natalie is coming to the estate today. You're going to love her! She will fit right in with us once this all blows over. Her dad's the CH accountant, so I guess he's coming up to work on the financial end of things. I can't wait for you to meet her!"

I looked over at Shari, and her fake smile was still plastered across her sweet, little face. Whoever told her she was a good actress was full of shit. When I didn't look away, I guess she finally decided she should say something. "Oh, that's great, Kendall. We can't wait to meet her. I guess you'll have to bring her down to rec time tomorrow or something since…well, you know, we're kind of being held hostage at the moment."

Sugary-sweet venom dripped from her voice as she patted me on the hand and smiled.

Okay, maybe the bitch can act.

Well, that's it. And here I was being nice…Maybe I shouldn't mention that Ryder's mother, Red Ridge's accountant, was going to end up in the jail cell as soon as Natalie's dad arrived, for the safety of the merger and all. Or maybe I should. I bet that little tidbit of information would wipe that fucking smirk off Shari's pretty face. Screw her!

Ignoring Shari completely, I turned to the only Red Ridge friend I knew I could count on. "Hey, Becca, maybe you can come over later and meet Natalie. I bet you two would really hit it off."

CHAPTER 25

Cami

As soon as I saw Teagan sitting under a tree, I knew something was up. She looked shaken, like something bad had happened. As I made my way over to her, I followed her gaze over to a picnic table several feet away, and I immediately knew the cause of the downtrodden look of her face. Kendall *Avery* Stuart.

What the hell was she doing here during Red Ridge's rec time? The ho-bag from hell had the nerve to hang around and chat it up with Becca and Shari, just like the good ol' days. Seriously?

"So what did she do?" I asked as I squatted down in front of Teagan.

She looked up at me and let out a small chuckle. "How'd you guess?"

I sat down next to her and glanced around to make sure so no one was within earshot. "We'll call it a hunch. Spill."

"Just Kendall being Kendall. I was on my way to find you and ran into her...literally. She offered her condolences about Aiden. Let's just say, it was extremely heartfelt."

Jeez, that girl was a piece of work. Hate didn't begin to describe how I felt about Kendall. "You know she's not worth getting upset about, right? Besides, we don't have much time, and we need to talk."

Teagan's eyes lit up as she said, "I know. That's why I was coming to find you. I have to know how Aiden's doing. It's driving me crazy. I miss him so much."

"That's what I wanted to talk to you about, but we need to talk to Lilly and Paul too." I looked around and spotted them nearby. Before I said another word, Teagan was up and headed that way, so I followed her lead.

Lilly and Paul said polite hellos as we approached, and we waited a moment for the CH guards to pass. As soon as the coast was clear, I said, "I talked to Cade, and Aiden is getting pretty sick because he is away from Teagan. I told them that I'd sneak her out of here tonight, so she needs to be ready. They are going to meet me right outside of the estate. I'm sure I can get in and out without being seen, but they are going to realize she is gone, and I'm sure there will be consequences."

Paul and Lilly began to speak at the same time, but Lilly let Paul go first. "Are you sure you can do this, Cami?"

"Yeah. I wouldn't put Teagan in danger if I didn't. There's always a chance something could go wrong, but I'm pretty confident we can do this."

"Then we'll do whatever it takes for Aiden and Teagan to be together. Lilly and I will just have to face whatever consequences these bastards have for us. We can't let Aiden suffer."

Paul turned to his wife, and she nodded her head. "Yes, we'll handle Crescent Hills in the morning. Just get Teagan to Aiden. Thank you, Cami. We can't thank you enough for doing this for our family."

*****

For the rest of the evening, Gavin and I watched the cameras like hawks, neither one of us wanting to say what was really on our minds. Gavin had been distant all day, and I knew it was because he was worried, but it was killing me. I wanted nothing more than for him to grab me and kiss me until my knees buckled, to run his hands over every inch of my body while his lips followed, to make me forget about all of the worries rolling around in my head. But instead, he just sat there in front of the surveillance screens, shifting from camera view to camera view and not saying much of anything.

When it was almost time to leave, I got up and left the room to get ready without saying a word to Gavin. After I threw on a sports bra, a long-sleeved shirt, a thick hoodie, and fleece-lined pants, I pulled my hair into a high ponytail. I forced down a banana and chugged some water. Then I looked at the clock.

I walked back into the safe room, and Gavin was standing right inside the door waiting for me. "Is it time?"

His dark eyes were so full of anguish that it made me want to curl up his arms and forget the whole thing, but I knew I couldn't. I had to do this. "Yeah, it's time. I promise I'll be fine, and I won't be gone long. They should be waiting right outside of the estate."

He took a step toward me, reached out, and pulled me into his embrace. My body molded into his, and as I laid my head against his chest, I could feel his heart pounding a mile a minute. He ran his hand down my back and whispered, "Please be careful."

Looking up at him, I tried my best to appear confident even though I was feeling less and less so as each minute passed. "I will. I'll be back before you know it."

Leaning down, his lips laid claim to mine as he kissed me fiercely. Cupping my face in his hands, he tilted my head to the side to deepen the kiss. It was hard and demanding and full of promise, the kind of kiss a girl could get lost in, and never in my life had I wanted to lose myself more than in that moment, but all too soon it was over, leaving me completely breathless.

When he pulled away, there was fire in his eyes as he said, "I'll be waiting here for you when you return. Please don't make me wait long." Unable to find the right words, I simply nodded my head and then turned to sneak out into the night.

I took the same route I did before to get to the Wrights' home, and Teagan was waiting at the mudroom door. Lilly and Paul couldn't hide the worry written all over their faces, but whispered *good luck* and *be careful* as we headed out.

It'd be a bit trickier getting all the way to the gates this time, and also having to worry about Teagan didn't help matters, but I knew the guards' routes by heart, and if they were anything, it was predictable, especially the night guards.

I checked my watch and motioned for Teagan to duck down behind a large bush a few houses down from the Wrights'. A guard would be passing through any minute, and sure enough, like clockwork, a flashlight lit up the road and the guard wandered by. After he was out of sight, we ran past a few more houses, staying as far away from the main road as possible. Then I motioned for her to follow me behind Ryder's home. This would lead us to the edge of the estate, and from what I could tell the guards weren't patrolling behind the houses nearly as much as the front.

Without any problems, we made it past my house, but were on the opposite side of the road. This was where it got a bit more complicated. The CH guards were keeping a pretty close eye on the entrance and exit to the estate. However, I didn't plan on going through there. All I could do was hope that Teagan knew how to climb a fence, a really tall fence, and quickly. We couldn't afford for her to have any girlie, I-can't-do-this moments.

When we ducked down in a covered area, I whispered, "We can't go through the drive-thru exit. The fence is our only option. Are you up for it? You have to be fast because this is the only area that the guards actually seem to be paying close attention."

Teagan nodded her head. "Yeah, I can do it. Trust me. Nothing is going to stop me from getting to Aiden."

Her eyes told me everything I needed to know. This girl was determined, and if she had to scale a damn mountain, she wouldn't hesitate. I glanced down at my watch. We had about three minutes before a guard passed through. "Okay, we need to wait here for a couple of minutes. Then on my go, run like hell for the fence, right there in that patch that is covered in darkness, and climb like a freaking chimpanzee on crack. Got it?"

Again she nodded, and after I watched the guard go on his merry way, I motioned toward the fence, and we took off running. That tough, little domestic beat me up and over the fence and was running into Aiden's arms within minutes. Aiden pulled her into the car and then turned to me to offer a weak, "Thank you."

Knowing they needed to get out of there as soon as possible, I told Cade to call the next night, and he too offered his thanks for my help as well. Seconds later, they were gone, and I was on my own. I headed back, but checked my watch first. I had about three minutes to get over the fence and back to my house before the guards made another pass.

Shit! That wasn't near enough time, but I had to make it work. I was over the fence in record time, and my feet barely had time to hit the ground below before I was running like the devil himself was chasing me.

CHAPTER 26

Gavin

My eyes darted back and forth between the surveillance cameras and the stopwatch on my phone. Cami had the trip planned down to the minute, so when the timer went off and I still didn't see her on the camera, I started to panic. Images of Cami being caught, dragged off to my father, and beaten in front of her pack, haunted my head and my heart. A sick feeling settled in my stomach. I had to do something.

Holding my breath, I watched the clock, determined to give her two more minutes to get here before going after her. It would be the longest two minutes of my life, but I couldn't go storming out of here prematurely. With thirty seconds left, I heard the back door open. I quickly grabbed the remote to the TV and switched to the interior camera system.

"Oh, thank God!"

I released the breath that I didn't even realize I had been holding when I saw her in the mudroom. I dropped the remote and raced out of the safe room. As soon as I saw her with my own eyes, I froze. I couldn't move; hell, I could hardly even breathe, but seeing her there, standing in front of me, all in one piece caused something inside of me to light up.

She was beaming, obviously proud of herself for safely delivering Teagan to Aiden. She wasn't the only one. I felt it too. I was feeling a lot of things: relief, pride, joy, lust…love. *Holy shit! I love this girl.* The realization probably should have scared the shit out of me, but it didn't. Not one bit. Because I knew in that moment that she was mine and I was hers.

I waited until Cami took her first step toward me to reach out and take her in my arms. As I pulled her to me and meshed her body up against mine, something strange happened. We had been living together for a while now, and sure I'd noticed Cami's scent, but for whatever reason, this time when it invaded senses it practically dropped me to my knees.

I breathed her in, and my were-senses went into a frenzy. I buried my face in her hair, trying to inhale all that sweetness. She smelled like coconuts and sunshine and fresh summer air, and I couldn't get enough of it. Needing her closer, I lifted Cami up and her legs immediately wrapped around my waist. I ran my hands under her shirt and felt her skin grow hot under my touch. As my hands roamed over her perfect back, the warmth of her body seeped deep into my bones.

We were face to face now, and I could tell that she was feeling exactly as I was. Looking into her eyes, holding her that close was killing me. I couldn't hold back any longer. I stepped forward until Cami's back was pressed against the closest wall and rubbed my face in her neck before my lips found hers.

Our kiss began as a slow and gentle tease as I slowly traced her lips with my tongue, tasting the remnants of her cherry lip gloss and Cami's own unique flavor. Letting my kiss say all the things that I was feeling but wasn't ready to say out loud, I took my time worshiping her soft, supple lips.

Cami's arms snaked around my shoulders and up to the back of my head. As her fingers toyed with my hair, chills shot straight down through my body. When she tugged my hair roughly, my lips pressed harder against hers, and our kiss took on a whole new energy.

Cami ran her hands around to my face. She cradled my cheeks in her palms, her touch soft yet demanding, causing our lips to part. The intensity in her eyes told me everything I needed to know. She wanted me too. Whether she loved me or not, I didn't know, but I'd spend every day for all of eternity trying to convince her that she should. I needed this girl. This girl somehow made me whole, and I didn't even realize anything was missing from my life until this moment.

The heat in her eyes seared my heart, and I couldn't look away. I was trapped by her gaze, yet I had never felt so free. Shifting Cami up higher on my waist, I walked us out of the room and up the stairs to her bedroom.

"I can walk, you know," Cami said, smiling.

I shook my head. There was no way I was going to let her go. Instead of putting her down, I kissed her again. In fact, I didn't stop kissing her until I had her lying on her bed, and I was hovering over her.

Damn, she is beautiful.

"Well, are you just going to stare at me or what?" she asked just before a wicked grin spread across her face.

"Maybe," I answered. "Maybe not."

I covered her mouth with mine and felt her body soften beneath me. Cami had me completely wrapped around her finger. I loved that she was so tough one minute and sweet and vulnerable the next. And how perfectly our lips melded together. And how the air in her lungs sort of whooshed out every time I got close to her.

I had to figure out a way to help her help her pack. The sooner this whole ordeal was over the sooner we could really be together. I was thinking of all the ways I could help when Cami's hand slipped under the waistband of my sweatpants. That was it. All coherent thought left the building. And there was only one thing left for me to do: just go with it.

CHAPTER 27

Kendall

To say all hell broke loose at the Red Ridge rec time today would be an understatement. I wasn't there of course since Drew practically lost his freaking mind when he found out about my little visit yesterday, but when the emergency sirens went off for the second time in a under a week, I knew some serious shit was about to go down, and there was no way in hell I was going to miss it.

I tugged on my boots and grabbed my coat before rushing out the front door of the place I now considered my own private hell. It wasn't long before I was in front of the lodge watching the members of Red Ridge being herding inside once again.

I spotted a guard I recognized, a sleazy douche bag who took every available opportunity to eye-rape me, and figured he'd be my best bet to figuring out what was going on, so I wandered over and turned on the charm. "Oh my God! What's going on? This is crazy!"

James or Jason or something that starts with a J looked me up and down as he flashed me a heated grin. Gross! "Hey, Avery—I mean *Kendall*. Word is that the little blonde domestic is missing. I guess she managed to escape. I'm sure we'll find out more here in a few, once Nathaniel addresses the pack."

Un-fucking-believable! Teagan Rhodes escaped! I certainly didn't see that one coming. Without bothering to reply to the creepy guard, I rushed off in search of Drew. I couldn't wait to see what he had to say about this. One thing was for sure. A shit-storm was brewing in Red Ridge.

After wading through the crowd, I finally made it through the lodge doors and caught sight of Drew just before he disappeared down the hallway. Where the hell was he headed? I took off in that direction and called out his name, but there was no reply. Once I made it to the hallway, I called out again, but I can't say I was all that surprised when it went unanswered.

I glanced in every open doorway as I made my way down the hall, but no one was around. Moments later, he walked out of one of the rooms at the far end of the hall carrying a stack of papers. "Drew! I've been calling your name."

"I don't have time for this right now, Kendall," he said as he stormed my way.

I stood there in the middle of the hall, knowing he'd either have to stop and talk to me or he'd have to literally move me out of the way to get past me. "What are you talking about? What's going on?" I asked, pretending I had no idea.

His pace slowed and his eyes narrowed as he looked down to meet my gaze. "Get out of the way. I mean it, Kendall. I don't have time for your shit right now."

Oh hell no! Drew stopped directly in front of me, but I wasn't backing down. I stared up at him and said, "I'm not going anywhere until you tell me why the sirens are going off."

His hand reached out and grabbed my arm. His fingers bit into my skin as he forcefully shoved me into the wall. He held me there and said, "I'm not fucking playing with you, Kendall. When I say to get out of the way, I mean get the fuck out of the way."

He let go and stepped past me, but this wasn't over just yet. Drew Barnes had pushed me too far this time. Taking full advantage of the element of surprise, I grabbed him by the back of the hair and pulled his head back until it was even with my mouth. "Now it's your turn to listen to me, you stupid piece of shit, because I'm not fucking playing either."

Knowing he could easily get out of this position, I took my other hand and grabbed him by the balls and squeezed until his legs gave out. He dropped to his knees, but I hung on tight because I didn't plan on letting go of his precious jewels until I finished what I had to say.

"Drew, you don't have to love me, you don't even have to like me, but you will fucking respect me. Do you understand? You're not going to push me around, treat me like your whore, or ignore me anymore. I will be the alpha female of this pack, and you are going to start treating me as such, or so help me God, I will cut off your dick, shove it in your mouth, and then slit your throat. After you're out of the way, I'll hook up with the next in line to be alpha and still run this pack. You will start treating me right, Drew, or I'll be the death of you. You can count on it."

Before I let go of his balls, I gave them one more good squeeze. Then I walked away. I didn't give him the chance to respond. He didn't deserve it.

CHAPTER 28

Cami

When the sirens went off this time, I wasn't shocked, but that by no means meant that I wasn't scared shitless. I may have known why my pack was being rounded up and forced into the lodge, but I had no idea what we were in for. Or what Nathaniel had in store for Mr. and Mrs. Wright—and that was what worried me the most. Surely, they would be blamed for Teagan's disappearance, and it killed me to think that they would have to suffer the punishment.

The last thing I wanted to do today was leave Gavin's arms, but there was no way I could skip out on rec time, and I knew it would only be a matter of time before one of the guards noticed the gorgeous blonde human was nowhere to be found. I'd seen a few of the guards drooling over Teagan like they couldn't wait to sink their teeth into her, and just as I'd assumed, only minutes after rec time began, the sirens sounded.

As I entered the lodge, I looked around for Mr. and Mrs. Wright, but didn't see them anywhere. I noticed all of the elders and the majority of the other higher-ranking members were being escorted off to the side and forced to sit in a specific area. The rest of us were directed to our usual spot.

Shari caught my eye and discreetly waved me over. Trying to appear as inconspicuous as possible, I focused on the ground and made my way toward her. Surprisingly, it worked. From one side of her mouth, she whispered, "What the hell is going on now? My parents were forced to sit over there."

I considered playing dumb, but if Shari was going to be a part of this, I needed to trust her, and thankfully, Becca was nowhere in sight, so I decided to just spill. "I snuck Teagan off the estate last night. I had to get her to Aiden before he got too sick."

Shari's face remained completely impassive. "Good for you, but Nathaniel's going to shit a freaking brick. Any word on what we're going to do to get out of this mess?"

"Not yet, but after this, I have a feeling we're going to have to figure something out quick or—"

Our conversation was cut short by the banging of a gavel. The ever-psychotic and exceedingly irate alpha of the Crescent Hills Pack took his place at the podium, but as soon as he began to speak, chill bumps broke out over my entire body. The man was far too calm, and as far as I was concerned, that wasn't a good thing.

With a clear and concise voice, the CH alpha began his speech. "People of Red Ridge, I have called you here today with a heavy heart. I very much wanted to work together. To join forces peacefully, without hostility or resistance or bloodshed. But it seems you leave me no choice. Again last night, another of your pack escaped. Teagan Rhodes, one of two domestics living on this estate, has disappeared, so I am quite sure that she had help. As a result, Paul and Lillian Wright have been detained in the cell below this lodge, and all other elders and high ranking members with a controlling interest in your pack's business are being sequestered.

"It is a shame it has come to this, but you leave me no choice. In three days' time, the Crescent Hills Pack will be in full control of this estate and your business. Suffice to say, there will no longer be a Red Ridge Pack. If you choose to stay, you will recognize me as your alpha and Crescent Hills as your pack. In three days, the Red Ridge Pack will be no more. From now until then, the members of Red Ridge will remain in their homes. There will be no rec time. And let me be clear; if anyone is caught outside of their homes, they will be shot on sight. If anyone else comes up missing, my men will be instructed to begin killing members of the council one by one, at the top of each hour, until the missing party returns. This is your last warning. If any more blood is shed on this land, it will be on your hands."

CHAPTER 29

Gavin

After watching what went down at the lodge after the sirens went off, I was all prepared to comfort a very upset girlfriend, but when Cami came through the front door of her house she was anything but upset. She was extremely pissed and more determined than ever to do something to stop Nathaniel. Her face was flushed, and a thin sheen of sweat glistened on her skin. I could tell that she was fuming mad, so I took a step back to give her some breathing room.

Cami didn't say a word as she stormed passed me. Hell, she didn't even seem to notice me standing there. She slammed her door shut, not bothering to lock it behind her, and all but ran into the master bedroom. Letting out a breath, I locked the front door and followed her into the safe room.

"Let me talk to Cade," Cami said, already on my phone and sitting on the loveseat. *Great. Hello to you too, Cami.* I walked over to the surveillance TV and began flipping through the camera angles, just to have something to do. Cami put the phone on speaker and set it down on the small coffee table in front of her.

"Cade, we've got to move and I mean now. We have three days, max," she said.

"Okay Cami. Tomorrow, during rec, get a message to Gage—"

"No good. As soon as they realized Teagan was missing, Nathaniel put us on house arrest. No rec time at all," Cami said cutting Cade off.

"Shit…"

"No kidding, but listen, I think I might have a plan. Can you meet me again tonight?" Cami asked.

"Cami, you can't be serious," I said, standing up and running my hands through my hair.

The look Cami shot me spoke volumes, but I wasn't about to back down.

"I have to say that I'm with Gavin on this, Cami. It's too risky to meet again so soon," Cade said, sending a rush of relief through me.

"We can't afford to wait, and you know it, Cade. We can meet farther from the main road this time since I'll be alone," she said.

She can't be serious about going out again. She just can't.

"We really need a way to communicate on the estate. Can you get me some phones?" she asked Cade.

"Yeah, I can go into town and get a few of those pay-as-you-go phones for you, but will you be able to get them handed out?" Cade asked, and my stomach dropped.

I couldn't sit there any longer and watch her eyes light up at the thought of yet another risky escape plan. I threw my hands down on the arms of my chair just a little too hard, earning another dirty look from Cami as I stood up and walked away. I didn't want to have this conversation with her again, and especially not with Cade listening in, but there was just no way I was letting her leave here again, especially after what Nathaniel threatened today. The man didn't make promises he didn't plan to keep.

"Of course I can," I heard Cami say from my new spot in the kitchen.

"I'll get one for you and Shari, and a few for Gage. He will need to get them to Sammy, Ryder, and Jake. How is Jake, by the way?" Cade said.

"Good as new, as far as I can tell. Listen, can you get the phones by tonight?" Cami asked, sounding impatient.

Still with tonight...fuck!

"Yeah, I'll get them. Let's meet at one a.m. This time near the cliff on the western edge of the estate. Do you know where that's at?" Cade asked.

"Yeah, I know the place. I'll see you at one then."

"Cami…thank you for doing this. I know what you are risking for our pack, and I couldn't think of anyone better for the job," I heard Cade say. "Luke wants to speak to you. Is that okay?"

I watched as the smile faded from her lips and her back straightened. What the hell was that about? A surge of jealousy rushed through me. I knew that Luke was mated to my sister, and Cami knew that as well, but Cade didn't put that look on her face…just Luke.

"Sure," Cami said biting down on her lower lip.

I held my breath and waited to hear what Luke had to say.

"Cami, are you okay?" Luke asked.

"I'm fine. Why?"

"Really? The truth?" he asked again.

Cami took a deep breath before answering, "Yeah Luke, I'm okay."

"You're going in human form tonight, right?" he asked.

"I'm going to have to," she said.

"There is a lockbox under the bed in the safe room. Can you get it?" he asked.

Cami jumped up off the loveseat and ran past me to the bedroom. "Got it," she said as she ran back into the room carrying the black, metal box.

"Good. The code is 06-11."

"Your birthday?" she asked.

"Yeah, my dad set it. Did you get it opened?"

I walked back over to the loveseat so that I could see what was in the box. My eyes widened when I saw the four tranq guns and several boxes of tranquilizers.

I couldn't help myself. The need to butt in on this conversation was too strong, so before Cami could answer, I said, "It's open."

"Oh, hey, Gavin," Luke said as if it hadn't even occurred to him that I'd been listening.

"Cami, can you get one of those to us, and one to Gage? Keep the other two for you and Gavin. You remember how to shoot, right?" Luke asked, and I wanted to punch the big lug in the face. He wanted *my* girl to not only sneak off the estate, but also carry guns with her. If she gets caught with weapons, even if they are just tranq guns, she's as good as dead. The whole idea was ludicrous.

"Of course, I remember. I'll bring them tonight."

"Okay, thanks Cami. You be careful," Luke said before giving the phone back to Cade.

I stopped listening at that point and went into the bedroom to lie down. Asking Cami to do that was wrong. Allowing her to do it was wrong. Why was I the only person able to see that?

A few minutes later, Cami walked in and sat on the bed next to me. I didn't say anything. I didn't even acknowledge her presence in the room. I knew that I was being an ass, but I didn't care.

"Are you okay with this? Do you want to talk about it" Cami asked.

That was it. I completely lost it. I climbed out of the bed and stood over her.

"Yeah, let's talk about it. Let's talk about how you storm in here and don't say a word to me. Let's talk about your asinine plan to smuggle goddamn guns off the estate on the same fucking day that Nathaniel warned everyone that he would begin killing members of your pack. You really want to talk about how you made all these plans and decisions without discussing anything with me beforehand? Really, because I don't think you want to know my opinion on the subject, Cami. And while we are at it, let's talk about why you got so nervous and timid when Luke wanted to talk to you, and don't deny it because I saw you with my own eyes."

I watched as the different emotions crossed her face: surprise, guilt, irritation, anger.

"You're right. I don't wanna talk about it," she said as she stood and began to leave the room.

Taking a deep breath, I said, "It's not safe. If you get caught, they will kill you. I will lose you, Cami. Can't you see that?"

Cami walked over to the surveillance equipment and ejected the latest video and grabbed a few from the desk.

"I'm sorry, Gavin, but I have to do this. I really hoped that you finally understood that," she said before leaving the safe room and me.

CHAPTER 30

Kendall

Not long after Nathaniel's supposed *final warning* was declared, the lodge mostly cleared out, but I decided to stick around for a while to see if I could overhear any new information about Crescent Hills' plans to takeover Red Ridge now that their alpha had declared a timeline. Obviously, no one intended to tell me anything, but I'd been learning how to be a fly on the wall. Right place, right time, and hidden from sight seemed to be the best recipe for success.

I needed to know if anyone else connected the dots regarding the reason behind Teagan's escape. Or was I the only one here smart enough to put two and two together? If so, these dumbasses needed me way more than they thought. If our great and powerful alpha had half a brain, he'd have realized that there was only one viable reason for the domestic to risk escaping the confines of the estate—to get to her mate.

There's nothing else out there for her beyond these gates, but if Aiden were still alive, she wouldn't have any other choice than to get to him before he became too sick. And if this was true, it only meant one thing. The rest of them were out there too.

Nathaniel may think he had the upper hand here, but he had no idea what the members of Red Ridge were capable of. There was no doubt in my mind that Cade, Aiden, and Luke were working on a plan to take back their pack, so Crescent Hills better make their move fast before it was too late. It's unfortunate that Nathaniel and Drew decided to keep me in the dark since our arrival because it only made my decision to return the favor all the easier. For now, this tidbit of information would remain mine and mine alone. Besides, they *should* be smart enough to figure it out on their own.

The meeting had only been over for a half hour or so before a sleek, black town car pulled up in front of the lodge. I knew it had to be Natalie and her family inside, and I was more nervous than ever about her being here. After what transpired with Drew earlier, I wasn't sure I could keep up the everything-is-fabulous façade, and Natalie was the last person in this pack that I wanted to know about my trouble in paradise. She'd love nothing more than to see me fall from grace and would most likely try to slide right into my place if things really did go south with Drew.

I watched from the window as my long-legged frenemy stepped out of the car. Her wavy, black locks shined like she just stepped off the set of a Pantene commercial, her makeup was flawless as usual, and even in a coat, her figure screamed *look at me, boys, because it doesn't get any better than this.* Yeah, I totally hated her.

Drew was there to greet her with a kiss on the cheek, and the way those two looked at each other made me wonder how many other not-so-innocent kisses they had shared when I wasn't around. Nathaniel, Brian, and Clayton chatted with her parents, leaving Drew and Natalie to "catch up" for a few minutes. Sure, I could have gone out there to join them, but I couldn't help but watch as my so-called closest friend and my boyfriend had their little moment. The sad fact that Drew said more to her in those few minutes than he had to me since we'd arrived wasn't lost on me.

When Nathaniel finally decided to lead the group inside, I knew I couldn't stay hidden forever, so I ran may fingers through my hair, smoothed out my clothes, and smiled like I couldn't be happier to see my bestie as I hurried over to greet them at the door.

As if on cue, Natalie squealed when she saw me, and like always, she grabbed me by the shoulders and pulled me for a kiss on the cheek. "Oh my God! Kendall! I've missed you so much! You look gorgeous as always, love. But have they been working you too hard around here? You look a little tired."

Her backhanded compliment didn't surprise me in the least. She'd perfected that little tactic and never failed to find a way to make anyone in her presence feel like shit while simultaneously telling them how "gorgeous" they were. I wanted to tell her what an evil bitch she was, but as expected, I kissed her back and said, "Natalie, I'm so glad you're finally here. I've been counting down the minutes ever since I found out you were coming."

During our little frenemy reunion, the men had continued walking and were now surely tucked away to converse away from prying eyes and ears, having the exact conversation I was hoping to hear. But alas, I was stuck making nice with the pack's head mean girl, a title I used to be a proud owner of right here on this very land.

To my surprise, only a few minutes passed before Drew came around the corner and was headed our way. I purposefully avoided eye contact, fearing the hatred lurking there would be my undoing. My heart rate soared to astronomical heights as he approached, knowing only seconds from now he was going to make me look like a complete fool in front of the girl he was probably screwing behind my back. And if he weren't hooking up with her, he'd most likely do it now just to spite me after the stunt I pulled earlier.

When he was only a few steps away, I braced for impact, but instead of totally humiliating me like I anticipated, a warm smile spread across his face. Then he wandered up behind me, wrapped his arms around my waist, and gently kissed my cheek before he said, "I hope I'm not interrupting you ladies, but my arms just felt so empty without my baby in them."

Natalie giggled and then gushed, "Oh Drew, aren't you just the sweetest thing."

Drew trailed a few kisses down my neck and pulled me tighter. "Not near as sweet as this girl right here."

Oh my God. Who the hell was this guy? It was like I'd been dropped into an alternate universe or something. If only I could read his mind, I'd love to know what little game he was playing. He was as fake as the wicked wench standing in front of me, who was smiling brightly as if she actually was happy to see me wrapped in the soon-to-be alpha's arms. I call bullshit…on both of them.

CHAPTER 31

Cami

Why did I have to be such a stubborn ass? It wasn't as if this was our first argument, but it was definitely our first fight since everything had changed between us. And it was my fault. I knew Gavin was just worried about me, and obviously, I should have included him in my plans before I busted in the house and called Cade, but my head was flooded with everything that needed to be done and what would happen if we missed our tiny window of opportunity to take back our pack.

Then when Gavin went all alpha-male on me, I knew I couldn't back down. My plan with Cade needed to happen, and it needed to happen tonight. Truth be told, the fear in Gavin's eyes was almost too much to take, and it wouldn't have taken much to convince me to change my mind. If it was him taking off in the night, I'd be freaking out too and begging him not to go, but there was no one else to do it, so what other choice did I have? Unless I planned on allowing my own pack to go down in flames, I had to do this. There was no other way.

Trying to ignore the overwhelming urge to run back into the safe room and throw myself into Gavin's embrace, I scrounged around the kitchen for something to eat, but there wasn't much to choose from. Didn't our captors realize that we needed to go to the grocery store every once in a while? Not that they gave two shits about what we had to eat. They probably figured we could survive a few more days on whatever we had stocked up before the attack. Only a few more days…

Three days before Red Ridge's time was up. At least we had an answer to the question of how much longer we'd be confined to the estate. But the most important question had yet to be answered and most likely wouldn't be until it was too late. What happened next?

I hoped we wouldn't have to find out. If nothing else, Red Ridge would go down fighting. There was no way Cade, Aiden, and Luke would sit back and let Crescent Hills not only steal their land and business, but hurt their pack as well. We could do this. All I could do was pray that we'd all get out of this alive.

After deciding that unless I planned on actually cooking something, a bowl of cereal would have to do, I shoveled it down and headed upstairs to get ready. I jumped in the shower even though I knew I'd probably need another by the time I made it back. I thought taking a few minutes to relax under the stream of hot water would help, but it wasn't long before everything that had happened and everything that could happen invaded my mind.

Suddenly, I couldn't breathe even though I sucked in as much air as possible over and over again. With my heart pounding in my chest, I doubled over and tried to slow my shallow breathing, but it was like I was suffocating, and before I knew it, I was on my knees sobbing as the water rained down on me from above. I sat back and let it all out figuring—hoping—that was what I really needed. I'd been holding it all in, all the worry, the fear, the pain, and the sorrow. I'd finally given in and let it out.

By the time I stood back up, the water had grown cold and my fingers were shriveled prunes, but I could breathe again and my tears had long dried up. After shrugging on some clothes, I blow dried my hair and pulled it up into a ponytail. I collected everything I needed to hand off to Cade and shoved it into a backpack. I'd have to do this on two legs, but I already knew it could be done, and I was going to do it again—for my family, for Gavin, for myself, and for my pack.

On my way out, I passed my parents' bedroom and wanted nothing more than to go inside, find Gavin, and have him wrap his arms around me and tell me that everything was going to be okay. I wanted to say I was sorry and that I'd be careful and not to worry. I wanted to feel his lips against my own, knowing they'd give me the strength I needed to get through this. But I didn't stop. Instead, I walked on by as a single tear slid down my cheek.

I couldn't risk him talking me out of going. One look from him could sabotage

my resolve, and it was a chance I couldn't take. This had to be done, and it had to be done tonight. Time was ticking, and I couldn't make decisions with my heart. All I could do was hope that he'd be waiting for me when I returned.

CHAPTER 32

Gavin

I kept hoping that Cami would walk back into the safe room and, at the very least, tell me goodbye and let me wish her luck, but she never did. Instead, I watched her through the surveillance camera as she finished packing her backpack and got ready to leave the house. As much as I tried, I couldn't take my eyes off of her. Watching as she moved around with such purpose and determination only managed to both piss me off and freak me out even more. I wanted badly to try to stop her one more time, convince her she was crazy, convince her to stay, or at the very least, let me go with her, but my pride wouldn't allow it.

I wanted her to choose to stay with me or want me to be with her when she left. I didn't want her to change her mind out of guilt but because she knew how important she was to me. And I wanted to be that important to her. Maybe that was the real reason that I didn't go after her even after I saw her stop and look toward the safe room. I needed her to come to me, to pick me, to stay safe for me, but she didn't.

She only looked my way for a second before turning and walking out the back door. What hurt most of all was that she didn't even care enough to stop and tell me she was leaving. Nothing, not a word.

I flipped to the exterior cameras so I could keep an eye on her as she made her way through the trees. Every time I lost her, my heart would stop beating and my lungs would freeze up. It was excruciating, and I didn't know how much more I could stand. Maybe it would be better for everyone involved if I just left. I could sneak off the estate and find Scarlett. At least then I wouldn't be stuck in this fucking room anymore. Why was I even here? What was the point? If it weren't for Cami, I would have been out of here days ago.

Just when I thought I couldn't take it anymore, Cami would appear through the trees. My breathing would return to normal again, and all thoughts of leaving her would vanish. I took advantage of her time on camera to calm down before I punched a hole through the wall of this goddamn safe house.

"Holy shit, Cami…," I said out loud when she got too close to one of Nathaniel's goons. Watching as she hid behind a tree, her chest heaving in fear, was the last straw. I couldn't do it anymore. I couldn't sit by and watch her put herself in danger. Not anymore. Before I knew what I was doing, I had grabbed my phone off the coffee table, put it on silent, threw on my borrowed coat and went after her.

After being locked up in the house for a few days, the cold January air was a shock to my system. I was assaulted by the abundance of scents and sounds that drifted through the night winds. Closing my eyes, I tried to focus on the one scent that I needed to find.

It didn't take long for me to pick it up, but the girl did a good job of spreading her scent around to keep wolves off her trail, so I had a hell of a time following it. I knew where she planned on meeting Cade. I just needed to figure out how to get there. What I needed was a marker; something that I could use as a guide through the estate. Since I wasn't all that familiar with the layout of the grounds, except what I'd learned by watching the surveillance video, the main road would have to work. If I followed the main road to the entrance then headed west, I hoped I'd pick up her trail.

I pulled my hood up over my head, breathed in deeply, and headed in the direction of the main road. I kept my head low, but my eyes wide open. Remembering that Cami's house was pretty close to the entrance, I picked up my pace a bit. Imagining Cami being caught by some asshole sent me into a full-on sprint.

Within minutes, I saw the line of trees that marked the main road into the estate. I should have felt relieved…should have, but when I got there, I had to look around to figure out which direction was the exit and which would take me to the lodge. I stood there wanting to kick myself for being so damn directionally challenged. I was probably the only werewolf in existence that got lost on a regular basis. As I stood there trying to get my bearings, I felt the presence of someone walking my way, and I knew it was too late to hide.

"Gavin? Is that you?"

Oh shit!

"Gavin? Oh my God! Gavin!" Avery or Kendall or whatever the hell her name was these days called out. I turned toward her voice in time to see her running my way.

"Hey, Kendall," I plastered a big, fake smile on my face. How the hell was I supposed to explain this? I didn't have time to think too hard about it before she was jumping into my arms. When I saw at how excited she was to see me, I almost felt bad for her.

"You don't know how incredibly happy I am to see you here, Gavin! Finally, I'll have someone to talk to. Drew has been such an ass. You wouldn't believe it," Kendall said, pulling back and linking her arm through mine. "How did you get here?" she asked as she looked around for my car.

I had to think of something quick since my car was hidden in someone's garage. Phillip thought that was for the best, and I didn't argue with him. "I had my roommate, John, drop me off down the road, and I walked from there."

"Omigod, Gav! You must be freezing. Let's get you to the lodge. I think your dad's there. He's going to be so happy to see you," she said as she rubbed her hands up and down my arms. Kendall reached up and hugged me again. Suddenly, she pulled back and looked me right in the eyes.

"Gav, you don't smell like yourself," she said sniffing the air.

It was a statement, not a question, but she was definitely expecting an answer. "That's weird. Well, I am wearing one of John's coats, and who knows where that guy's been," I joked, trying to make light of what could be a nightmarish situation since she probably either smelled Luke's scent on this coat or Cami on me. By the time we reached my father, maybe the wind would help get rid of their scents a bit.

Kendall shrugged. "I guess. Anyway, come on. I have so much to tell you." She took my hand and started dragging me down the road toward the lodge.

CHAPTER 33

Kendall

With my heart pounding wildly in my chest, I tried desperately to play off just how excited I was to see Gavin here, but seeing him, touching him, just being near him again, I couldn't suppress the ear-to-ear grin on my face. He was back, finally, and I didn't want to let him go.

No, I wanted to pull him into the thick brush and trees and, under the cover of darkness, show him just how much I missed him, but I knew him too well. He was one of the good guys and wouldn't lay a finger on me as long as I belonged to Drew. Little did Gavin know, as much as I'd fought it, a part of my heart had always belonged to him.

Gavin pulled me to a stop, knocking all of the dirty thoughts of our writhing naked bodies out of my head. "Ave—Kendall, wait. I don't want to see my father right now. I just came to find Scarlett. I know something must be wrong, or she would have returned my calls days ago. Do you know where she is?"

Dammit! I should have known he was here for her. When my eyes met his, and I saw the sorrow and fear that filled them, it wasn't difficult to mirror those feelings in my own, and once again, the years and years I'd spent spouting bullshit at the drop of a hat came in handy.

Unlinking my arm from his, I let out a sigh as if what I was about to say was painful to admit. I ran my hands up his long, sinewy arms and then pulled him into a tight embrace. Standing on my tiptoes, all the while reveling in how his height always made me feel so petite, I wrapped my arms around his neck and ran my fingers through the back of his hair. When he hugged me back, I couldn't help myself from melting against him.

Without letting go, I said, "Oh, Gavin, honey, I didn't wanted to be the one to have to tell you this. You know how much I care about you, and it kills me to see you hurting." I pulled away to look at him, but only slightly, keeping my hands locked behind his neck.

"The truth is she's gone. She hooked up with some Red Ridge Pack member named Luke, and when your father told her that she wasn't allowed to be with him, they just took off without a word to anyone. That Luke guy must have really gotten into her head if she is refusing to speak to anyone, even you."

Gavin's eyes grew wide with disbelief, and then he quickly looked away. When his arms dropped to his side, and he started to take a step back, I did the only thing I could think to do. I pulled him to me, molding as much of my body as possible to his, and hugged him tightly. Breathing him in, I pleaded, "Come here, baby. I know you're upset, but she'll come back soon, and if she doesn't, I'll help you find her. I promise. Everything will be okay now that you're here."

There was that scent again. I knew that smell, but I couldn't place it. There were two things I was sure of. One, it didn't belong to a guy; it was definitely a girl's scent, a werewolf girl. And, two, I'd smelled it before. Inhaling again, I desperately racked my brain to connect that scent with a face, but just as quickly, all thoughts were lost when Gavin's arms enveloped me once again. His hands rested low on my back, only millimeters away from my butt, and I wanted badly for him pull me in even closer so I could feel if I was having the same effect on him that he was having on me.

How would he react if my hand released his neck, slid its way down his chest, past his stomach, and cupped him hard on the outside of his jeans? A few strokes would have him wanting me, needing me too, and I wouldn't deny him. I'd let him take me right here, right now.

When his lips pressed lightly against my forehead, I forced my fingers to remain locked behind his head before I made my dirty, little fantasy a reality. Making it even more difficult to contain myself, his gravelly voice sent giddy, little tingles coursing crazily throughout my body. "Thanks, Kendall, but I have to go. I can't face my father now. I just need to find my sister. Can you get me out of here before anyone sees me?"

No! He couldn't leave. Not when I finally had him here and in my arms. My heart plummeted when he let go of me and stepped away. Looking up at him, I felt my eyes burn, threatening to fill with tears, so I looked away. Then Gavin grabbed my cold, lonely hand and linked his fingers through mine. I couldn't take my eyes off our perfectly joined hands as he started to gently stroke my palm with his thumb.

"Kendall, please. Help me get out of here so I can find her. I'll come back. I promise. I just have to know she's okay."

I didn't know what to say. If I said no, he'd hate me, but if I agreed, he'd be gone. I knew everyone here believed Scarlett to be dead, but my gut told me she was still alive and hiding out with the rest of them somewhere outside of Red Ridge. I had to give him an answer, but…

A voice rang out, causing us both to jump. "Hey, Gavin! Holy shit, man. I can't believe it's you. I've been wondering when you'd show up."

Our eyes connected briefly once more before we turned to find out who had spotted us. One of the many guards, whose name I couldn't remember, was heading our way. He pressed a button on the intercom clipped to his shoulder and spoke into the receiver. "Gavin Reed has just shown up. Be expecting him soon."

Oops! I guess Gavin won't be going anywhere now.

CHAPTER 34

Cami

After a close call with a CH guard, I finally made it up and over the wall and could now see Cade's SUV parked a little ways down the road. I would have thought I'd be relieved, but seeing his car door swing open only caused my rapid heartbeat to intensify. No matter how hard I tried to act as if I wasn't scared to death, I couldn't deny that until this whole thing was over, I wouldn't feel even a tiny bit of relief. Only when Cade and the rest of them were back and Crescent Hills was defeated would I be able to breathe easy. And the only chance of that happening rested solely in my hands.

Swallowing down the lump in my throat, I jogged over to Cade and handed over my bag. "This is all the surveillance footage from the time Crescent Hills arrived until now. Review it carefully. The guards pretty much stick to their same route each night, so it's not too difficult to avoid them if you know what to expect. You got the phones?"

Before responding, Cade pulled me into his embrace and hugged me tightly. "Thank you, Cami. We wouldn't have a chance to get through this without you. And what you did for Aiden…he owes you big time. We all do."

A tremble tore through my body as my eyes filled with tears, and I silently cursed myself for being too weak to hold it together. Cade pulled back and looked at me. "Hey, everything is going to be okay. We can do this. You can do this. Do you hear me, Cami? We're going to take back our pack."

My gaze dropped to the ground and I wiped away the few escapee tears. "I hope so, Cade. But we are running out of time. We have to act fast. Their alpha is a freaking psychopath and won't hesitate to kill anyone who stands in his way."

Cade, appearing as confident as ever, assured me once again. "We can do this, Cami. This is our pack and no one is going to take that away from us." Then he turned to throw the bag I'd handed off into the front seat and pulled out another one. "Here are the phones. There is enough for all of you, and my number is already programmed in each of them. Whatever you all do, keep them hidden. We will review the footage and figure out a plan. We'll contact you as soon as possible, and if you need anything or if anything changes, you call me."

I so badly wanted to believe that this would work. It was our only shot, but I suddenly had a bad feeling about the whole thing. My gut told me that it was going to take a miracle to pull this off. I looked back up at Cade and knew he didn't need to hear that my confidence was slipping away. He didn't need to know that I had serious doubts about pulling this off.

So instead, I nodded my head and replied, "I got it. The major players are scattered throughout the estate. They've taken over quite a few of the homes since our elders and high-ranking members have been taken into custody. Their alpha, Drew, and Kendall are in the guesthouse. Brian and your mother are still at your house, and Clayton is at the Petersons', which is where all the guards are staying. Just review the footage carefully before making any moves."

"Don't worry, Cami. We will. We don't want anyone else hurt. Now, you better get going, but be careful. We can't lose you. We can't do this without you. Get the phones handed out and tell them all to be ready. When the time is right, we will take back what is ours. I guarantee you."

The determination in Cade's eyes told me he believed whole-heartedly every word he spoke. As for me, all I could do was hope that he was right. After a brief goodbye, I headed back to the wall. I needed to move fast, not only to avoid getting caught, but because I needed to see Gavin. I needed to be in his arms, needed to feel his lips against mine, needed him to help me forget how much danger we were in even if it was only for a little while. There was only one person who could make me feel as if we weren't buried under a six-foot pile of shit, and I needed him now more than ever.

I made it over the wall and halfway back to my home when I noticed a guard up ahead. Immediately, I dropped to the ground, thankful for the nearby bushes that provided cover. This was the second guard tonight that wasn't where he was supposed to be. Had they decided to change routes? If so, this would not bode well for our own attack. The guards' predictability was the one thing on our side.

Keeping my body flush against the ground, I remained perfectly still and tried desperately to slow my breathing. The smallest noise would give away my location. Hearing his footsteps only few feet away, I froze and held my breath, and within seconds a second set of footfalls joined his.

I couldn't see them but knew they had both stopped nearby. An unfamiliar voice spoke first. "I didn't think you'd come." He sounded breathless and...nervous maybe?

A sultry female voice replied, "I told you I'd be here. And now that I am, whatever are you going to do with me?" Flirting? Really?

"Baby, if only you could read my mind right now. Let's get out of here. I can't wait to show you just what I plan to do to that fine-ass body of yours." Definitely flirting.

They hurried off towards the trees to do God knows what, and finally I could breathe again. I silently thanked my lucky stars for horny teenagers and secret rendezvous as I snuck back to my home.

Once safely inside, I headed straight for the safe room, but as soon as I opened the door and didn't see Gavin sitting at the surveillance screens, I knew something was wrong. I called out his name and searched the small area. Nothing. I hurried back out and did the same, searching every square inch of my home, but Gavin was nowhere to be found.

He was gone. But why? I dropped to my knees in the middle of my bedroom, unsure of what to do now. How could he just be gone? Did they find him? Did he go after me? Could he be lost out there somewhere? Nothing made sense.

Suddenly, it dawned on me that there was only one way to find out. Scrambling to my feet, I took off out my door, almost tumbling to the ground again in my haste. Within seconds, I was in front of surveillance screens shifting from camera to camera in search of any sign of him.

It wasn't long before I found the view of the outside of the lodge. A loud gasp escaped my lips as my hand flew up to cover my mouth. No way! No fucking way!

Clenching my eyes shut didn't stop the tears from sliding down my cheeks. It didn't shut out the image that would forever be burned into my brain. And it certainly didn't prevent my heart from shattering into a million tiny pieces right then and there.

Cautiously I opened them again, if for no other reason than to confirm what I already knew I'd seen. Kendall and Gavin, arm-in-arm, were walking up the steps of the lodge. Together.

CHAPTER 35

Gavin

I had to fight back the bile rising to my throat as I walked past pack members that I once considered family. Everyone who saw me smiled and welcomed me home. Home, as if they had any right to call this place their home. Kendall, who kept her arm wrapped in mine during the whole walk here, quickly let go when Drew came into view. He was standing next to the one person I didn't know…not anymore.

"Son!" my father said with enthusiasm as he left Drew and walked over to me.

I could hardly look at him. He'd tried to kill my sister, his own daughter, for Christ's sake. What kind of monster would do that? Standing before me was not the man that raised me. He had become what everyone assumed he was. His reputation as the cruel, heartless Fixer was now well deserved in my eyes. My mother would have killed him with her bare hands if she were still alive. Seeing him just confirmed what I already knew: Scarlett was the only family I had left.

"I'm glad you decided to come and join us," he said looking back and forth between Kendall and me.

"I couldn't get Scarlett on the phone, so I decided to come in person," I said flatly.

"I was just telling Gavin about how Scarlett ran off with that Luke guy. It's just horrible. And now she won't even return Gavin's calls either," Kendall jumped in. My father's face tightened at

Kendall's lie. It was a good cover, I thought. It's not like he would ever tell me the truth anyway.

"It was a shock to us all. I never imagined she'd do something like this. Well, you know how sensitive she is. We got into one small argument, and she bolted with that meathead," he explained, and I did my best to look surprised.

"Well, I have to go," Kendall said suddenly. She gave me another hug and this time she whispered, "I'm so glad you're here." She started to pull away but stopped. She pressed her nose right up to my neck as she breathed me in.

It was more than obvious what she was doing. I mean really obvious. She took a whiff of my neck right there in front of my dad. Right there in front of Drew. I could see the wheels turning in her head. She was trying to figure out what, or rather who, I smelled like. Quickly I stepped back out of her reach and tugged my jacket tighter.

Kendall was a bitch, but she wasn't stupid. Sooner or later she would figure it out. I needed to figure out a way to get Cami's scent off of me before all hell broke loose. The look Kendall gave me as she let her hands drop to her side could only be described as frightening. She wasn't going to let this drop.

"Thanks for finding my boy, Kendall," my dad said to her before she walked away leaving us alone. I stood there just staring at my dad. I had no idea what to say to him, or what I should do. I wanted to tell him to go fuck himself and walk out the door, but I knew that would never fly.

"I want to talk to you. Let me tell Nathaniel that I'm leaving. Give me a minute," he said. I stood there with my hands in my pockets and waited while Dad spoke first with Nathaniel and then with Noel. Seeing him with Noel made me sick to my stomach. I wondered then if she was the reason for all of this. Would my father go through all of this, put his own children in danger, all because of this woman?

The ride to my "dad's house" was nearly silent. He asked me only two questions: 1) how did I get here, and 2) where was my bag? He didn't bother mentioning anything about what he'd been doing since he left home weeks ago to come here and destroy people's lives or ask about what I'd been up to during all that time. No mention of the fact that he'd been the driving force behind ambushing and taking over another pack. He just wanted to know where my luggage was. Seriously?

So, I told him, in as few words as possible, that John dropped me off at the main entrance and that I wasn't planning on staying. I reminded him that I had only come to see Scarlett and then planned to leave.

He didn't say anything after that, but once we were inside the house, he turned to me and said, "I want you to stay a few days, Gavin. We are taking full control of this pack very soon. I want you here for it."

I shook my head. There was no way I was staying for that. I needed to get back to Cami and get both of us off this damn estate.

"Do this for me, Gavin. Do this, and then I'll help you find your sister."

Just hearing him talk about her made me want to kill him. There was no way in hell I could live under the same roof as this creep, especially since as far I knew he still believed Scarlett was dead.

He saw the answer on my face, and he didn't like it. How did he manage to trick the Red Ridge Pack for so long? He was a terrible actor.

"It's late. At least stay the night, and you can make your decision in the morning," he said. I didn't want to stay, but I couldn't leave the estate without Cami, so reluctantly, I agreed.

"Let's get something to eat. I'm starved," Dad said throwing his arm over my shoulder and leading us into the kitchen. Remembering Cami's scent on me, I replied, "Why don't you throw something together for us while I take a quick shower. It's been a long day."

Dad seemed to like that idea. If I was going to have to stay and spend time with him, I might as well see what kind of information he would freely hand over. It'd be nice to have something of importance to take back to Cami. I was going to have to leave the estate one way or another now that I've been seen. I was hoping to convince Cami to leave with me. Maybe having some information to take back to Cade would do the trick. I just needed to figure out a way to get to her before I had to leave.

CHAPTER 36

Kendall

I left Gavin at the lodge with his father and hurried home, hoping Drew wouldn't be there yet. I looked down at my watch when I saw that his car wasn't there. Not that the time mattered. He never seemed to show up at the same time. Could be hours. Could be minutes. But if I hurried, I may just be able to jump in the shower and at least pretend to be fast asleep before he made it to bed.

The last thing I needed was for him to smell Gavin on me. As much as I tried to hide my feelings for Gavin, Drew had his suspicions and had, on more than one occasion, accused me of cheating. But he knew as well as I did that it was all bullshit. Little did he know, I'd be with Gavin without a second thought if he wasn't such a good guy, but as soon as Drew and I got together Gavin had made it clear that we'd never be more than friends. Damn him for being such a freaking saint.

After a quick shower, I wrapped a towel around my body and brushed out my wet hair. I considered just going to bed with it wet but decided to blow out most of the moisture and then braid it. At least then it wouldn't be a ginormous frizz-ball in the morning, and it would only take a few minutes.

With my hair taken care of, I headed out of the bathroom to grab something to wear only to have my heart practically leap out of my chest. "Damn it, Drew! You scared the hell out of me!" I shrieked, keeping a death-grip on the towel covering my body.

Sitting on the edge of our bed, Drew shot me a lazy grin as he eyed me from head to toe. "Sorry, baby. I was hoping to catch you naked. But this look…this look is definitely working for me." Desire filled his eyes, and I knew exactly where this was headed. Then his eyes locked with mine and visibly hardened as he demanded, "Come here."

I walked over, and once I was in reach, he grabbed my wrist and pulled me over so that I was standing between his legs. He remained seated as he ran his hands up my thighs and under my towel. With his teeth, he tugged at the corner of the towel that had been tucked in above my chest so that it would stay in place. It didn't take much effort to pull it loose and within seconds I was standing before Drew completely nude.

He ran his tongue up my body, from my belly button, up between my breasts, to my collarbone. "God baby, you make me so fucking hard. I don't want to fight anymore. I'm going to make you feel so good that you forget all the bullshit that's been going on between us since we got here."

He didn't wait for a response before he pulled me down to the bed and covered my body with his. As he kissed me everywhere but my lips, I closed my eyes and tried to imagine I was somewhere else. Only that didn't work as I had hoped. Instead, it was suddenly Gavin's lips ravishing every inch of me, Gavin's body hovering above mine, readying himself to stake his claim. In my mind, it was Gavin, not Drew, and I couldn't help but lose myself in the moment even if it was only a fantasy.

For the first time since we'd arrived in Red Ridge, that night, I went to sleep with a smile on my face.

*****

My fantasy, full of lust and desire, continued into my dreams. It was one of those dreams where somehow I knew I was dreaming, but I didn't care and refused to wake up. Gavin was all mine, and I didn't want it to end. I wanted nothing more than to remain right there for as long as possible. With his long, hard body covering mine, I wrapped my legs around him, reveling in the feeling of having him so close. My greedy hands gripped his hips to guide him to his destination as I inhaled deeply, taking in his scent. But it wasn't his scent. It was *hers*.

My eyes shot open, and I sat up in bed. No! It couldn't be. Could it? How? Why? There was no way it was *her*. It was just a dream, right? Either way, I was going to find out. It was time to pay Cami Moore a visit.

CHAPTER 37

Cami

I lay in bed and stared up at the ceiling last night in complete and total shock. Somewhere around 4:00 in the morning, I'd finally fallen asleep after tossing and turning for hours, so when the doorbell rang at 8:00 a.m., the last thing I wanted to do was drag my emotionally battered body out of bed, so I just continued to lie there, mulling over the same crap I did the night before.

Why in the hell would Gavin betray us...betray me? All this time, he had me believing that he was on our side, that he wanted to help us, but now I wasn't sure of anything anymore. Had he been playing me all this time? Was that why he didn't want me sneaking out? Maybe it wasn't because he was worried at all. Maybe the truth was that he didn't want me helping my pack.

Could he have really had me so fooled? Did he realize that we were getting too close to finding a way to save Red Ridge and finally decided it was time to bail? None of it made sense. But then again, he didn't come to Red Ridge to help us. He came to find his sister, and just by happenstance ended up stuck inside our safe room when his pack attacked. He had no allegiance to Red Ridge.

The sad truth was that I didn't even really know him, what he was like back home, how strongly he was committed to his pack, what he truly wanted after all this was over. But his sister was with us, on or side. Would he betray Scarlett? My gut said no. He loved his sister. That much I knew. But maybe that was all a sham too.

How could I be so stupid? So blind?

When the doorbell began to ring with vengeance, I threw back the covers and gave in. Obviously, not answering wasn't an option.

What if it was Gavin? What would I say? No, surely he wouldn't come, not after what he did, which meant one of two things. Either it was time for a surprise raid on my home, or it was the very last person I wanted to see right now, Kendall Mega-bitch Stuart.

On my way down the stairs, the doorbell rang again and again and didn't stop until my hand hit the doorknob. Before I unlocked the door, I looked through the peephole and sure enough, there she was, looking refreshed and gorgeous as always.

I opened the door but didn't bother with my usual fake pleasantries. I just didn't have it in me. "Kendall, what do you want now?"

Pushing her way inside, she replied, "Now Cami, that's no way to greet one of your best friends." She stopped in the foyer and turned around to look me up and down. "My goodness, girl. You look like shit. Ever heard of a shower? Makeup maybe? At least run a brush through that rat's nest on your head."

Still standing at the door, I repeated, "What do you want?"

I'd never hated Kendall more than in this moment, and that's saying a lot. I wanted to tackle the skank to the ground, rip out her perfectly shiny hair, and then strangle her half to death.

She still didn't answer as she turned on her heels and headed into the living room. After looking around at nothing in particular, she made her way to the kitchen.

"Kendall!" I warned.

"Oh, calm down. I have a message for you from your parents." She continued her search for God knows what, but didn't bother to elaborate.

I followed her into the kitchen and asked, "What? What did they say?"

With a stupid, little smirk on her face, she sidestepped me and then sighed. "Maybe you should consider apologizing for being so inhospitable first."

I figured she was headed back into the living room, but she didn't stop there. She wandered over to the stairs, as if she had all the time in the world, and marched her way up and into my room.

Again, I followed behind, stopped in my doorway, and waited patiently as she scoped out my room. When she sat down on my bed and grabbed my pillow, I'd had enough. "What the hell are you doing here, Kendall? Either give me the damn message or get out!"

Watching as she squeezed my pillow against her chest and inhaled deeply, sent my gut spiraling into red-alert mode. I marched toward her, ready to snatch my pillow out of her hands and suffocate her with it when she released her grasp and tossed it back into its place.

She stood and threw her hands up in surrender. "Okay, okay. Relax. No need to go all rabid dog on me. I'm just trying to be helpful. They wanted me to tell you that they are fine and not to worry. And that all of this will be over soon. To just sit tight and do what we say."

Eyeing her wearily, I called bullshit. She stepped around me again and headed back downstairs. "Believe whatever you want, Cami. Like I said, I was just trying to be helpful."

Once we were both downstairs and standing in the foyer by the front door, I asked, "Why are you really here?"

Kendall opened the door, and I thought she was actually going to leave without replying, but that wasn't Kendall's style. She always had to have the last word, so I waited for the sucker punch that was sure to come. And she didn't disappoint.

With an evil glint in her eyes, she said, "Oh, did you hear? Scarlett's brother showed up last night. Guess Gavin finally decided to take his place at the table and help out. I knew he would come to his senses sooner or later."

She stood there and watched me as her words sunk in, surely trying to gauge my reaction. Trying my damnedest to hold on to a mask of indifference, I didn't respond. After a few excruciatingly long seconds, she smiled and said, "Well, see you later. I'll tell your parents you said hi." And with that, she closed the door behind her just before my legs gave out, and I dropped to my knees.

CHAPTER 38

Gavin

I was hoping to leave the house before my dad woke up, but luck was not on my side. Just as I was about to go, my father walked in the front door and stomped the fresh snow off his boots.

"You weren't about to leave, were you?" he asked, already sounding pissed off.

I shivered as the cold air reached me, and I shoved my hands into my coat pockets. "I was, actually. I need to find Scarlett, and school's starting soon," I said, trying to step around him.

My grand plan was to first get off the estate and then to call Cade and hope to hell he would come pick me up. Then I needed to get Cami's new number and let her know where I was. After a lot of thought, I figured that would be my best shot of getting out of this mess, even if it meant I wouldn't be with Cami.

With my father's feet planted directly in front of mine, he eyed me up and down. "I want you to stay until after my meeting with Nathaniel. You said that you would. I thought you were a man of your word."

"I would have had no problem staying here if you hadn't run my sister off," I threw back.

Dad ran his hand through his hair and turned to head into the living room. "Look, I already agreed to help you find Scarlett. I don't know why you are so worried about her. She's with Luke. That's where she wants to be."

Dad lowered himself into one of the chairs by the fireplace. "You're already here. Just go to the meeting with me. I want Nathaniel to know that you are with us. I need one of my children to appear to be on my side. If you still want to leave after the meeting, I'll ask Avery, or Kendall, or whatever she wants to be called these days, to drive you back."

I wanted nothing more than to leave the estate, but I knew that I shouldn't miss the chance to hear firsthand what Nathaniel had in store for the Red Ridge Pack. I agreed to stay through the meeting, but I reinforced the fact that I was leaving immediately after. Just being in the same room with my father was more than I could stand. If I stayed any longer than that, I would surely explode and either end up killing him or letting something slip. Then he would know the truth about Scarlett.

"What time is the meeting?" I asked.

"We need to leave here soon. I'm going to grab a cup of coffee. Do you want one?"

Really? A cup of coffee? I wouldn't put it past my father to slip a little rat poison in there and be free of his parental responsibilities forever. Hell, for all I knew, that could have been his plan all along. Dad and Noel already thought that Cade and Scarlett were dead. What was to stop them from getting rid of me, too?

"No thanks. I'll just wait for you outside."

The moment I stepped out onto the front porch I regretted it. Not only did the wet, cold air instantly invade my bones, but an overly cheerful Kendall was headed my way.

"Don't you just love the snow?" she asked, holding her hands up to the sky.

"Not really. I'm freezing."

Kendall laughed as she tugged my hand free of my pocket. "Don't be such a baby. Anyway, I'll keep you warm."

I pulled my hand from hers and shoved it back into my pockets. I thought that she would be pissed, but she simply shrugged. "It's the high altitude up here. You will get used to it soon."

I looked her straight in the eye. "You know that I'm not staying here, right? I only came here for Scarlett. In fact, I'm leaving today. I'm only staying long enough to go the meeting with my Dad."

Kendall's smile faltered, but only for a moment. "We'll see about that," she whispered.

"I mean it, Kendall. I'm not staying."

Kendall took a couple of steps toward me, and it took every ounce of strength I had not to move back. She smiled. I realized then that she was playing some kind of game with me. She wanted me to retreat. She wanted to be in control.

"Gavin, where have you *really* been for the past few days?" she said softly.

My eyes widened. "I told you already."

"Don't insult my intelligence or my desire to know the truth when it comes to you. Where have you been?" she asked again, more firmly this time.

"I don't know what you're talking about."

"You are going to stay here, Gavin," she started.

"You know I can't," I said cutting her off.

"You will. You will stay here or I will tell everyone where you have been. It would be a shame if something happened to Cami. Don't ya think?" she said as she threw her hair over her shoulder and walked away. Once I picked my jaw up off the snow, I had to run to catch up with her.

CHAPTER 39

Kendall

"What do you want, Kendall?" Gavin asked as he followed a few steps behind me.

"Hmmm. What *do I want?*"

"Yeah, Kendall. You heard me. What do you want?" Gavin asked, his eyes full of emotion, a bit of fear and worry mixed with a whole shit-ton of anger. I had him right where I wanted him…sort of. I didn't exactly want him pissed at me, but I didn't have another hand to play, so this would just have to do. He'd get over it, eventually.

Channeling my inner innocent girl in need, I looked up at him beneath my lashes and said, "What I want is you here. I don't want you to leave. Everything is a mess, and I need you, Gavin. Just having you here will…I don't know. I just don't want you to go. So I'll keep your little secret. You can trust me as long as you agree to stay."

Gavin let out a deep breath and looked away before he ran his hand though his hair and snapped, "Fuck, Kendall! I'd finally almost gotten the hell out of this Godforsaken place and now you're blackmailing me into staying?"

Wait! What? I knew for sure Gavin was involved somehow with Cami. His scent was all over the place, and the look on that bitch's face before I left her house confirmed everything I'd been suspecting. It was time to get to the bottom of whatever the hell had been going on between the two of them.

"Come on; let's go for a walk. We need to talk," I insisted as I linked my arm through his. Gavin didn't argue, so I headed down to the pier, so we could sit and talk in private. We walked in silence the whole way there, and as the pier came into view, I realized I hadn't stepped foot near that thing since I found Cade and Allison there hooking up. Without meaning to, I shuddered.

"You okay?" Gavin asked, and in that moment, I realized why I needed him around so much. No one else around here, not Crescent Hills, not Red Ridge, gave a damn about me. But Gavin, whether he realized it or not, cared. He felt something. I knew he did, and if it weren't for Drew, Gavin wouldn't be so adamant about keeping his distance.

I looked over at him and smiled. "Yeah, I'm fine." I led him over to the swing, and we sat down before I began asking all the questions that had been floating around in my head. I needed answers. "You said you were trying to get out of here, right? Why don't we start with what you were doing here in the first place? Why were you at Cami's?"

Gavin turned his body toward mine and placed his arm over the back of the swing. It wasn't exactly around me, per say, but close enough. "If I tell you this, Kendall, you have to promise it stays between me and you. I could be in some serious trouble if anyone finds out about what I'm about to tell you."

More than anything, I wanted to reach out to him, to touch him in any way I could, but I resisted and just nodded instead. "Yeah, you can trust me. You know I don't want to see you hurt."

He gave me a small smile before he began. "The truth is that before the ambush, I was worried about Scarlett. I hadn't heard from her in a couple of days, and I thought that someone may have found out about her involvement here or that we had Phillip or something, so I drugged Phillip and brought him here to trade. Phillip for Scarlett."

Oh my God. What a stupid thing to do! But so brave. And for his sister…No wonder I was practically obsessed with this guy. I fought the urge to tell him what an idiot he was. That they'd kill him if they found out it was him who helped Phillip escape, but I didn't want him to stop talking, so I just nodded again and said, "Okay…"

"Anyway, once Phillip came to, he convinced me to stay, that he would protect me from my father while Cade and the rest of them went to get his mother back. I agreed because I wasn't sure what else to do until Scarlett got back and we had a chance to talk. I should have never let her go with them…"

He trailed off, and this time I did reach out. I placed my hand on his knee and assured him, "I'm sure she's fine. Don't worry. We'll find her."

"So when all hell broke loose around here, Phillip pawned me off on Cami and told her to keep me hidden. And well, I've been stuck there ever since. That is until I finally tried to escape and you caught me and dragged me here. Guess you've figured out by now that I wasn't sneaking in. I was trying to sneak out."

Why the hell would Phillip make Cami hide Gavin? That part didn't make sense. I wanted to believe him, really I did, but it just didn't add up.

"So what's going on between you and Cami? And don't lie to me."

He raised his eyebrows as if he was shocked and then chuckled like I'd just said the funniest thing in the world. "You've got to be kidding me, Kendall. Me and Cami? No way. That girl is a bossy, know-it-all brat. I can't believe I survived being there as long as I did. She was driving me crazy. I had to get out of there before I strangled her. Seriously, tell me you weren't friends with that girl."

He laughed again, but this time when he did, the hand that was resting on the back of the swing moved and his fingers swept my hair away from my shoulder. Suddenly, his eyes were serious again as they met mine. The moment his hand landed on the top of my back while his fingers gently ran up and down my neck, he had me. Right where he wanted me. I didn't want to believe him, but how could I not when he looked at me like that?

CHAPTER 40

Cami

I locked myself in the safe room and sat down in front of the surveillance screen. I messed around with the buttons until I remembered how to review older footage. I needed to see for myself what had really happened.

After what seemed like forever, I finally found what I needed. From what I could tell, Gavin left the house to follow me. For a moment, I thought, maybe he really did just get caught when he was just trying to make sure I was safe. But then out of nowhere, he left the path that I had traveled and walked right out to the main road like he was waiting for someone. My heart clenched in my chest, because I knew before she showed up on the screen the person for whom he was looking. And just as I'd suspected, Kendall arrived.

Tears welled up in my eyes again, but I swallowed back the urge to break down. There was no time for that now. I pulled up the camera view of my front door so that I could keep an eye out for unwanted visitors. I had a call to make that couldn't wait, and I didn't want to take any chances.

After Kendall's little visit, I couldn't ignore the panic bubbling up inside of me. I had to talk to Cade now. My fingers trembled over the keys as I dialed his number, and while I listened to ring after ring, my heart drummed wildly in my chest. To make matters worse, my breathing wouldn't slow no matter how hard I focused on not sounding like a manic crazy person when he finally answered. I needed to keep my cool, but I was fighting a losing battle.

Finally, he answered, and I couldn't control the word vomit from spewing out of my mouth. "Cade, he's gone. Gavin is gone. He went back to his pack. He's flipped sides, and somehow Kendall knows that he's been here. She showed up here today and—"

"Cami, slow down. What do you mean he's flipped sides?"

"Gavin, he's betrayed us! And Kendall was here snooping around as if she was looking for something, and then when she left, she made sure to tell me that Gavin was here and that he's finally decided to take his place at the table, whatever the hell that means. He's a traitor, and I have no idea what he's told them. They could know you are all alive and that we're planning something. We have to do something! We can't wait any longer!"

By the time I was finished, I was huffing and puffing as if I'd just run a marathon. Apparently, I wasn't the only one because I heard Cade take a few deep breaths as well before he spoke. "Okay, Cami, listen. I need to you calm down and tell me exactly what happened with Gavin."

I started to explain but then heard Scarlett panicking in the background. After a bit of commotion, I heard her say, "What do you mean what happened with Gavin? Is he okay? Let me talk to her, Cade!"

Cade must have shaken her off because she continued. "No, Cade! I need to hear it. Is she saying *he* flipped sides? There is no way he would betray us. Something must have gone wrong. He would never turn his back on me. Never!"

Cade told her to calm down as well, that he was sure there was some explanation, and that he needed a minute to hear me out. With his attention back to me, he said again, "Cami, tell me what happened."

I told him how Gavin didn't want me to go meet them and that we had gotten into a fight and how when I got back, he wasn't here.

That he was with Kendall. That I'd seen it with my own two eyes. He was a traitor!

Again, I was trying to catch my breath and somewhere along the way, tears had begun streaming down my face, so I fiercely wiped them away.

Then I heard Scarlett shout, "He's not a traitor, Cami! Take it back! You're wrong! You have to be."

It sounded like Luke was trying to console her, and I couldn't risk Cade believing her, so I warned him again. "It's true, Cade. I promise." And even though it killed me to say it, I admitted, "I've seen him with Kendall, and they looked a little too friendly. I watched last night's footage, and he took off after I went to meet you. He left to go meet up with Kendall. He lied to us all. We can't sit around any longer. We have to do something. Who knows what Gavin's told them?"

"But we aren't ready yet. We haven't reviewed all the footage. We haven't gotten in contact with everyone. We have to have a plan, Cami. It's the only way this will work. It has to be a well-planned sneak attack or there's no way we can defeat them with so few people. We need more time," Cade explained.

Then it was over. What was the point in trying now? We'd been played. I'd been played. Gavin had used me, and now it was over. When I didn't respond, Cade asked, "Cami, are you there?"

I took a deep breath and tried to speak, but a sob escaped instead. When I finally found my voice, it didn't even sound like me. "But they know…It's really over, Cade."

Cade sounded far away when he spoke again. "Scarlett, you said Gavin wouldn't betray us. How sure are you? And before you answer, remember the safety of us all, the livelihood of my pack, depends on it."

Scarlett swore that he'd never go against us. She pleaded with Cade to believe her, to believe that there had to be some other explanation. "Cami, can you hear her?"

"Yeah, but she didn't see him. Why would he be with Kendall?"

"I don't know, but Scarlett's right. There may be a good reason. Either way, we aren't ready. We need at least another day to make this work. I need you to keep an eye on Gavin. See if he does anything else that makes you think he's really flipped sides. Watch the others and see if they are preparing for a battle. Any sign that they know we are coming, you let me know."

I agreed, but I didn't know what to think anymore. Everything inside of me just felt so defeated, so hurt, so wronged. I trusted Gavin, and he turned on me. Everything I thought we had was all a lie. As I hit the end button on the phone, I laid my head down on the table and cried.

After a long while, when my tears had finally dried up, and I looked back up at the screen and toggled through camera views until I landed on Gavin and Kendall walking into the lodge, arm-in-arm. As I watched the door shut behind them, it felt as if my heart was being ripped from my chest, and I knew right then that there was no misunderstanding of what I was seeing. It was over, and I was the fool who let it happen.

CHAPTER 41

Gavin

"Shit—this was a complete waste of time," I thought to myself as I sat and listened to Nathaniel go over the guard schedule for the day. I leaned back in my chair and looked around the table. My father was there, of course, along with Noel.

A hand snaking across my thigh caused my thoughts to scatter. I should have known better than to sit next to Kendall at the huge conference table. Her hand kept wandering over to my leg throughout the meeting, and every time I had to remove it without anyone noticing. Oddly enough, she seemed to like my refusal. Her relentless pursuit of me was obviously a game to her.

Trying to block her out, I listened for anything that would be of any help to Cami, but I learned absolutely nothing. I should have skipped the meeting altogether and used the time alone to get a hold of Cade. He needed to know that Kendall was really close to figuring things out, and I had to find a way to protect Cami without anyone knowing the truth about us.

I should have known that Nathaniel wouldn't reveal anything important with so many of us "regular members" in the room. But I was surprised when he told us that things would start moving fast, so we needed to keep our ears open for further instructions. That didn't sound good.

They were planning to end this charade, and it was happening soon. I needed to call Cade and tell him to figure something out ASAP. After only a half hour, Nathaniel excused most of us and asked only a select few to stay behind. Of course, I wasn't all that surprised that I didn't make the cut for his little inside circle, but that was just fine by me. At least now, I would have some time alone without my dad around so I could make some calls. I hurried out of the room, passing Kendall, who looked like she was ready to spit nails. When she hung back to speak privately with Drew, I took the opportunity to get the hell out of there.

"Gavin, wait up!" Kendall yelled as she jogged to catch up with me. Shit! I shouldn't have led Kendall on at the lake. It only seemed to encourage her, but I needed her to believe me. Why the hell was this girl so hung up on me? Apparently, Kendall Avery Stuart wasn't used to the word 'no.' Somehow, she was going to have to get it through her thick skull that there was no way in hell I'd ever touch her, and not just because she was with Drew. Besides, Cami was the one I wanted—the only one. Not that I could tell Kendall that.

"I need to get back to my dad's, Kendall," I said, hoping that she would get the hint.

"I'll walk with you," she replied as she linked her arm through mine and then pushed open the door to the lodge. We walked in silence for a while, but I knew that wouldn't last. Kendall wasn't the type to keep anything bottled up, and I knew something was bothering her. As we approached my dad's place, I tried again to get rid of her, but, big surprise, she ignored the hint.

"You're not mad at me for making you stay, are you?" she asked, pushing me up against the front door and pressing her entire body against mine. I fought the urge to shove her away and tell her exactly how I felt about her. I wanted to see her face as I told her how much she repulsed me, how her touch made my skin crawl, and her scent made my stomach turn. But if I did that, Cami would be the one to suffer. So, I held my breath and reached behind me to open the front door. With the door open, I could back away from her.

"I get it, Kendall. I know that you're lonely here, but you're only thinking of yourself. And yes, I'm a little mad that you're blackmailing me into staying here. You know this is the last place I want to be."

Unfortunately, my frankness didn't deter her. Instead, she followed me into the house, pushed the door shut, and locked it. As she turned my way, her face had softened a bit. I couldn't lie. Kendall was one of the prettiest girls I had ever seen, and in that moment, I knew why she was used to getting exactly what she wanted. She was gorgeous, and tempting, and she never hesitated to go after what she wanted. Most men would do anything she asked of them, but I was not most men.

"I'm sorry, Gavin. Don't be mad. Trust me, I can make you very happy again. Let me make it up to you," she said as she reached out and slid my coat off my shoulders. I couldn't keep backing away from this chick. Every time I did, it seemed to encourage her as if she just thought I was playing hard to get or something.

I put my hands on her shoulders and gently moved her back. "It's fine, Kendall. Really, I mean it. You should probably get back to Drew."

"You are so clueless," Kendall said before grabbing me by the back of my neck and pulling my lips to hers. It took a second to realize just what she was doing. When I didn't kiss her back, she jumped into my arms and wrapped her legs around my waist. I turned my face, breaking her lips from mine, but that didn't stop her. She had the audacity to continue her assault on my neck.

With her body still firmly attached to mine, I walked her over to the couch, unwrapped her legs from my waist and her arms from my neck, and put her down. "Dammit, Kendall! Why did you do that? Are you trying to get me killed?"

She avoided eye contact as she sat there still and silent. "Kendall, I like you, but we can't do this. You're Drew's girl. You're going to be the next alpha female, so this is never going to happen," I tried again.

I left out the part about me belonging to another, or how much Kendall disgusted me. She *was* blackmailing me after all. I needed to play it safe.

"I know. I'm sorry, but I don't love Drew. Drew doesn't make me feel the way you do," she admitted, looking up at me through her eyelashes. I sat down on the other end of the sofa and leaned my head back. How the hell did this happen? As soon as I rubbed my hands over my face, Kendall pounced. She was straddled on my lap, her hands in my hair, and her face only inches from mine as she whispered in my ear, "The last time Drew and I were together, it was you I was thinking about. Only you."

"Oh, holy hell," I muttered.

"Oh yeah, Gavin. You are the one I want, the one I need. I have to be with Drew, but you are the one I love," Kendall said holding my face in her hands. I had to get away and figure out what to do with this wolf in heat.

I lifted Kendall off my lap and stood up. "Kendall, will you give me a minute? This is just a lot to take in." To ensure her cooperation, I reluctantly leaned down and pressed my lips to her forehead, and thankfully, I felt her relax under my touch. This girl really did have it bad.

"Sure, baby. How about I wait for you in the guest bedroom? But you better hurry. I want you so bad it hurts," she said as she slipped her jacket off and headed for the stairs.

As I walked off, an idea hit me. As the Fixer, my dad always traveled with a supply of drugs and hypodermic needles. I hurried to my dad's bathroom and began rummaging around for something that I could use to knock Kendall's crazy ass out. Desperate times called for desperate measures.

CHAPTER 42

Kendall

Perfect! With Gavin out of the room, I had just enough time to make this one memory he wouldn't soon forget. I hurried to make sure all the curtains were drawn, dimmed the lights, and got out my phone to turn on my love-song playlist. Then I stripped down to my black lacy bra and matching panties. When I heard his footsteps coming up the stairs, I stretched out on the bed in my most seductive pose. *Yeah, good luck resisting this.*

When his eyes met my half-naked body, he stopped in his tracks with a look of complete shock on his face. I shot him a scandalous smile, knowing I could turn his scared-shitless expression into one of lustful desire as soon as I got my hands on him.

"Come here, Gavin. I won't bite…much," I teased.

He continued to stand there frozen in place. "Kendall, this is not a good idea. As I think I mentioned before, I do not have a death wish. If word got back to Drew, he would kill me without question."

Jeez, why did he have to be such a good guy? I knew he wanted me. Who wouldn't? Gavin just needed a bit more convincing. He needed to realize that this would so be worth it. I stood up and walked over to stand before him. His eyes roamed over my body and then back up to my face. Yeah, he wanted me. There was no denying it, so I took his hand in mine. I brought it up to my lips and kissed his palm before I guided it down my neck, over my chest, and then placed it on my breast.

His breathing slowed, but his heart rate increased, and I knew without a doubt that he was into this. His scent and pure desire washed over me as I molded my body to his. Looking up into his eyes, I slipped my hands under the hem of his shirt and then took my time allowing my fingertips to trace the hard, defined muscles of his abs and chest. Needing to feel his skin against my own, I lifted up his shirt, and he helped me pull it over his head.

My eyes took in his perfectly sculpted body, and I couldn't take it any longer. I needed this man. I needed to feel his hands all over me. I needed to feel his weight on top of me as he claimed me for the first time. My arms wrapped around his neck, and I pulled him closer. His lips finally met mine, and this time he kissed me back, gentle at first and then...

Ouch! What the hell was that?

I pulled back and looked up at Gavin, but immediately my vision began to blur and my legs turned to Jell-O. Then I think I heard, "I'm so sorry, Kendall," before everything faded to black.

CHAPTER 43

Cami

I'd hardly left the safe room all day. After my call to Cade, I decided to make it my life's mission to observe every move made by the Crescent Hills' elite, memorize every guard's patrol path, and figure out how to beat this pack at their own game, all the while ignoring the fact that Gavin and Kendall had yet to come out of his new home.

By ten o'clock the hunger pangs in my stomach became too much to ignore, so I begrudgingly left my post in search of food. There wasn't much left to choose from, but I knew my mother had a secret stash of ramen noodles hidden in the pantry. She'd never admit it aloud, but it was her favorite stress food. Some people gorged on chocolate, others drank wine. My crazy mother ate ramen in the dead of night when no one was around all because she was too snooty to just admit that she loved the cheap, nasty, dried-up noodley brick. Tonight, I was quite thankful for her dirty little secret.

It wasn't long before I was right back in my chair shifting through camera angles, looking for anything and nothing. The only camera view that never changed was the one directed at Gavin's place. I briefly wondered if Kendall left while I was gone. No, surely not. She was most likely taking full advantage of his return.

My mind wandered to a place where I took off out of this house, marched right over to his house, threw open the door, and caught his two-timing ass in the act. Before I knew it, I was switching camera views to check out the perimeter of my house, so I could time my grand escape.

I stopped and started laughing at myself for my moment of insanity. I was *not* going to sneak out of here and risk my life for that no-good sack of shit! Not a chance! What the hell was I thinking?

It wasn't long before my laughter turned to tears, and I was cursing myself for being so damn pathetic. As I wiped away the evidence of my weakness, movement on the camera outside of my house caught my attention. I sat up and took a closer look.

"Holy Mother of God! That freaking asshat," I muttered as I watched Gavin sneaking around to the back of my house. "He going to get himself killed!"

I jumped up from the chair and hurried to the back door to rescue him from his own stupidity. Sure, he deserved to fry for his transgressions, but if anyone was going to kill him, it was going to be me. Not Crescent Hills!

I threw open the door just before he approached. Shock registered across his face as I grabbed his arm and pulled him inside. I let go as soon as he was safely in doors, and without a word, I marched straight to the safe room, knowing he would follow.

Halfway there, he said, "Cami, listen. I have to—"

I stopped in mid-stride, keeping my back to him, as I cut him off. "Don't even try it, Gavin Reed. You don't get to try to feed me your line of bullshit just yet, so you best just save it until I'm damn good and ready to listen. You'll be lucky if I even give you the chance." When he didn't reply, I kept walking.

Once inside his former little home, I turned around and laid into him. "Are you fucking kidding me right now? What the hell are you even doing here?"

He reached out for my hand, but I jerked it away. His sad gaze hit the floor as he spoke. "Cami, you don't understand. I—"

"Don't understand? Oh, I understand just fine! I saw you! I saw you meet up with Kendall. Kendall, for Christ's sake! I trusted you, and you turned on me. On all of us!"

"No! That's not what happened."

Gavin reached for me again, and I shoved him away with every ounce of strength I could muster. "Don't touch me, you sick son of a bitch! You're a liar and a traitor, and you used me! Was it all just bullshit? You were just using me to find out what we were planning, weren't you? Oh my God! I can't believe I was so stupid!"

This time he just didn't reach for me; he wrapped his long arms around me, and no matter how hard I fought, he wouldn't let go. I struggled against him, but he just held me tighter. "Let go of me!" I cried as tears streamed down my face. "I hate you, you evil piece of shit! You and Kendall deserve each other!"

"Stop it, Cami. Just listen to me. Please! You have this all wrong. I promised you I'd never betray you. Never."

I stopped resisting, but he still didn't let go. With my face buried in his chest, I muttered, "Liar. I know you're lying. Why are you even here?"

He kissed the top of my head and said, "I'm here for you. I had to get back to you. The truth is that I screwed up, and I got caught, Cami. I was an idiot and tried to follow you that night. I wanted to make sure you were safe."

"No, that's not what happened. I watched the footage. You walked out to the main road. I saw you meet up with Kendall with my own two eyes."

Still wrapped up in his embrace, I couldn't see him, but I could feel him shaking his head. "No, that may be what it looked like, but she caught me and then blackmailed me into staying. I walked out to that road because my dumb ass got lost. I lost your trail and knew the only way I would find the gates was if I followed the main road out. But Kendall spotted me. And after she realized that I'd been with you this whole time, she threatened to tell the pack and said you would be the one strung up on a tree next. I couldn't let that happen."

It was my turn to shake my head. I wanted to believe him. My heart was begging me to trust him, but I couldn't. My head told me again and again that he was a liar, a traitor; he was the bad guy. But what I couldn't figure out was why he came back. If he had really betrayed us, why come back?

Slightly releasing his grip, Gavin pleaded, "Cami, please look at me."

I looked up into eyes full of pain and regret. Again my head started to shake back and forth. "No, Gavin. It's not going to work. I saw you with Kendall. I saw you two, arm in arm. That was *not* the picture of blackmail. I know you're—"

Before I could finish, Gavin's lips crashed into mine. With my head in his hands, he kissed me hard then pulled back to say, "I know what you saw, and I'm sorry. I did what I had to do to keep you safe. I wasn't going to let Kendall hurt you even if that meant playing into her hand, but I swear to you, Cami Moore. I'll never lie to you. I'll never betray you. And I'll never leave you again because I love you. You're mine and I'm yours, whether you like it or not."

CHAPTER 44

Gavin

By the look on Cami's face, I could see that she was just as shocked by my confession as I was. I wasn't even sure where the words came from. The feelings were there and had been for a while, but I never tried to put a name to them. Not love, and not so soon anyway. It was real though, and I meant it with every fiber of my being.

Cami stood completely still; her eyes locked on mine. I released my grip on her and took her hands. They trembled, and I thought for a second that she might try to pull away, but she didn't. Gently, I placed her shaking hands on my chest and admitted, "I mean it, Cami. You're it for me. I don't know how or when it happened, but it did. I love you."

Holding my breath, I just stood there and waited for her reply. When she didn't speak, I reached out and tucked a strand of her hair behind her ear and said, "Say something."

She took my hand again, and my heart stopped beating. "Gavin, I...I," Cami started, but when she couldn't find the words, she kissed me. We were only apart for a single day, but when her lips touched mine, the agony of being without her flooded into my soul. I hadn't realized just how much I needed her. Her touch filled me with such warmth, my insides erupted into flames.

Pulling her body flush against mine, I deepened our kiss and took my time exploring her mouth, memorizing the shape of her lips and savoring the delicious taste of her kiss. But as each second passed, my control began to slip. Just kissing Cami wasn't enough anymore. I needed her intoxicating scent all over me, and I needed it now.

I had to have a moment to clear my head. I pulled away, breaking our kiss, but the desire in Cami's eyes told me everything I needed to know. She felt the same way I did. Taking her by the hand, I led her into the small bedroom inside the safe room. When I paused to shut and lock the door, Cami stopped in front of the bed and turned to face me.

Without uttering a sound, Cami pulled her shirt over her head and tossed it to the floor by her feet. I was entranced. She was so beautiful, and she was all mine. I had to be the luckiest guy in the world.

As I walked over to her, my eyes never left hers. Cami smiled up at me as she slid my jacket off my shoulders and lifted my shirt up. Reaching behind me, I grabbed the neck of my shirt and pulled it over my head to help her remove it.

She ran her fingers down my chest, searing a trail on my skin, and I sucked in a breath as my muscles tightened. When she licked her lips, I nearly came apart right then and there.

"You are so beautiful," I said as I ran my fingers down her face. She closed her eyes, completely absorbed in the moment. In my touch. I kissed her again, gently at first, but quickly gave in to every ounce of need and yearning coursing through me. I backed Cami up until her legs hit the bed behind her. She broke our kiss but only to ease back on top of the bed. Wasting no time, I climbed in after her. My lips returned to hers as my hand skimmed up her side to find her breast. She moaned into my mouth when my thumb teased her peak.

As if she could read my mind, Cami pushed me up so that she could reach behind and unfasten her bra. As soon as the silky fabric was gone, my mouth watered for a taste. I trailed kisses down her neck, stopping to pay special attention to her beautiful breasts, and then worked my way down her flat stomach.

Cami's unique scent mixed with the smell of desire was like a drug that I couldn't get enough of. As I kissed my way back up to find her mouth again, she reached down and slipped out of her yoga pants, sending my lust-fueled mind into overdrive.

Our hands and lips were everywhere and becoming increasingly desperate with each passing second. Unsure of how far she wanted to take this, I knew I needed to slow things down before my brain shut down all together and pure instinct took over.

Easing off of Cami, I was rewarded by a moan of frustration as she grinded her core against my throbbing shaft. At that point, all reasonable thought was lost, and with my lips still on hers, I slipped my hand inside the silk of her panties. Cami whimpered against my mouth as my fingers sought out her warmth, and hearing my name cross her lips while she rocked her hips back and forth made me desperate to be inside of her.

Again, as if our minds were somehow connected, Cami grabbed my shoulders and pushed me down beside her. Before I knew it, she had climbed on top of me. "I love you too, Gavin," she whispered as she unfastened my jeans, "and I want you. All of you."

*****

I woke up sometime in the middle of the night with Cami still wrapped around me, warm and completely naked. I thought she was asleep until I felt her soft, swollen lips gently kissing my chest.

"I need to get to my room. Just in case," she told me. Nodding, I kissed her forehead. "I know. I was about to wake you."

Cami started to get up, but I grabbed her and pulled her back on top of me. "Tonight was incredible," I whispered.

Cami chastely kissed my lips and smiled. "I love you," she said, snuggling up in the crook of my neck. I squeezed her tighter before telling her that I loved her too, and then I reluctantly let her go, knowing that she wasn't safe in my bed.

I propped myself up and allowed myself the pleasure of watching Cami get dressed. "Did you find anything out from your dad that we could use?" she asked before she smiled, surely at the needy expression on my face that I couldn't have hidden if I'd tried.

Shaking away the dirty thoughts running rampant in my mind, I said, "Nothing definitive, although it did sound like they were planning on ending this charade very soon. Whatever 'ending' means. In any case, we need to move fast."

Cami leaned down, kissed me, and said, "I like that you said *we*." I took her hand and pulled her down to sit next to me on the bed just before she finished her thought. "I know you're with me, Gavin. I was just so sick about it yesterday. It's nice to hear again," she admitted, looking down at our entwined fingers.

"I go wherever you go from now on. I won't let anyone come between us again," I told her, lifting her chin so that she could see the promise in my eyes.

"I spoke to Cade earlier. After Kendall left here the other day, I got a bad feeling, so I told him that we needed to hurry. He agreed and told me to be ready. We are making our move within the next twenty-four hours."

"We'll be ready," I assured her.

She nodded her head and smiled. "I'd better go. Goodnight, Gavin," she said before she kissed me once more.

She was almost out the door when a thought occurred to me. "Baby, you better go take a shower. Kendall could smell you on me earlier, and I'm guessing she would definitely smell me on you now," I said with a wink. "I have a feeling she might be paying you a visit as soon as she wakes up. I kinda had to knock her out in order to escape. Let's just say, my father's medical kit actually came in handy."

"You didn't!" she exclaimed with a smile.

"Yeah, I did."

CHAPTER 45

Kendall

My brain felt like mush when I slowly opened my eyes to find the morning sun filtering in through the curtains. Wiping away the disgusting drool that had dribbled across my cheek, I sat up and glanced around the empty room. My mind flooded with images of last night as it tried to piece together what had happened and how I'd ended up passed out in the guest room of Gavin's house.

I reached up and touched my neck. *That bastard!*

Standing up on shaky legs, I found my balance, got dressed and slipped on my shoes before I snuck down the stairs and out the front door. There was no need to search the house. If Brian were there, what would I say? Besides, I was sure Gavin was gone. And there was only one place he could possibly be if he was still on the estate.

Halfway to Cami's house, I regretted not using the bathroom or grabbing a bottle of water before I left. My mouth felt like sandpaper, and I was quite sure I could drink a gallon of water and still not quench my thirst, but it was too late now.

I banged on Cami's door with vengeance, more than ready to lay into the stupid whore, but I had more important things to attend to, and when it didn't take her long to answer, I almost thanked her before I pushed my way in and practically ran to the nearest bathroom. Thankfully, she had mouthwash.

When I came out, she was standing there waiting with her arms crossed over her chest. "Well, good morning to you too," she scoffed.

Staring her down, I demanded, "Where is he? I know he's here!"

Not backing down one bit, the snarky little bitch replied, "What the hell are you talking about, Kendall? I'm the only one here."

I picked up a lock of her hair and took a deep whiff, surprised to not find a trace of Gavin's scent on her. But her smirk gave her away. So she was smart enough to shower; maybe she wasn't as stupid as I thought. Who was I kidding? It was probably his idea. "You're not fooling me, Cami. I know Gavin's been here. Where is he?"

Before she had a chance to deny it, I shoved her out of the way and began my search. She followed behind me every step of the way, assuring me that she hadn't seen him since he'd run off.

She even had the nerve to pretend to be pissed at him. "Seriously Kendall, even if he had shown back up here, I would have told him to get the hell off of my property. That is if I didn't kill him first for being a lying piece of shit. He's a traitor to both your pack and mine. You really think I'd let him back in after what he did?"

I stopped and turned to face her. "You're actually going to stand there and call Gavin a liar? I may not smell him on you, but I can sniff out bullshit like nobody's business. And Cami, you're full of shit, and we both know it."

"I'm not lying, Kendall. Feel free to turn this place upside down. You won't find him here."

I searched every inch of her home, feeling more like a fool every step of the way, but I wouldn't dare let her know that. Finally, giving in to the fact that he wasn't there, I headed for the door, but before I left, I had one more thing to say. "If you think for one second that I'm not going straight to Nathaniel to tell him that you've been holding Brian's son hostage here this whole time, you'd be wrong."

Cami strutted over and stood right in front of me. "Go right on ahead. But what proof do you have? Gavin is gone and said nothing about being here before he left, so it's just going to make you look pathetic and desperate for attention. You know…the usual."

Un-fucking-believable!

"Keep it up, Cami. You'll be strung up on that tree, just like Jake, before sundown. Only I'll make sure you don't walk away from it."

Fear flashed in her eyes, which was enough to make me feel at least a tiny bit better, so I turned and walked out the door without bothering to shut it behind me.

CHAPTER 46

Cami

After Kendall's not-so surprising visit, I spent the rest of the morning wrapped up in Gavin's arms. I hated to admit it, but I was more than a little shaken by Kendall's threat. I shouldn't have egged her on, nor should I have called her out on running off to her new alpha and throwing me under the bus.

I knew Kendall well enough to know that she would do it in a heartbeat just to see me beaten half to death, especially if it would give her a leg up in her pack. All I could do now was pray that her lack of proof would keep her from ratting me out for the time being. I hoped we wouldn't need much more time.

Gavin caught me glancing at the phone once again and kissed me on top of the head before assuring me once again, "Don't worry. He'll call. Besides, I'm not going to let anything happen to you. If someone comes looking for you, they'll have to get through me first."

My heart clenched at the thought. There was no way in hell I'd let the CH guards, or anyone else for that matter, anywhere near Gavin. I lifted my head from his chest and looked up to find eyes full of concern. That combined with his resolute tone told me that he meant every word that he said. Reaching up, I kissed him lightly and then warned him, "Don't even think about it. You are not being a freaking martyr for my sake. If we have to, we will hide out in this room while they ransack this house before I give you up. You hear me?"

Letting out a small chuckle, Gavin replied, "Yeah, I hear ya. But let's just hope it won't come to that because Kendall is going to keep her mouth shut, and Cade *is* going to call."

As if on cue, the burner phone rang, causing us both to jump and then simultaneously breathe a sigh of relief. We moved over to the table as I answered the phone, and after putting it on speaker, I laid it down between us.

"Hey, Cade. You're on speaker with me and Gavin," I said before I realized that he had no idea that Gavin had returned. "He's a...back."

"Back, huh? Glad to hear it. Gavin? Wanna fill me in?"

Gavin explained what had gone down with Kendall, but before he could even finish, Scarlett must have grabbed the phone straight out of Cade's hand because with no warning whatsoever, Gavin was interrupted with his sister ranting about what an idiot he was and how happy she was that he was okay.

Cade took back the phone, but we could still hear Scarlett in the background shouting something about if he ever pulled that shit again that she would kill him herself, but that she loved him and couldn't wait to see him. We couldn't help but laugh at her bipolar fit.

"Sorry about that, guys. Scarlett's kind of had a rough twenty-four hours," Cade explained. "Anyway, we have figured out our plan of attack. You guys ready on your end?"

Gavin and I looked up from the phone and into each other's eyes. Smiling, we both answered at the same time. Me with an "Of course," and him with a "Hell yeah."

"Okay, so after reviewing the tapes, we decided the best time to begin is at 1:45, a.m. of course. There is a shift change with the guards at two, so the ones on shift are basically waiting around to go home and the others are just showing up to the lodge."

"And?" I said when Cade paused to take a breath. I knew there was more, but my impatience was getting the best of me.

"And...I'll be calling the others to give them their part in the plan and where they need to be, but you two will be in charge of taking out the guards on the path to the front gate, so that we can get in. You still have the tranq guns there in the safe room, right?"

"Yeah," Gavin and I answered in unison.

"Okay, well you two will tranq every guard you come across, and then Sammy and Ryder will be coming behind you to collect the guards' weapons and take them to the cell to lock them up. Luckily, Gage had a spare key to Luke's and was able to secure some more tranq guns, so he and some of the other guys will be in charge of taking care of the guards that are already at the lodge. Once the rest of us are inside, we will rendezvous at the jail and begin part two."

After a more-than-detailed explanation of the rest of the plan and assurances that Gavin and I could handle our part, we hung up the phone and both turned our attention to the clock. We still had well over twelve hours to wait before we took back our pack.

"Looks like we have a while before we have to get ready," I casually mentioned.

Gavin glanced my way with a wicked glint in his eyes. "Well until then..." Without bothering to finish his sentence, he was up out of his chair, and when his lips found mine, every bit of anxiety I'd been feeling all morning faded away within an instant and was replaced with nothing short of an overwhelming, all-consuming desire that I had no doubt was about to be filled...and then some.

CHAPTER 47

Gavin

"Cami, baby, it's almost time. Are you about ready?" I asked as I finished lacing up my boots. When she didn't answer me right away, I went in search of her. I found her sitting in the dark curled up in a chair in her parent's bedroom with her knees pulled up to her chest and her arms wrapped around her legs.

I walked over and sat on the bed, facing her. She lowered her legs and scooted up closer to me. Taking her hands in mine, I asked, "You okay?"

She shrugged. "A little nervous, I guess."

Cami was always so sure and confident about everything, so seeing her there with her nerves so visibly getting the best of her just about killed me. Knowing I had to hide whatever doubt I was feeling inside and be the strong shoulder that she needed to lean on, I lifted her chin with my finger and said, "Hey, look at me."

I waited to see her beautiful brown eyes before I continued. "You are going to do great. We are going to do this together. Remember I told you, wherever you go, I go. As long as we are together, there is nothing that we can't do."

"You are so cheesy," she teased, surely trying to make light of her fear. "But, I love you for it."

I pulled Cami onto my lap and wrapped my arms around her waist. She snuggled into my arms and buried her face in my chest. I was both warmed by her affection and alarmed by her sudden lack of assurance in herself. We couldn't afford for Cami to stop believing in her own ability. If anyone was capable of getting the job done, it was Cami.

"Baby," I whispered as I lifted her chin again so that I could see her face. "What's going on in that head of yours?"

Cami breathed in deeply before she climbed off my lap and sat facing me on the bed. "I just have a bad feeling about all of this. So much could go wrong."

"Like what? Since when is my little badass scared of anything?" I asked with a small smile.

"Make fun, I don't care, but shit could go wrong, Gavin. What if we get caught? What if someone sees you with us, and they mark you as a traitor? We're using tranq guns, but those guards out there, they aren't. They're using real guns, Gavin, with real bullets. What if someone gets shot? Oh God! What if you get shot?" She carried on until she was a bubbling mess of tears.

I didn't know what to say. She was right. It wasn't like we were trained mercenaries; I was barely out of high school. Damn, Cami was *still* in high school. She was right. Any one of those things could happen, and whether I wanted to admit it or not, chances of something going wrong were pretty damn high. It wasn't like any of us had any training in any of this.

What would I do if something happened to her? I may not have known Cami for long, but now, I couldn't live without her. I wouldn't. I'd been the one all along telling her that she was being reckless, taking too many risks. I had always known what my father was capable of. Unfortunately, for Cami, it finally sank in on the one day that we couldn't afford to be scared.

"We can't think like that, Cami. If we go out there scared, we are as good as dead," I said, trying to get her to focus.

"I know…I just can't stand the thought of losing you," she said through her tears.

I stood up and helped Cami off of the bed. Taking both of her hands in mine, I raised them to my lips and gently kissed her fingers. "You won't lose me...ever."

She smiled, but it didn't quite reach her eyes. There was no way around the thought that this might be our last day together. As much as I tried to hide my own fears, and as much as I tried to fight hers away, they remained.

"Let's just trust each other. Let's watch each other's backs. Let's try and stay focused and not think about the what-ifs," I said.

"You're right. I know you're right. I'm being stupid."

"You're not being stupid, Cami. Not being nervous at all, now that would be stupid." She took a deep breath, and I wiped the few remaining tears from her face. "We have about ten minutes before we have to head out, and I plan to spend the next nine minutes and forty-five seconds making out with the sexiest werewolf I have ever seen."

Cami smiled and pulled me to her for a quick kiss. "What are you going to do with the last fifteen seconds?" she asked.

I lifted Cami up so that we were nose to nose, and she wrapped her long legs around my waist. "The last fifteen seconds I will spend putting my coat on. Girl, it's freezing out there," I teased.

Cami rolled her eyes at me. "You are such a romantic, Gavin Reed."

"I know," I agreed. "Now, please stop talking. You are cutting into my make-out time."

CHAPTER 48

Kendall

I'd been lying in bed in the weird state of half sleep for what felt like hours. Unsure if I was actually asleep or not, one thing was for sure: my mind had been running on a hamster wheel, and I was quite sure I could open my eyes at any moment and be wide awake, but for whatever reason, my eyes remained sealed. Maybe I was asleep after all.

I tried desperately to clear my mind, to think of nothing, but it wasn't working. I couldn't get past the ominous feeling inside of me that something bad was going to happen. Gavin never returned, not that I really expected him to, but I couldn't help but wonder where he ran off to or what he'd gotten himself into. Was he still here somewhere? Did he go find Scarlett? Would he be stupid enough to get wrapped up in whatever plan Cade must be cooking up to take back his pack? God, I hoped not. Unless he had a death wish.

Why couldn't I just shut down my brain and finally fall asleep? Or was I asleep? Or was I simply stuck in a nightmare where my overactive brain refused to behave?

Then a strange noise outside shot my eyes wide open and my internal debate finally came to an end. Instinctively, my head turned to the side to see if Drew had heard it too. Nope. There he laid, the man who so quickly became the bane of my existence, sleeping soundly. Lightly snoring, even. Gross. *I bet Gavin doesn't snore.*

I slipped out of bed and tiptoed over to the window. Pulling the curtain aside just the slightest bit, I peeked outside. Even with the light from the moon, I didn't see anything. By this point, I was sure I'd imagined the whole thing, but I wasn't ready to get back on the hamster wheel just yet.

I snuck out of the bedroom and down the stairs. Bypassing Nathaniel's bedroom, I headed toward the front door. I considered opening it to take a look around, but that ominous feeling was suddenly back with a vengeance, so I just checked that the door was locked instead. While I was at it, I checked the back door as well, but before I made my way back upstairs, I stole a quick glance out the crack in the curtains of the living room window.

Nothing out of the ordinary. Just one of the CH guards roaming aimlessly back and forth out in the near distance, probably counting down the minutes until the shift change. I watched for a moment wondering how these pseudo-guards would actually match up against Red Ridge at its best. Sure, they look all tough with their automatic weapons and camo, but we're wolves for God's sake. Not a damn military. When did they forget that? We have claws and teeth. Why did they feel the need to strap a small arsenal to their chests? Pathetic.

Just as I began to turn away from the window, he went down. The guard literally dropped to the ground like he'd been shot, but there was no shot fired or any blood from what I could tell from where I was standing. My heart drummed in my chest as I surveyed the area. Someone was out there.

And then there *he* was, causing my pulse to race even more. Out in the brush, I saw him. I couldn't see his face, but I knew it was him. I'd memorized his stature long ago, the shape of his body, the way only he carried himself. Gavin was out there, and I couldn't stop the smile that spread across my face.

And so it begins.

Before I could talk myself out of it, I turned around and headed back up the stairs and into my bed. I scooted as far away from Drew as possible, closed my eyes, and waited.

CHAPTER 49

Cami

Ready as we'd ever be, we had taken off into the night, all geared up and ready to take out the guards one by one. Gavin and I stayed within sight of one another, neither of us willing to separate. With Gavin's words of encouragement, I forced myself to put aside my fears and just get on with it, and after the first guard was down, thanks to my tranq, I finally found the confidence I was lacking. I could do this. We could do this. Together.

Like seasoned spies in our own little version of espionage, we stealthily moved through the cover of darkness, seeking out our next target. With a head nod as his warning, Gavin took out the next guard. Two tranqs used, two guards down. I'd say we were off to a good start. We couldn't afford not to be. One wrong step and the whole plan could be over.

We continued down the path perfectly synchronized. I covered his back as Gavin led the way. CH's biggest weakness was that we knew exactly where they'd be, which meant our only downfall would be if one of the guards changed course, but from what we'd seen so far, they were as predictable as they come. Not to mention lazy.

We slowed up as soon as we came upon the area we expected to find the next guard, and just as expected, he was there, checking his watch and barely paying attention to his surroundings. Giving me his signal, Gavin took his shot, but the tranq whizzed right by the guard. He'd missed, causing the guard to immediately duck. But I was ready. Taking one step to the side to keep Gavin out of my line of fire, I aimed and pulled the trigger. Down he went, and I was rewarded with a sigh of relief and a smile from my guy.

The next few guards went down as easily as the first, and we had actually made it to the gate unscathed. There were still four guards surrounding the gate, but we had gotten there just in time. They were all together, loading up their Jeep and awaiting the next crew's arrival. If all had gone as planned with the others, no one would be showing up any time soon, and every guard standing between us and opening that gate were sitting ducks.

Knowing we had to take them out as quickly as possible, the plan was to fire off our first shots at the same time and then immediately do it again, hopefully getting all four of them knocked out before they had the opportunity to either run or fire back, and we both knew it wouldn't be tranqs they'd be shooting. It was risky, but it was our only option.

We waited patiently for just the right moment, and when one of them pointed out something in one of the bags in the Jeep, Gavin gave the signal, and we fired off our first shots and then the next almost immediately and perfectly in synchronization. All four guards were down before they even had the chance to wonder what was going on.

Once we had the gate open, Cade, Allison, Aiden, Teagan, Scarlett, and Luke hustled inside. After Gavin and Scarlett's brief embrace, we all squeezed into the tiny guard shack and Cade, being in the ultimate alpha mode, took over. "Everyone find some camo and put it on. If there's not enough, someone needs to go strip down the guards out there before Sammy and Ryder make it over here to collect them."

Without question, we began grabbing whatever camo we could find. While we dressed, Cade continued, "We're going to drive back to the lodge, just as the guards would have for shift change.

Hopefully, everyone is still asleep, but just in case, it will look less suspicious if we look like guards. Girls, make sure you find a hat and stuff your hair up inside. Once we get to the lodge, we'll have more time to talk. Let's just get through this part for now."

Moments after we were all dressed, Ryder and Sammy arrived and handed us all a weapon, a real weapon. "Just in case," Sammy said when my eyes went wide. "We'll see you back at the lodge." Then he turned his attention to Cade and said, "So far, so good, Boss."

Just as instructed, we loaded up in the Jeep and headed toward our next destination. With my mind in overdrive, I focused on taking long, deep breaths in an attempt to cool my nerves. I hadn't seen my parents since the night this all began, and all I could do was pray they were still alive and well. Until this point, I hadn't allowed myself to believe otherwise. They had to be.

I'd convinced myself days ago that if Crescent Hills had hurt anyone they'd been holding hostage, they would have made a public showing of it. Nathaniel got off on instilling fear in others, and surely he wouldn't pass up the opportunity to show us just how much power he had over us all. Yeah, they would be fine. Worried…scared maybe, but alive.

As if somehow sensing the anxiety pouring off of me, Gavin wrapped an arm around me and pulled me close. "It's all going to work out, Cami. No worries, okay?"

I nodded my head and offered a weak smile just as we pulled up to the lodge. With no time to hesitate, we were in the lodge and down to the jail before my mind had time to register any of it.

All I could see were my parents standing before me, my mother with tears in her eyes and my father's arms reaching out for me. I may have resented the hell out of them for smothering me to death for the last seventeen years, but none of it mattered in that moment. I loved them and had never been more relieved in all of my life to see them.

"Dad! Mom! Thank God," I cried as I fell into my father's arms. I reached out for my mom as well, and Dad pulled her into our embrace.

Grabbing my face in her hands, my mother ask, "Baby, are you okay? We've been so worried."

Nodding my head, I assured her, "I'm fine. Really. I'm just so glad you're okay." I looked around the small room, watching as Luke, Aiden, and Alli all reunited with their parents. "I'm just so glad all of you are okay."

Then my attention shifted to Cade. He stood there witnessing it all with a cold, distant look in his eyes, and my heart sank for the loss he had suffered from all of this. Not only was his father dead, but his mother betrayed him in the worst of ways. Her hate for her husband allowed her to turn her back on her only son. Cade could deny it until the day he died, but it was killing him inside.

Thankfully, Alli finally noticed and reached out for him, but it seemed it was too little, too late. With murderous rage in his eyes, Cade practically roared, "Let's get on with this. We can celebrate once this is over."

Cade began handing out ammo and weapons to each of us as he explained, "We need to break up into three groups. One will take down Nathaniel's place, one will go to Clayton's, and I'll be heading to Brian's. I have a score to settle with that man."

Phillip's head popped up, and he looked around at the group of us. It was clear he had something to say to his new alpha and was weighing his options of how best to go about broaching the subject. He laid down his weapon and placed his hand on Cade's back. "Son, first let me say that I have all the respect in the world for you and your plan. This is your mission, and I'm here to follow orders, but I think it would be in all of our best interests if we did what we could to keep our emotions out of this. For the safety of everyone—"

"What the hell are you saying, Phillip? That I can't lead this pack without my emotions getting in the way? Are you fucking kidding me right now?"

"Just hear me out, Cade, and if you disagree, we'll do it your way. Everyone's emotions are running high right now, mine included. We have mates here, parents that were just reunited with their children, and a whole lot of hate for the people who did this to us. I just think we may want to be smart about who we group up and who storms whose house."

Cade was about to interrupt again when Luke cut in. "I think he's right, Cade. As much as I want to slaughter Drew right now for what he did to Scarlett, we need to be thinking with our heads right now, and I know I can't do that when every fiber of my being is shouting at me to take off right now, shift, and rip Drew to sheds. Trust me when I tell you, I'm struggling with this too, man."

Cade nodded his head at his new second in command and then turned to Phillip. "So what are you suggesting?"

"First, we separate the mates. I know you want to keep them close, but we need you all completely focused, and you can't do that with one eye on your mate." My gut immediately twisted as his words registered. But then again, Gavin wasn't my mate. Maybe we wouldn't be separated.

Addressing the group as a whole, Phillip continued, "Second, I think Cade should lead the group to Nathaniel's. Naturally, he should be the one to take down the alpha, and it would probably be best if he stayed away from his mother and Brian during this. Gavin should keep his distance from his father as well, so he should be with the group that goes to Clayton's. Unfortunately, that leaves Luke heading up the group going to Brian's." Phillip turned to his son and asked, "Do you think you can handle it?"

Pulling Scarlett against him, as if he needed the support, Luke simply nodded.

Cade took over from there and split us all into three groups. When it was all said and done, Gavin and I were separated after all. After plenty of kisses between mates, hugs between children and parents, and countless calls of "Be careful" or "Good luck" amongst friends, we moved into our groups.

Standing with Luke, our leader, and Allison, Sammy, and Vince, I looked over at Gavin and offered him my most reassuring smile. I wasn't so sure it was convincing, but I tried anyway. With a smile and a wink, Gavin appeared more confident than ever. He never ceased to amaze me. The guy was gearing up to invade the most dangerous area, the home that housed all of the off-duty guards on the estate, and he didn't even flinch. But when I looked over at the guys standing with him, Aiden, Phillip, Dane, Jake, Logan, and Nick, I knew his crew would do whatever it took to take back our pack.

The last group, led by our new alpha, was the first to leave. Cade opened the door and Gage, Scarlett, Ryder, and Shari followed. It was time. With one last look at my parents, who were staying behind to guard the lodge, I took my leave, praying luck would be on our side.

CHAPTER 50

Gavin

Armed with only a tranquilizer gun and my were-senses, I followed Aiden and his team into the darkness. I was assigned to go with Luke's dad and some guys that I had just met. Although Jake, Dane, Logan, and Nick all seemed like good guys, I felt like an outsider among them.

It probably didn't help that my father was public enemy number two around here, or that Cami personally threatened each one of them that they'd have to answer to her if anything happened to me. They assured her that I would be fine but then each shot me a grin that said that they now had all they needed on me to make my life hell from here on out. If tonight went as planned, and we are all safe in the morning, I had a bad feeling that I would be the brunt of many jokes for weeks to come, maybe even longer.

Our mission: go to the house where the guards were staying, take them down—all of them—and bring Clayton in alive and conscious for questioning. I didn't like being separated from Cami, but I was kind of glad she wasn't here for this. The seven of us were up against all of the off-duty guards, guards that had real weapons—not tranq guns. If any mission had the chance of going very wrong, it was ours. There were at least twenty guards inside that one house. I had just met these guys, and I was already putting my life in their hands and vice versa.

We moved fast at first, keeping to the shadows and moving one at a time. We took turns watching each other's backs as we moved from tree to tree. It didn't take long for the house to come into view. Phillip signaled for us to stop and gather around.

"We need to split up now," Phillip said, nodding to Aiden for him to take over.

Aiden didn't miss a step. "Jake, you and Logan go around and enter through the back door." Jake and Logan nodded before leaving the group. We all watched as they disappeared around the side of the house. "Phillip and I will go in first through the front door. I want Gavin to take the far side of the house," Aiden said and then looked right at me. "Stay at the front. Watch for guys trying to escape out the windows. When you see me, Phillip, and Dane make it all the way inside, you come in through the front." I nodded in understanding.

I stood there and listened as he told Nick to do the exact same thing on the other side of the house, except he was supposed to enter through the back door.

"Shouldn't one of us, at least, have a real gun?" Dane asked. Surprisingly, I was relieved that he asked because I know I was thinking the same thing. Aiden looked to Phillip, who answered, "I have my gun." He pulled back his jacket, revealing a very real handgun holstered around his chest. "I don't want to have to use it though. Most of those men inside are not much older than any of you and are just following orders. Cade made it very clear that there are to be as few casualties as possible, and remember, we are not cold-blooded killers. We will, however, do what we have to do to protect our pack," Phillip said as he concealed his weapon once more.

Aiden told us all to take our positions, so I cautiously made my way through the trees to the far side of the house. I found a spot between two large pines. From where I was, I couldn't be seen from any direction except directly behind me. I saw Aiden, Phillip, and Dane take their positions on the front porch and watched as Phillip raised his hand. With his fingers, he counted: three...two...one.

Things happened so fast after that. Phillip opened the door, and Aiden went in shooting. Aiden was followed inside by Dane, and then Phillip. I could hear the shots fired and the commotion from where I was in the trees. I waited like I was supposed to, but it took every ounce of restraint that I had. No one tried to escape out of the windows, but I did see a guy try to climb down the balcony. I waited until he was almost all the way down before I shot him.

A wave of panic and guilt swept through me when I realized the guy I shot was a buddy. His name was Trey. We had grown up together, and he wasn't a bad guy. Phillip was right; he was just following orders. Trey had a girl back home and a baby on the way. Having a baby at nineteen was hard enough without having to deal with this crazy shit. Suddenly, I was very thankful that Cade wasn't as cold and ruthless as my father and Nathaniel. If he were, I would have just killed a friend.

Shaking the thought away, I hurried inside to catch up with the others. I stopped in my tracks as soon as I stepped into the main room. Bodies lay everywhere. There must have been ten guys lying unconscious on the floor. I could feel the bile in my stomach rising up to my throat. I knew in my mind that every single one of these guys, all of whom I had known my whole life, would be okay. I knew that they weren't dead, but they looked it. They really did look dead.

I could hear Aiden yelling in the other room and shots still going off upstairs. I ran into the room where Aiden was, and he looked to have everything under control, so I went back to help whoever was upstairs. I'd only made it up the first few steps before I saw him. Clayton. He was standing in the hallway eyeing the balcony, which was being searched by Jake, who was apparently occupying Clayton's chosen route of escape.

Jake's back was to Clayton, but Clayton's back was to me, so I continued up the stairs as quietly as possible. I was sure I could reach Clayton before he made a move, but like the heartless assassin that he was, Clayton raised his gun and pointed it right at Jake's back. He was going to shoot Jake in the back like a coward. Without a second thought, I raised my own gun and fired, hitting Clayton right in the back of his neck. Immediately, his gun dropped to the floor.

Hearing the shot, Jake turned around and saw what had happened. I knew in that moment, by the way Jake looked at me, that I had just made a friend for life.

We were supposed to bring him back awake, but to hell with that. He would be a lot easier to transport this way anyway. Logan came around the corner and told us that the upstairs was clear. Together, Jake and I dragged Clayton down the stairs.

By the time we got downstairs, Aiden, Phillip, Dane, and Nick were all busy moving the unconscious men into the living room and tying their hands and feet together with zip ties.

"Cade said awake," Aiden said, pointing to the limp body of Clayton, "but I like him better that way." We all kind of laughed. It wasn't that funny, but it did lighten the mood tremendously. Our mission was a success. It was amazing how much the element of surprise could help you out.

After all the Crescent Hills guards were tied up, Aiden told Logan and Nick to stay at the house. Phillip assured them that we would send reinforcements as soon as we were back at the lodge. Jake and I carried Clayton to one of the trucks parked outside and threw him not so gently into the bed. Aiden and Phillip climbed in the front, while Jake, Dane, and myself jumped into the back. Just an hour or so ago, I had felt like an outsider. After that mission, whether or not I belonged was no longer an issue. This was where I was meant to be.

CHAPTER 51

Kendall

I was lying in bed with my eyes wide open when I heard them enter the house. While I had no idea who comprised "they," I knew someone was coming, that it had only been a matter of time. While the anticipation had been killing me, my body still jerked at the sound of the front door opening.

I'd had it all planned out in my head. I'd leave Drew sleeping and quietly surrender, pledging to help Red Ridge take back their pack in any way I could. Screw loyalty. Drew had never been loyal a day in his life, and I was by no means putting my life on the line for him or his pack. And that was exactly what it was. *His* pack.

Looking over at Drew, I said a silent prayer that Gavin was among the intruders and then slipped out of bed, ready to face whatever destiny had in store for me.

But as soon as my fingers touched the doorknob, pure terror struck. What the hell was I thinking? What if it was Cade down there? He'd be less likely to take pity on me than the Devil himself. After what I did to Allison, I'd be lucky if he didn't kill me on the spot. Who was I kidding? Did I really think they'd just take me back?

I turned back around and looked at Drew, contemplating whether or not to make a break for it alone or to take him with me. In the end, my fear of doing this alone won out, and I rushed over to the bed. "Drew, wake the fuck up!" I whispered as I shook him relentlessly.

"Someone's here! I think it's Red Ridge. We have to get out of here! Now!"

I grabbed a pair of sweats for myself and threw a pair of pants at him just as he shot up in bed. "What? What's going on?"

In seconds, we were both partially dressed, and I grabbed his keys off the dresser. "They're here! And if we don't get the hell out of here now, we won't be going anywhere! Not alive, anyway."

I rushed over to the window and opened it as wide as it would go. Never had I lived anywhere that I didn't have an escape route, and little did Drew know that I'd picked this room for a reason. With an awning over the porch just below us, it wasn't a far jump. I might get a twisted ankle along the way, but it wouldn't be fatal. "Come on! This is the only way."

"You want to jump out of a second-story window? Are you freaking insane?"

I turned back to the man I obviously should have just left sleeping, and replied, "You do whatever the fuck you want. I'm out of here." And with that, I made the first jump. I landed on the awning with ease, but the jump to the ground would be a bit trickier.

Just as I was about to go for it, Drew landed beside me. "You know this would be a whole hell of a lot easier as wolves."

I huffed and replied, "No shit, Sherlock. But then we wouldn't be able to drive out of here. And if we did, we'd be naked. Not really up for that in January. You really do think I'm an idiot, don't you?"

Without waiting for him to respond, I leapt to the ground. This time I didn't stick my landing. Instead, I fell to the side and took quite the tumble. Thankfully, nothing was broken, sprained, twisted, or otherwise. Of course, Drew had no problems with his landing. Bastard!

With our bodies practically plastered to the side of the house, we made our way toward the driveway, and as luck would have it, no one was outside. We made a mad dash to his car and got in, careful not to slam the car doors. "Leave the headlights off until we're out of here," I said as he turned on the ignition.

"No shit, Sherlock," he mocked as he backed out the driveway. "You think you're so damn brilliant, Kendall! You're not the only one with a brain, you know."

"Oh really! Is that so? Well, try this on for size, Mr. Brainiac. I'm guessing you nor anyone else in your oh-so-brilliant pack had any clue that Cade and the rest of his crew were still alive, did you? Because I did, and I'm gonna go out on a limb here and guess that's who's in your house right now, most likely taking your alpha hostage."

Slamming on his breaks, right there in the middle of the main road, Drew roared, "What? You knew they were alive and didn't bother saying anything? What the fuck, Kendall?"

I turned toward him, gifting him with my wickedest grin, and said, "Well, all you had to do was ask."

CHAPTER 52

Cami

With Luke as our fearless leader, Allison, Sammy, Vince, and I headed straight to the Walkers'. Thankfully, only Brian and Noel were there, but we all knew Brian put the *D* in dangerous, not to mention the *S* in scary and *P* in psycho, so needless to say we proceeded with extreme caution.

As we approached the door, Luke whispered, "Remember, if at all possible, Cade wants his mother awake. Let me handle Brian, and you all take care of Noel. Get her restrained, and do your best not to shoot her, but if all else fails, do what you have to do. Cade will just have to wait if you have to tranq her."

We all nodded as Luke gently slid Cade's key in the lock. We all visibly cringed listening to him turn the knob and push open the door. The entire house was dark and eerily silent as we entered one by one. Luke signaled Sammy to make a search of the downstairs while the rest of us headed up.

With a tranq gun in my hands and a real one in the back waistband of my pants, I'd never been so nervous. Images of Brian and Noel awaiting our arrival flashed through my mind, and I had to clench my eyes shut for a moment in hopes the nightmarish vision would go away. All I could think was whether or not something had gone wrong at one of the other houses. What if Brian had been warned? They could be standing in their room ready to gun us down the moment we showed up.

Luke halted the bad scenario playing out in my mind once we arrived at the top of the stairs. Stopping to listen for any movement coming from the master bedroom, we all froze, even Sammy, who was now halfway up the stairs. Satisfied, Luke motioned us to move forward, but stopped us again outside of the bedroom door to listen again.

Relief flooded my insides at the sound of muffled snoring coming from the other side of the door. I knew Luke well enough to know that he wouldn't waste any time taking out Brian. He may be an enforcer, but he'd never had that I'm-the-toughest-guy-in-the-room complex that most enforcers seemed to have, and Brian, apparently being a step up from an enforcer, needed the world to know what a badass he was. Luke was smart enough not to give Brian a chance to prove it, of that I was sure.

Before I had time to psych myself out any further, the bedroom door was open, revealing two bodies sound asleep in bed, and I could hardly believe our luck. Just as I had suspected, Luke took about five steps into the room raised his tranq gun and fired twice, both shots hitting Brian in his bicep. Startled, he shot up in bed, but only had time to glance around the room before he passed out cold.

Noel, on the other hand, flew out of the bed the moment the first tranq was fired. With her eyes wild with fear and fury, she backed herself into a corner, knowing her only exit was blocked, but she grabbed the lamp off of the night stand and held it in front of her like a shield or a weapon.

And then suddenly it was like someone had pushed pause as we all just stood there. No one moved. No one spoke. We all just stared at Noel, watching her frantic eyes as they scanned over each of us. It was Luke who finally said something. "Noel, you're going to have to come with us. No one wants to hurt you, but one way or another, you will be leaving here in our custody."

"Just tell me one thing first." A sob escaped her lips as she spoke. "Oh my God, Luke," Noel cried. "Is my son...is Cade alive?"

Before Luke could answer, Noel fell to the ground, a sobbing mess of tears and remorse. The lamp fell from her hand as she wrapped her arms around her knees, dropped her head, and let out everything she must have been holding in since she'd heard that her son's SUV went over a bridge and into the water below.

I'd be lying if I said my heart didn't hurt for her in that moment, but I had to remind myself that the sad pitiful woman before me killed her husband and turned her entire pack over to Crescent Hills, who had caused what she believed—up until only moments ago— the demise of her only son. Noel Walker was a hateful bitch. There was no denying that, but no one could fake that kind of pain.

As Luke and Sammy walked over to pick up Noel, I glanced at Allison and noticed tears welling up in her eyes, but her expression was cold and hard, and it was pretty obvious she was struggling with the conflicting emotions colliding inside of her.

While the guys restrained Noel, I walked over and took Allison's hand. I led her out of the room, down the stairs, and then offered her the only thing I could. A hug. There were no words for what that woman had done.

Allison and I were waiting downstairs when Vince came down with Brian over his shoulder. Sammy, Luke, and Noel were following close behind when Luke's phone rang. He stopped midway down the stairs to answer, and everyone stopped to stare at him as he took the call.

"They what?"

"Dammit!"

"Yeah, we got 'em both"

"We're leaving now."

Luke looked up at his captive audience, a grim expression on his face. "Slight change of plans. Kendall and Drew escaped."

CHAPTER 53

Gavin

We had just made our way out of the driveway when Aiden suddenly pulled the truck over. Phillip opened the truck's cab window so that we could hear what was going on. Aiden was on speakerphone with Cade, and he was talking so fast that I could hardly make out what he was saying. Luckily, Aiden repeated the news. "Kendall and Drew escaped? You have got to be fucking kidding me."

The words had hardly left his lips when a car came barreling down the road toward us. I leaned over the edge of the truck bed, and as soon as I saw the asshole's Mustang, I jumped out of the back.

"It's them," I yelled from the middle of the road. I heard Aiden tell Cade what was going down, and then he pulled the truck up sideways, right behind me to block the road. They all got out and joined me in the road making a makeshift roadblock in front of the truck, and we stood frozen, watching as Drew and Kendall got closer and closer.

We knew the moment they saw us. Drew slammed on the brakes, and his Mustang skid to a stop, momentarily blinding us with his headlights.

"Watch for them to make a run for it," Phillip shouted, squinting his eyes to block out some of the light. For what seemed like forever, they just sat in the car. I thought they were just going to give up, but then both doors flew open at the same time, and Kendall and Drew had shifted into wolves by the time they made it out of the car. They immediately took off in different directions.

"Phillip and Gavin, take Drew. Dane, you stay here. Jake come with me. Now…fast," Aiden ordered before shifting and taking off after Kendall.

Phillip was halfway into the woods before I'd even started to move. Hurrying to catch up, I finished shifting on the run. Phillip might be faster on the takeoff, but on the run, I had him beat. In a full-out sprint, there weren't many wolves out there who could outrun me. Drew always hated that about me when we were young. As much as he tried, he could never beat me in a race.

I flew past Phillip and picked up on Drew's scent immediately. Drew was never really one for using his brain and trying to cover his tracks. He would be an easy catch.

It felt good to run, to stretch my body and let the wolf inside me take over for a while. It had been too long since I'd completely let go. Drew's scent was getting stronger and stronger, so I knew I was getting close. As I ran through a small clearing, a sliver of the moon shone down, lighting my way, showing me exactly who I was looking for.

Cutting to the right, I caught up with Drew within seconds. I jumped. My front paws came down hard on Drew's back. My claws dug into his thick fur, touching first, and then digging into his flesh. I heard a sharp yelp right before he fell to the ground in a heap. I was about to sink my teeth into the bastard's throat when Phillip showed up and put himself between us. In that moment, I hated Phillip for getting in my way. I wanted more than anything to put an end to Drew's miserable existence, and Phillip was stopping me.

I shoved at Phillip with everything I had in me. He barely moved, but it was just enough for me to get to Drew. I lunged for the prick, but before I got to him, he had changed back to his human form. Again, Phillip shoved me out of the way. More pissed off than ever, I stood there on all fours, growling and baring my teeth. It took a few moments and a couple of deep breaths to clear my head enough to make the change from wolf to man. I'd never wanted to kill someone so much in my life, but I knew Phillip was right. This wasn't the way to do it.

"I knew you didn't have it in you. You're too much of a pussy," Drew said standing there behind Phillip.

I could feel my face burning with rage. My hands clenched as I tried to rein in my temper. Phillip grabbed Drew's hands and held them behind his back, "You should count yourself lucky that I was here to stop him."

"He's not worth it, anyway," I said looking directly into Drew's eyes.

After spitting on the ground at my feet, Drew replied, "Keep telling yourself that, buddy."

CHAPTER 54

Kendall

Fuck. My. Life.

There was no way in hell I was going to be able to out run these two brooding, testosterone-fueled wolves of fucking fury. I was done for, and I knew it, but I was not going down without a fight. I was Kendall Avery Stuart for fuck's sake, and these boys needed to remember that.

I'd say I ran like my life depended on it, but well, it kind of did, so I guess the saying loses its meaning when the crazed werewolves chasing you want you dead. There was certainly no love lost between Aiden and I after I tried to kill his sister; and being that Crescent Hills just recently strung ol' Jakey Boy up to a tree and practically beat him to death, I was guessing he wouldn't be taking much pity on me either.

Yeah, I'm totally screwed.

But that didn't stop me from running like hell, from swerving right, from swerving left, from faking left and turning right again. I was actually gaining ground until karma shot straight up from the ground and bit me square in the ass. Karma in the form of a massive tree root covered in snow, that is.

I took quite an impressive tumble, and before I could regain my footing, Aiden and Jake were close enough to pounce. The chase was over. It was all over. The way I saw it; I had two options: submit or fight, which would most likely result in my untimely death. I went with option one.

Against every instinct within me, I sank to the ground and lowered my eyes, showing the big, bad wolves that I'd given up. Aiden jerked his head to the side signaling me to follow them. At least, they weren't going to make me march back to their Jeep naked. Even I could be thankful for the little things.

With Aiden in front of me and Jake behind, I followed orders like a good little prisoner. I wasn't foolish enough to think I could escape without a head start, and I had a good feeling Jake was looking for any reason to *accidentally* rip my throat out.

Once our car and their Jeep were in sight, I saw Drew in the back of the Jeep. He was wrapped in a blanket with his wrist handcuffed to one of the bars, and Cade had a gun aimed at his head. Both Drew and Cade turned our way when they heard us approach, and surprise, surprise, both guys looked equally disgusted when they saw me. Interesting. I seemed to have that effect on alphas.

But then as we approached the vehicles, I was completely caught off guard, when the last person I expected to see stepped into view with a blanket in his hand. Gavin hardly looked my way as he held out the blanket, and as I shifted back, he completely turned his head. I took the cover from his hand, and when my fingers grazed his, he flinched and yanked his hand away from mine.

As I wrapped myself in the blanket, he started to walk away, but I couldn't let him leave like that. "Gavin, please. Talk to me. I'm so sorry. I didn't want to run. I didn't want to get mixed up in all of this. You know that. You know me. You're the only one who really knows me."

When he heard those words, he turned around and looked at me. The sadness in his eyes completely shattered me. "Gavin, please! He made me! I never wanted to hurt anyone. You have to help me."

Looking me square in the eyes, Gavin said, "Kendall, I'm sorry, but this time, you're going to have to help yourself."

CHAPTER 55

Cami

Before we'd even loaded up the Jeep, Luke received another call from Cade, who told him that Gavin's group was taking care of the Kendall and Drew situation and that we were to report to the lodge. On one hand, I was relieved to know that Gavin had made it out of his mission safely, but on the other, he was now facing Drew, the most sadistic bastard I knew, which in turn, would leave me a massive ball of nerves until I saw him again.

Over and over again, I reminded myself that Drew and Kendall were completely outnumbered, and Gavin would be fine, but it did nothing to calm the overwhelming panic threatening to pull me under. The ride to the lodge passed by in a blur, and once we arrived, I couldn't seem to make myself move. Somewhere along the way, I'd pulled my knees up to my chest and wrapped my arms around my legs, and despite my best efforts, I couldn't stop shivering.

Though I heard someone speaking, I couldn't quite make out the words. Then, suddenly I was being shaken, and Luke's face was in front of mine. "Hey, Cami! You okay? We're here."

Trying my best to pretend I wasn't a complete mess, I managed to snap out of it and said, "Yeah, just cold, I guess." I waited as the guys unloaded Brian and Noel and then followed behind as they made their way down to the cell.

Once we arrived in the room that housed the jail, Luke addressed the group. "Cade is backing up Aiden's group, who is taking care of Kendall and Drew as we speak. They should be back with the two of them and Clayton and Nathaniel soon. We need to make room in the cell for all of them, plus Brian and Noel. As you can see, it's already getting a bit crowded in there. So, I need you all to help me move these guys around to make some room. Everyone will probably be unconscious until morning, except Noel here, but we'll just sit her on a bench, and I'm sure she'll behave herself. Right, Noel?"

Luke shot her a perfectly condescending smile, causing Noel to roll her eyes. The whole scene almost made me laugh out loud, and I could have thanked Luke right then and there. That was the first time I'd smiled all day. My God, that woman was evil.

We got to work moving bodies around, and by the time we were finished, it looked kind of ominous, like we were getting the bodies ready for a mass burial or something. They all just looked so dead. Well, everyone except for Noel, though she did look like she'd been to hell and back. Instead of being lined up on the cold, hard floor with the rest of her pack, she was sitting at the end of a bench, zip-tied to one of the cell bars. Personally, I thought Luke should have made her lay there on the ground, but unfortunately, no one asked my opinion.

When we heard the door open upstairs, everyone stopped what they were doing and immediately reached for their weapon just in case. As we listened to the footfalls tromp down the stairs, my heart drummed in my chest, my stomach churned with unease, and even in the dead of winter, my palms began to sweat. I just needed to see him. I needed to know that Gavin was okay. Only then would I be okay too.

The door opened, and I watched as one by one members of our pack filed in, all safe and none wounded, but I didn't take my eyes off that door until I saw him. And then I did. See him. Gavin Reed walked through that door, and his eyes immediately found mine. A smile broke out across his lips as his legs carried him across the room and directly to me. Scooping me up in his arms, he buried his nose in the crook of my neck, spun me around, and said, "You have no idea how happy I am to see you. Thank God you're all right."

"Not as happy as I am to see you," I replied. When my feet hit the ground below, his lips found mine, and I pulled him close, savoring the all-too-brief kiss. There would have to be a whole lot more of that once this was all over.

With our arms still wrapped around each other, we looked around, watching as mates reunited. Everyone congratulated each other on a mission well done while Clayton and Nathaniel were brought in and laid on the ground along with the others, and then Luke led Kendall and Drew through the door and instructed them to sit on separate benches away from each other and Noel.

As they walked through the cell door, Drew, being the evil douche bag that he was, said, "Hey, look Cade, your mom's here. Small world."

Immediately, a silence settled over the room, and all eyes landed on Cade, who had finally acknowledged that his mother was sitting in the jail cell only a few feet away.

CHAPTER 56

Gavin

I couldn't even begin to imagine what Cade must have been feeling. To be betrayed by your own mother? Don't get me wrong; my father was a total bastard, but he had pretty much been one his whole life, and he never pretended to be anything but. My mother, on the other hand, was just about as perfect as a mother could be.

She would have had a shit-fit if my father had even entertained the idea of getting involved in this asinine plan of Nathaniel's. Bastard or not, my father had been a different man when she was alive. And my mother loved me. She loved us. She would have never betrayed my sister or me. It had to be killing Cade to have to confront Noel after everything she'd done to him, and, to make matters worse, he had to do it in front of everyone.

"Baby, let me explain," Noel said to Cade as she tried to stand, but the zip-tie kept her pinned to the bench.

Cade held his hands up and took a step back, away from her. His eyes closed for the briefest of moments before he said, "Don't. Just don't. Don't call me baby."

Cade turned his back on her and walked over to his mate, Alli. She placed her hand on his cheek and smiled up at him. It was obviously just what he needed because his shoulders visibly relaxed.

Noel turned on the waterworks and looked down to the floor. "I'm so sorry, Cade. You have to believe me. I love you, honey. You're my child. I'm your mother."

The entire room filled with even more tension than before. Cade's jaw tightened, and his fists clenched. Alli's hand dropped from his face, and she shot Noel a look that brought new meaning to the term "death stare."

Cade walked over to his mother and said, "Okay…let me hear it. Tell me all the reasons you had for killing my father, for joining up with a pack that was out to take us over, for letting your asshole boyfriend over there try to kill me, my mate, my brother, my enforcer, and his own fucking daughter. Tell me how you thought that was a good plan."

"I didn't know," Noel cried.

"Bullshit! You knew. You knew that night in the rain when you apologized to me and walked away. Well, at least now I know what you were apologizing for. So, don't tell me that you didn't know. Just stop lying!" Cade shouted.

Noel's tears flowed down her cheeks and splashed onto the concrete floor at her feet. Seeing her chin quiver, it was difficult not to feel sorry for her, but I shook that feeling away. She deserved every single cruel word Cade said to her…and more. Most packs would have already killed her for her vile acts of betrayal. She was lucky to even be breathing.

"But I didn't know that they were going to try to kill you. When I thought you were dead…" Noel broke off crying. She sniffled away the sobs and continued, this time looking directly into his eyes. "When I thought you were dead, it nearly killed me. You have to believe that. You are my only son. My baby boy."

Cade held his mother's eyes for an uncomfortable amount of time. What passed between mother and son was just too personal to watch; I had to look away. I squeezed Cami's hand and tugged her closer to me. I only looked back up when I heard Cade finally speak. "I'm not your son. Not anymore."

A small gasp escaped Noel's lips as she closed her eyes and bowed her head in acceptance. I could see the grief and regret on her face, but that look was nothing compared to the hatred and disgust on Cade's. Nothing more was said between the two of them before Cade turned and left the room.

"Someone should go talk to him. Don't you think?" Cami asked looking up at me.

"It's probably best to give him a minute," I offered.

I hadn't even noticed Luke and Scarlett standing behind us until Luke spoke up. "I'll give him a minute, but only a minute. We still only have two guys guarding Clayton's men. We need to move them, or at least send some more reinforcements," Luke said in a calm and matter-of-fact tone. He had slipped into his role as enforcer seamlessly.

The hands on the clock slowed as Luke anxiously watched them. When we had finally been standing there in silence for two full minutes, Luke decided that Cade had enough time alone to cool down.

"Mind if I tag along?" I asked Luke as he turned to go find Cade. I wasn't sure if it was the best time, but at some point, I wanted to talk to Cade. It was my father that his mother was with. I needed to make sure Cade knew that my allegiance was to him and to his pack, to Red Ridge and to Cami. Cade needed to know that I would never return to Crescent Hills, and that as far as I was concerned, I was no longer my father's son either.

Luke just nodded and motioned for me to follow. Cade wasn't difficult to find. He was standing by the front door to the lodge looking out into the darkness. He turned to face us as soon as we approached.

"You okay?" Luke asked.

Cade nodded his head and asked, "What's up? I know you didn't just come out here to check on me."

Luke smiled. They must know each other pretty well, contrary to what Cami had told me about them. "Logan and Nick are still over at the guest house with Clayton's men. I'm sure the guards are still unconscious and tied up, but we can't bring them all here. There is no room left in the cell. Logan and Nick will need a break. And some backup once they start waking up."

Cade thought about it for a while before he asked me, "All the men were accounted for, tranqed and tied up?"

I nodded.

"Then they should be fine until morning," Cade stated flatly.

My eyes darted to Luke to see if he looked as stunned as I felt. Sure enough, he didn't like that idea any more than I did.

"It wouldn't be a big deal to find a few more volunteers to help out over there," Luke added.

"Logan and Nick have weapons, correct?" Cade snapped.

"Yes, but they have been up—"

"Then they'll be fine," Cade interrupted.

Visibly stiffening, Luke asked, "You sure about that, man?"

Cade stepped closer to Luke, not intimidated by the big guy at all. "Are you questioning my judgment, Luke?"

I backed away from those two, suddenly regretting my decision to tag along. Definitely not the time to have a heart to heart. Luke held his hands up in surrender, but the look in his eyes said it all. He was most definitely questioning Cade's decision. So was I, but I wasn't about to say anything.

"You're the boss," Luke said as he turned and walked out leaving me standing there like an idiot. Shoving my hands into my jean pockets, I turned and hurried to catch up with him.

Luke went immediately to his father, and I went back to Cami and Scarlett. I walked up behind Cami and wrapped my arms around her waist. Scarlett smiled. "So, you two are together then, huh?"

I squeezed Cami tighter, knowing that Scarlett's comment had made her uncomfortable. "I like it," Scarlett said smiling.

I was about to tell her thanks, when Cade walked in the room and addressed us all. "I want everyone to go home and get some sleep. You deserve it. We will meet back here at 7:00 a.m. for a pack meeting. I want the rest of our family to see what we were able to accomplish tonight. I want to thank you all for your help and commitment to your pack. We did a good thing here tonight."

He didn't stand around and wait for any comments or suggestions that would have surely come. He just walked over to Alli, took her hand, and left the room.

CHAPTER 57

Kendall

I'd spent the night zip-tied to a cell bar while sitting on a wooden bench and leaning up against a concrete wall. Needless to say, I didn't get much beauty sleep. I hadn't been here long when my favorite frenemy Natalie and her father were hauled in. Natalie was still awake, but her dad was out cold. Apparently, Red Ridge either didn't know they were here or had forgotten about them, but when they tried to escape, somebody out there must have seen them. Poor Natalie. *Not.*

Red Ridge members took shifts watching us like hawks even though Drew, Noel, Natalie, and I were the only ones awake for most of the night. I couldn't be sure of the time, but I would have guessed it had been four or five hours when a couple of the CH lackeys started waking up.

The guards on shift at the time, Ryder and Sammy, ensured that we didn't speak by threatening us with tranq guns, which was actually quite brilliant on their part being that we all knew they wouldn't actually kill any of us, but they wouldn't hesitate to knock any of us out, some of us for a second time. Of course, Drew made sure to let them know that the only reason he was *choosing* to stay quiet was because he wanted to be awake for whatever their pack had in store for us.

After four of the CH guards were awake, Sammy called Cade, and it wasn't long before the whole damn crew was back. There was a cold, calculated look in Cade's eyes that I'd never seen before, and for the first time, I was actually nervous about what was to come. Maybe he wasn't just going to give us all a firm talking to and send us on our way after all. Was Cade Walker actually capable of more drastic measures? The scary thing was that after what had happened to his father combined with his mother's betrayal, he might just be.

Cade stood in front of the cell, and though he was looking at his prisoners, he addressed his pack. "Sammy, Ryder, keep your guns trained on the men who are awake. The rest of you, get in there and zip-tie everyone's hands behind their backs. We will be moving them soon."

Obeying orders, they got to work, and within a few minutes, everyone in the cell was restrained. "Now we need some water. Buckets full. A little cold water should wake the rest of these guys right up," Cade instructed, as if he did this kind of thing every day.

Fortunately, I was already awake, so when Luke, Aiden, and the rest of the guys started dousing the sleeping CH members with ice-cold water, I did my best to stay out of the way. Drew, on the other hand, wasn't so lucky. Luke made damn sure that a bucket of water was left solely for him.

After a great deal of confusion, warnings, and threats, we, the prisoners of Red Ridge, were all lined up and herded up the stairs and into the lodge's great room like cattle, just as we had done to them not so long ago. Even I had to admit, it seemed fitting. The other shoe had dropped, and Crescent Hills was finally going to get what was coming to them. Now, all I could do was hope that Cade hadn't completely lost his mind and didn't plan on slaughtering us all.

Cade ordered us to line up along the front wall of the lodge, strategically placing Nathaniel in the middle, with Brian and Clayton on each side of him. Drew stood next to Clayton and I next to Drew, and then Noel was placed next to Brian with Natalie and her father on the other side of him. While the Red Ridge members all had real weapons in their possession, they still had their tranq guns aimed at the lot of us while we stood there in a line as if they were preparing to gun us down at any moment.

Cade stood directly in front of Nathaniel and said, "Instruct your pack to get down on their knees."

Nathaniel's steely gaze hardened as he glared at Cade, refusing to comply with his request. "Nathaniel Barnes, if you want any chance, any chance at all, to walk out of this place alive, I highly suggest you order your people to get down on their knees. After what's been done to me and my pack, a smart man wouldn't test me right now."

Cade pulled the handgun from the back waistband of his pants and pressed the barrel against Nathaniel's forehead. Luke and Aiden moved in to back him up just as Nathaniel relented. "Okay, okay. Do what he says. Down on your knees everyone."

Taking a step back, Cade tilted his head to the side and said, "See? Now how hard was that?" Then he turned to Luke and ordered, "Sound the alarm."

It wasn't long before the rest of the Red Ridge Pack began filing into the lodge, and as expected, upon seeing us all lined up along the wall, they cheered and chattered, and hugged and celebrated until Cade stood up in front of his pack, banged his gavel, and for the first time, called his pack to order.

As if he'd been in control for years, silence fell over the room and his people took their seats. With more confidence than I'd ever seen him possess, Cade addressed his pack. "Members of Red Ridge, this is a day to rejoice, a day to celebrate, a day to remember because today is the day that we are taking back what is rightfully ours."

Applause erupted throughout the room, masking the sound of the door at the back of the room opening, but Cade saw it. And all the members of Crescent Hills saw it too. Old Man Larson, Jake's grandfather, entered the lodge and marched down the center aisle with murderous rage brewing in his eyes. Cade stepped out from behind the podium to stop him, but it was too late. Larson came to a halt halfway down the aisle, pulled a shotgun from his trench coat, and blew a hole through Nathaniel's chest.

Almost immediately, another shot was fired from somewhere in the room. While everyone was distracted by his grandfather, Jake had pulled his gun too, his real gun, and shot Brian right between the eyes. The two men fell face first to the ground while the rest of the room was shocked into silence.

CHAPTER 58

Cami

The moment the shots were fired, both Jake and his grandfather placed their weapons on the ground in front of them and got down on their knees as a sign of submission. No one had time to react, much less recover from their shock, because the back door flew back open once again. This time, it wasn't one of our own entering the premises.

A Crescent Hills guard, carrying the bloody shirts of whom I could only assume belonged to Logan and Nick, who had been left to watch the CH guards, stood in the doorway and shouted, "You didn't really think it would be that easy, did you? Let's do this right this time!"

He tossed the shirts aside and held the door open as the room flooded with the rest of the guards, now in wolf form, before he shifted as well. I glanced back to the front of the room, realizing in horror that at some point the CH leaders had all shifted too, but just as quickly, the majority of my own pack was no longer in their human form either. Crescent Hills had given us no other option. The fight was on.

I was just about to shift when I noticed Teagan, her body flattened against a nearby wall, and Aiden, in wolf form, trying his damnedest to protect her from the chaos surrounding them. Somehow in the midst of our own little Werewolf Armageddon, I managed to grab Teagan's arm, and despite Aiden growling at me, I pulled her out of there and down the stairs. We couldn't have been luckier than to have been standing near the hallway leading down to the room that housed the jail cell.

Pulling her down the stairs, I shouted, "Come on! We have to get you somewhere safe. I'm sorry, but right now, there is only one place I can think of."

"What?" she asked, clearly panicked.

By then, we'd made it down to the jail, so I turn to her and calmly explained, "I promise as soon as this is over, I'll be back. I won't even lock it, but if anyone else comes down here, you shut this door and stay away from the bars. Got it?"

Teagan, with tears in her eyes, nodded her head and got inside the cell. I pulled the door of bars almost shut, but as agreed, I didn't close it all the way. Then I turned around and headed for battle. Before I made it to the stairs, I heard Teagan over the growing noise from above.

"Hey, Cami. Thanks."

I smiled before I shifted and took off up the stairs.

Peering around the corner, I surveyed the lodge. To say that all hell had broken loose would have been an understatement. I'd never seen anything like it. Wolves had no other way to fight than to rip each other to shreds or to submit but that tactic didn't really work during a freaking Battle Royale. I considered shifting back and trying to tranq as many of them as I could, but in this form, I had a hard time telling who was who.

Honestly, I wasn't sure what to do. From this vantage point, I couldn't even tell if we were winning or losing. It just looked like one big-ass wolf fight. Growling, baring of teeth, and clawing, all I could see all around me was a massive collision of beast against beast. It was brutal and bloody and like nothing I could have ever imagined happening here on our land.

The only thing I did know was that I needed to find Gavin, and this time luck was not on my side. In the short time we'd been together, I'd never seen him in wolf form, so I had only one thing I could rely on. My nose.

Fighting through the crowd, I sought out the scent I'd grown to love in such a short period of time. Despite my best efforts to ignore it, fear crawled its way up my spine as all-consuming panic settled into my gut when I couldn't find him at first. I knew how pack wolves worked. Revenge would be on the forefront of their mind, and Gavin, being that he had been working with us, would be considered the ultimate traitor. There was no doubt in my mind that they would hunt him down and make him pay for his betrayal. Without help, there would be no way he could make it out of here alive.

CHAPTER 59

Gavin

From the second the shit hit the fan, I was fighting off assholes right and left. I'd taken my eyes off of Cami for just enough time to shift, and leave it to her to up and disappear on me. I wanted nothing more than to find her to make sure she was safe, but my old *friends* from Crescent Hills were making damn sure that I didn't go anywhere, including the current dickhead, apparently dead-set on killing me.

By thrashing my head as hard as I could to the right, I was able to throw the attacking wolf off balance long enough to get the advantage. Once he was off of me, I snapped my jaws down on the wolf's neck, not hard enough to cause any permanent damage, but enough to get him to stop trying to bite my head off.

It was only then that I realized who the wolf was: Clayton. Instantly, rage flowed throughout my body. But along with that rage came a certain amount of confidence. I had just taken down an enforcer, a man that brought fear to nearly everyone who met him. Knowing full well he was the most dangerous man left in the room, I had to do something, so I grabbed him by the neck again and slammed his head as hard as I could into a nearby metal pole. Watching as his eyes rolled back in his head, I felt better knowing that he would be unconscious, at least for a short while.

Then I raised my head and bared my teeth ready to take on the next opponent, but my newfound confidence quickly waned when I became aware of my grim situation. I looked from one pair of narrowed eyes to the next, from one set of sharp, white teeth to the next, from one growling wolf to the next. I was surrounded by five wolves, and they were closing in. I took a step back, and then another, but with every inch that I put between us, they tightened their circle and stepped even closer to me.

These wolves were crazed and full of bloodlust. No doubt that they saw me as the traitor to their pack, a turncoat, and they wanted me dead. It was clear they were ready to tear me limb from limb for what I'd done.

They walked slowly in a circle around me as they took turns snapping their jaws at my legs, teasing me, testing my resolve. They wanted me to fight them. They wanted me to give them one more reason to rip me apart.

As their circle grew smaller and tighter by the second, my life flashed before my eyes. Somehow, I saw the shock on my own face as my father was shot right in front of me and felt the mixed emotions I had experienced pass through me again. No one could argue that the man had done maliciously evil things and probably deserved everything he got, but he was my father, and it hurt like hell to see him fall like that, though I'd never admit it aloud.

Then, I saw Scarlett when she was a little girl looking up at me like I was her favorite person in the entire world. I saw my mother standing in the laundry room of our old house laughing at my lame jokes while she folded our never-ending piles of laundry.

The last face I saw belonged to the only other woman who ever held my heart. Cami's fierce attitude and soft smile, the perfect combination of fire and ice, was forever seared into my brain. Seeing her face gave me all the courage I needed to go out fighting.

I let out a growl that was so loud and fierce that it sounded more like a roar as I reared back onto my hind legs and attacked with more force than I knew I was capable of. There was no way in hell I could fight all five of them, but dammit, I would die trying.

I swiped at the first one and ducked down low to escape the bite of another. I didn't know if I was too slow, or there were just too many of them, but I couldn't stop the yowl of pain when I felt his jaws clamp down on my arm.

I didn't see them coming, but I definitely heard them. The members of Red Ridge truly were on my side and came to my rescue just in time. Two wolves I didn't recognize, Kendall, and a wolf I immediately knew had to be my girl, Cami, came barreling through the crowd surrounding me.

The sounds of teeth snapping and bones breaking filled the air. With Cami's help, I was able to fight off the wolf the closest to me while Kendall and the other two easily took care of the rest of my attackers.

As things cleared, Cami pulled me out of the mess to safety. She rubbed her head into my neck and pressed herself against me. I tried to reassure her, to show her that I was okay, but she wasn't having any of it. I gave up and let her take care of me.

Gradually, the snarls and yelps stopped. The Crescent Hills wolves had been beaten at their own game. I watched as the ones that could still get up ran away. They ran as fast as they could and didn't look back; all of them except one. Noel. Noel turned around and looked at her son one last time. With eyes full of both love and regret, she lowered her head slightly, apologizing in the only way she could…before taking off and leaving him and the estate for good.

Cade motioned for us to block the exits and not let anyone else escape. Jake and Aiden took the front doors, and Dane and Phillip took the back exits. Luke shook out his fur and moved to stand next to Cade. My wounded arm was already healing, so Cami and I walked over to join them.

Looking around, the lodge reminded me of a bad horror flick. The wounded wolves lay on the floor shivering and howling in pain.

A few unlucky wolves lay motionless…soundless. I tried to be hard and not let my emotions get the best of me, but at one time, those lifeless wolves were my pack, my family. They were definitely in the wrong, and they were trying to kill us, but it still hurt me to see them like this.

A loud crash came from the back, and we all turned to see Phillip growling and forcing one of the Crescent Hills wolves back into the main room. I knew exactly who it was. Looking around, I realized there were only two Crescent Hills members remaining…Drew and Kendall.

CHAPTER 60

Kendall

Well, this didn't exactly turn out how I thought it would. Sure, I knew Red Ridge had the home-court advantage and the numbers on their side, but I *had* planned on tucking tail and running for the damn hills long before this battle was over.

Yet, here I stood, surrounded by Red Ridge's finest—with Drew by my side, no less. I was so screwed. Royally screwed. My luck had finally run out. Kendall Avery Stuart's time on this earth was up. If only I could go back in time and do it all over again…

I watched as Cade disappeared down a hallway, and then in human form, covered in only a coat, came back in the main room and told the majority of this pack to report to the infirmary if they were seriously wounded or to head home to rest and heal if not. Then before he shifted back, he turned his attention to Drew and me and said, "We have a pressing matter to attend to."

As soon as the lodge cleared out, I did the only thing I could think to do, the one and only thing that might give me the slightest chance of surviving this little debacle I'd found myself in. I shifted back to human form. Even Cade would have a harder time killing me as a human than as a wolf, and he hated me more than any of them.

Quickly, I grabbed the nearest coat I could find and shrugged it on. No one should have to plead for her life completely naked. It just didn't seem right. Even with a body as perfect as mine, there was something completely humiliating about standing before your judge, jury, and executioner in the nude.

Surprisingly, Drew followed suit, but apparently not for the same reason as me. As soon as he had the ability to speak again, he immediately started yelling, but not at Red Ridge wolves. At me. Standing right in front of me, staring me down like one of his minions, Drew cruelly unleashed his wrath.

"You stupid, stupid bitch! This is all your fucking fault! I should have known better than to get mixed up with a Red Ridge cast-off whore like you!"

I grabbed the nearest coat I could find and threw it at Drew, hoping he would cover himself, as I shouted back, "My fault? How is any of this my fault? Look around, Drew! Your pack did this! Your desperate attempt to take over this place failed, and you have no one to blame but yourself. You're the alpha now. At least for the next few minutes, anyway, because I seriously doubt either of us are walking out of here alive!"

Drew reached out and grabbed me by the hair. Wrapping a chunk of it tightly around his fist, he pulled my hair up, forcing me to face the wolves surrounding us. "Look at them, Kendall. Where is he? Which one? You know exactly where he is, don't you?"

Tightening his grip, he moved my head around to slowly scan the area and then stopped our search when he found the wolf he was looking for. "There he is. Gavin fucking Reed. Your hero! *That* is why this is your fault. Do you really think I didn't see you help save his sorry ass? Do you really think I don't know how you feel about him? How you've *always* felt about him. You sad, sorry slut! You love that stupid piece of shit, and he doesn't give a rat's ass about you! He never has. He used you! He used you for intel, and you gave it to him! And then you fucking saved him! You're pathetic."

Tears welled up in my eyes, and I hated myself more than ever for letting his words hurt me. A single tear slid down my face as I closed my eyes, refusing to look at any of them.

Drew released his grip on my hair, and I almost fell to the floor, but he caught me before my legs could buckle. Using my body as a shield, Drew wrapped his forearm around my neck and said, "But you aren't useless. You, my dear, are my ticket out of here."

My eyes shot open as Drew tightened his grip, and instinctively, I clawed at his arm, which only made him chuckle like the madman that he was. Speaking to the wolves encircling us, Drew warned, "We *are* walking out of here alive. Don't test me. This girl means nothing to me, and I won't hesitate to snap her neck like a fucking twig if you make a move. Do you hear me? I will kill her!"

This was it. My last few moments here on this earth. I was going to die at the hands of Drew Barnes, which would have probably made me laugh if I would have had enough air to do so, because somehow I'd always known that it would be him that would kill me. Somehow, someway, I just knew that Drew would be the death of me. And this was it.

But before I left this world, I couldn't stop myself from taking one last look at the only guy that I'd ever truly cared about, maybe even loved. My eyes connected with Gavin's. He held my gaze, and for the first time since all of this began, I felt something I hadn't felt in a long time.

Peace.

CHAPTER 61

Cami

We'd formed a semicircle around Kendall and Drew and were slowly closing in. Panic surged inside of me, knowing it would only take half a second for Drew to kill Kendall, and as much as I hated Kendall Stuart, I didn't want to stand here and witness her death. Even she didn't deserve to die, especially not at the hands of that psychotic prick.

But Drew was right. Kendall was his one-way ticket out of this room, and if he killed her now, there would be no way he'd make it out of here. Drew needed her alive in order to survive.

But then it happened. Kendall's eyes met with Gavin's, and as soon as they did, I knew this wasn't going to end well.

They held each other's gaze for what felt like an eternity. I watched as a small, sad smile crossed her face. It was as if she was apologizing to Gavin with that smile. But it wasn't until Kendall scanned the room looking at all of us, her former pack, her former family, with the same expression on her face, that I realized what she was about to do.

"Kendall, No!" I screamed inside my head, but being in wolf form, what came out of my mouth sounded more like a cry. Then Kendall just snapped. She started kicking and clawing savagely at Drew's arm as she screamed, "You stupid motherfucker! I'm going to kill you! You're a dead man, Drew Barnes! A dead man. I hate you. I fucking hate you."

Our circle grew tighter as Drew tried to gain control of Kendall in her fit of rage, but even as he did, Drew warned, "I'll do it. I'll kill her right here. I swear it! Even if it means I'm dead too. I'm taking this bitch down with me. So stay back. I mean it. Stay back or she's dead!"

Kendall continued her rampage, her claw marks leaving trails of blood down Drew's arm, as she shouted every profanity known to man, repeating her hatred for him over and over again. She even added in what a lousy lay he was and that his dick was the size of a prepubescent boy's. Kendall knew how to cut to the core, and if I could have laughed, I just might have.

When I noticed Gavin stepping back and walking around behind the circle, I followed. Gavin had positioned himself directly behind Drew. Kendall's eye's shifted to the side and met mine, and I nodded my head, trying to let her know that Gavin was ready to do whatever he needed to do.

Doing the most un-Kendall-like thing imaginable, she actually mouthed the words *thank you* to me just before she let out an ear-piercing shriek and threw her head back, hitting Drew squared in the nose.

Drew released the hold he had on Kendall and stepped back as the room grew quiet. Drew and Kendall stood only a foot away from each other. The obvious hate they harbored for each other flowed off of them in reeking waves that threatened to turn my stomach. Drew's nose was bleeding, but the sinister grin on his face told me that he didn't feel a thing.

Before anyone even realized what he was doing, Drew snatched Kendall by the bicep, spun her around to face Gavin, and snapped her neck.

I held my breath, as her lifeless body crumbled to the ground near my paws.

The angry growls from the wolves around me grew to a deafening roar as we tightened our circle around Drew. With a howl from Cade, Luke snarled as he stepped forward, forcing Drew back. Gavin reared up on his hind legs and attacked. His front claws landed on Drew's shoulders as his teeth clamped down onto the side of his neck. Luke attacked from the front at nearly the same time.

Kendall's body lay under all the horror, her eyes still open as if she was watching the devastation. Quickly, I clamped my teeth around the coat that she was wearing and drug her away. When I turned back, the bloody scene was almost too much to witness.

The others had moved in, and within seconds, Drew Barnes had been ripped to pieces.

CHAPTER 62

Gavin

I didn't know what came over me, or why I felt the need to avenge Kendall's death, but I did. Maybe it was because she came to my aid when I needed it. Or maybe it was because deep down I had always thought that Kendall wanted to be a better person than she was. Either way, I certainly didn't want to see her dead.

I couldn't say the same about Drew, although I wasn't proud of the fact that I was the one that led the attack that ended his life. Unlike my father, I never wanted to have anyone's blood on my hands or their deaths on my conscience, but I saw an opportunity and I took it. This wasn't how I expected it to end, but now that it was over and Drew was dead, I felt nothing but relief.

Seeing that some of the pack had already started changing back to their human forms, I quickly followed suit. There was a fresh stack of folded blankets on a chair near the front of the room that Teagan had brought in once Aiden had released her from the cell downstairs.

I immediately went over and grabbed one to wrap around my waist. I stood there by the chair and looked around the room. The lodge looked like a war was fought inside of it. I guess there kind of was.

Blood stained the walls and the floor. My father's body was still where he had fallen. I wanted to feel something for him. At least, I thought that I should—sadness, regret, guilt, but there was nothing. Anything that I might have felt for my father didn't die with him, but died the moment he decided that my sister was expendable. There was grief and sorrow on some of the faces in the room, and I wondered if anyone could tell that I felt void of those emotions. Would they think less of me if they knew?

Over by the wall, Kendall's body lay all alone. Her arms were by her side and her eyes had been closed. She looked nothing like the strong, fearless girl she once was. Suddenly, I felt incredibly sorry for her. No one, not even her, deserved to die like that, alone in the world, at the hands of a madman. And not in Red Ridge, a place she once called home.

As I turned away, my eyes finally found the one I was looking for. Cami had just shifted, and Scarlett walked over to hand her a blanket. Watching as Cami quickly covered herself, I couldn't force my feet to move. I just stood there while Cami spoke softly to my sister. I couldn't tell what they were talking about, but she looked…well, she looked unreadable, and I didn't like that. When Scar walked away from her, I expected Cami to look my way, but she didn't. She stood there, squeezing her blanket around her so tightly that I could see the white in her knuckles.

I realized that she was probably sorting out the day in her head. All I knew was that she was okay. She was okay, and she was mine. In that moment, something inside me flickered. It was as if someone flipped on the light switch, and I was coming out of the dark. Colors grew more vibrant. The sounds in the lodge were even sharper than before. My eyes filled with unshed tears. I hadn't realized what I could have lost. My mate. Somehow in the midst of all of this madness, the most beautiful thing in the world was suddenly clear. Cami really was mine. We belonged together, and it was a forever kind of thing.

My girl was safe. My sister was safe. I had everything that I would ever need right here in this very room. It was hard to believe that the hell we'd been through was finally over.

Unable to stand the distance between us any longer, I forced my legs to move, and I walked over to her side. When I took her hand in mine, she wouldn't look me in the eyes. Instead, she looked down at our fingers entwined together, and she began to shake. I released her hands and lifted her chin with my fingers. Her beautiful brown eyes were shimmering with tears. It was like a knife in my heart to see her so vulnerable. I needed her to know that she was safe; that she would always be safe with me. I pulled her into my arms and held her tight. I could feel her sobs, her body trembling. I held her tighter.

"Shh, baby, it's okay. I've got you," I whispered.

She pulled back and looked up into my eyes. I couldn't resist any longer. I lowered my lips to hers, kissing her with every ounce of fear, hurt, loss, anxiety, and hope that I had experienced in the last twenty-four hours.

"How is your arm?" she asked when she finally pulled away. I shivered as Cami ran her fingertips along my arm, careful not to touch my already healing wound.

"I'm good. I'm good…now that I have you in my arms," I said, wrapping her back up in a hug. "It's over, baby. It's over." I didn't know if I was trying to comfort her with those words or myself, but it didn't matter. It really was over, and I was going to make the most of my new beginning with my mate.

CHAPTER 63

Cami

Sitting in my window seat, I stared out at the empty street below. It seemed like a lifetime ago since I'd sat here just thinking and watching as our once quiet little pack carried on with their everyday lives.

It was all just so surreal. As the events of the morning flashed through my mind once again, I closed my eyes, unable to believe it all really happened. Any of it. And now it was just over, and we were all supposed to just go back to our normal lives. Just like that, we'd all be expected to just go back to school again like normal teenagers.

Gavin would have to go back to school too. He would be leaving. He had a normal life to live too. And as much as I wanted it to be, his life wasn't here.

A knock at my door tore my eyes from the window. Trying to keep the sorrow out of my voice, I said, "Come in."

Gavin opened the door and smiled. "You ready to head to the lodge?"

Cade had called an evening meeting after he'd sent everyone home this morning. I figured he wanted to address the situation and assure the pack that he had everything under control, but at this point, I just wanted to crawl into bed, cover my head, and pretend it was all a bad dream.

I returned Gavin's smile, but knowing he'd be leaving soon, it was a bullshit smile, and Gavin probably knew it.

"You okay?" he asked with a furrowed brow.

Yep. He knew it.

I nodded my head. "Yeah, I'm fine. Let's get this over with."

When Gavin and I walked into the lodge, my jaw dropped. "Oh my God. How did he do all this?"

"I guess they've been busy since we left," Gavin answered as he looked around the room that had somehow been completely transformed over the course of the day. Not only had the room been completely cleaned up, and I mean completely—no remnants of the bloodshed that had taken place could be seen—but all of the pews had been moved out. Instead of rows of pews all facing the alpha's podium, tables and chairs filled the space, and the podium, which had always been the focal point of the room, was now gone.

Our pack stood around talking, seemingly unsure of what to do. A few minutes after our arrival, Cade spoke up over the crowd and said, "Everyone, have a seat. Let us begin. We have a few things to discuss."

Like it was the most natural thing in the world, everyone settled in at a table. Gavin and I were about to sit with my parents when Luke waved us over to their table. My father nodded his head as if to say *go ahead,* and we took our seats at a table with Allison, Aiden, Teagan, Luke, and Scarlett.

Cade stood next to the empty chair beside Allison, and with unwavering confidence, began his speech. "First, I want to apologize to each and every one of you for the hell you've all been through, and I want you to know that I will do everything in my power to never let anything like this happen to our pack again. If there is a silver lining, it is this. We now know where our weaknesses lie. We now know how we can better defend ourselves. And most importantly, we now know that in order for this to never happen again, we must stand together as one, united, and truly depend on one another so that we can be an even stronger pack than we once were."

As the room erupted in applause, Cade looked around the room, nodded his head, and a small smile broke out across his face. Still clapping, Aiden stood up, and almost immediately, Luke joined him. Then one by one, the elders stood too, and before long, we were all standing and still applauding, as if we were officially welcoming Cade into his new role as alpha.

Tears sprang to my eyes, and as I looked around, I noticed that I wasn't the only one touched by what was happening. When Aiden reached out to shake Cade's hand and then pulled him into a hug, I seriously thought I was going to turn into a blubbering mess right there, but then Cade thanked us all for our support and we took our seats again, which gave me a moment to reel in my girly shit. Then when Gavin reached over and squeezed my knee, I was suddenly all choked up again.

Cade finished his speech, assuring us all that with the elders and his new enforcer, Luke, he would be working toward creating a new system of defense, and he made it clear that though he was young, he was ready to be this pack's alpha and with his elders, Luke, Allison, Aiden, and Aiden's parents at his side, he felt confident that the transition would be a smooth one. There was no doubt in my mind that he was right. Red Ridge was in good hands, and we were all going to be okay.

After the meeting, Gavin and I stayed and talked to Scarlett and Luke. It was good to see Gavin reunited with his sister, and I couldn't help but be happy—very selfishly happy, but happy nonetheless—that Scarlett and Luke were true mates. It meant that even though Gavin may leave, Scarlett would stay, so Gavin would still hopefully visit.

Jeez, I'm pathetic. So very, very pathetic.

"Hey, Cami, you okay?" Luke asked.

Did I really suck that bad at hiding my emotions? Lovely. I probably had *the love of my life is leaving me, and I'm so pitiful and sad* written all over my face. "Yeah, I'm fine. Just tired, I guess."

Luke didn't buy it. He gave me *the look,* the one that told me that he knew I was full of shit. A change of subject was in order, so I asked the only thing I could think of, and it actually was a question I'd been wondering about. "So, what happened to all the CH members that didn't escape?"

Thankfully, Luke took the bait and answered. "The ones who had healed enough to leave were escorted off the premises, and the ones who were badly wounded are still in the infirmary. They will be sent on their way as soon as they're able to leave."

Just as we were about to head out, Luke stopped us and said, "Stop by Cade's house in about an hour. We're having a little get-together, and you both should be there."

CHAPTER 64

Gavin

Cami was quiet—too quiet. I could tell that something was on her mind, but when I asked her about it, she just shrugged. It wasn't until we had left the lodge that she looked up at me and said, "Gavin, I think we need to talk."

I took her hand and pulled her closer to me. I didn't like the tone of her voice or the distance that she was trying to put between us. "Come on, then. Let's go for a walk," I said as I pulled her jacket together and zipped her up tight.

We walked down to the lake and out on to the pier that stretched out over the water. I followed Cami all the way to the end to where a small swinging bench sat overlooking the lake. I sat down and pulled Cami onto my lap, but as soon as I did, she scooted off and sat next to me.

I sat there waiting for her to say something, but she didn't. She just stared out over the water. I knew where this was going, so I leaned back and prepared myself.

"I want you to know that it's okay," she finally said in almost a whisper.

"That what is okay?" I asked. I placed my hand on top of hers and when she didn't move it right away, I picked it up and held it in mine.

She looked at me for a moment before saying, "Look, I'm just going to say it."

I closed my eyes and waited for her to try and break up with me.

"I just want you to know that it's okay. I know that you have to go back to school, and I don't want you to worry about me, or my feelings. I mean…I understand that you have to leave," she said, not looking at my face, but at our hands on my lap.

"It's not like we're ma—I mean you're not even my boyfriend or anything. Maybe we can see each other when you come back to visit Scarlett, or we can at least be friends," she continued.

"It's been a crazy week, and I totally understand if our…if we were just a fling, or whatever," she continued to ramble.

I smiled. I couldn't help myself.

Cami let go of my hand and stood up. I followed her. She was still hiding her face from my sight as she spoke. "It's just okay. Let's not make a big deal about it."

I couldn't take it anymore, and I laughed out loud. That got her attention, and she finally looked up at me. "Are you seriously laughing at me right now?" she asked with her hands on her hips.

"Baby, shut up," I said still smiling down at her. She started to say something else, but I stopped her the best way I knew how. When my lips first touched hers, she flinched and froze, but I wasn't deterred. I knew that she would eventually give in and kiss me back. And good Lord, did she kiss me back. I wrapped my arms around her waist as she wrapped hers around my neck. Her lips parted, giving me what I wanted most, what I craved more than anything, a taste of her.

The kiss wasn't rushed. It wasn't demanding or needy. It wasn't at all selfish. It was an acceptance. A claiming of what was mine, and I knew she felt it. It was as if the heat from her mouth was branding me as hers for all the world to see.

Slowly, our lips stopped moving, and Cami rested her head against my chest. I smoothed her hair with my hand and kissed the top of her head. "I'm staying," I whispered.

Her eyes immediately shot to mine, "But—"

I stopped her. "I'm staying. There is only once place that I want to be, and that's right here with you. Cami, I love you, and I dare anyone to try to keep me away from you."

"Really? You're staying?" she asked with tears in her eyes.

"For as long as you will have me."

"That could be a really, really long time," she teased. That beautiful smile of hers was back on those beautiful pink lips—back where it belonged.

"I certainly hope so," I said.

"You feel it, don't you? In here," I asked as I gently touched her heart. She gave me a puzzled look, so I continued. "The tightness in here when I'm close to you. The ache in here when I'm not. Cami, I know you are my mate, and I'm yours. Forever."

I watched as the realization crossed her face. A nanosecond later, she threw her arms around my neck and attacked my face with feather-light kisses. Suddenly, she stopped and said, "Of course, I feel it too. But how can we be sure?"

"Well, there's only one way to confirm it, but I never plan on leaving your side long enough to find out. Besides, I just know. I love you, Cami, more than anything in this world. That's all the proof I need."

"I love you, too," she said in between a kiss to my forehead and a kiss to my cheek.

*****

When we walked into Cade's house later that day, the mood in the home was surprising. Everyone was casually sitting around the family room smiling and talking. Scarlett winked at me from her spot on the loveseat. She was lounging against the arm of the sofa with her legs propped up in Luke's lap. Aiden and Teagan were snuggled up next to each other on the floor, their backs leaning against the loveseat that Scarlett was in. Alli sat in Cade's lap in a big, oversized chair. There was a smile on his face that didn't quite reach his eyes. He had been through so much, but I knew that he would be able to handle anything now.

"Our heroes!" Teagan cheered as Cami and I moved to sit on the open couch. The rest of them joined in. Cami blushed bright red, but she really was a hero. What she had done for her pack was beyond brave, and I was so proud of her. I wasn't sure why I was being congratulated. I just went along because I had to. I had to do whatever I could to protect Cami.

"So, Gavin, you sticking around?" Aiden asked.

"If you'll all have me," I said, looking to Cade.

Cade looked around the room, smiled at me, and said, "Wouldn't have it any other way, man."

The look on Cami's face was worth everything I had gone through since I'd hijacked Phillip and took off to Red Ridge. She snuggled up next to me, and we all just sat around and talked like everything was normal, but deep down we knew that it wasn't.

We had all lost friends or family members. Life in Red Ridge would never be the same, but looking around the room, I could tell that this pack was going to be okay. Better than okay. They would rebuild and be stronger than ever. The lies and betrayal of those who came before them had been laid to rest. Today marked a new beginning for the Red Ridge Pack.

ABOUT THE AUTHORS

Sara Dailey and Staci Weber have been friends and coworkers for so long that they finish each other's sentences and answer to either name. They both have an addiction to romance novels, sweet white wine, and sexy rock stars. They both live in League City, TX, with their husbands and kids. *End of Lies* is their sixth novel together.

Did you enjoy this book? Drop us a line and say so! We love to hear from readers, and so do our authors. To connect, visit www.boroughspublishinggroup.com online, send comments directly to info@boroughspublishinggroup.com, or friend us on Facebook and Twitter. And be sure to check back regularly for contests and new releases in your favorite subgenres of romance!

Are you an aspiring writer? Check out www.boroughspublishinggroup.com/submit and see if we can help you make your dreams come true.

www.ingramcontent.com/pod-product-compliance
Lightning Source LLC
Chambersburg PA
CBHW072210170626
46813CB00003B/881